Praise for the ‘   ’
Susanna Carr

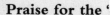

"Be sure not to miss out on this one; after all, being wicked and being in love can fall hand in hand. This is a keeper, definitely."
—*The Romance Reader's Connection

"Entertaining. *Confessions of a 'Wicked' Woman* proves that not only is being wicked good, but shows us how much fun it is."
—Romance Reviews Today

"Delightfully humorous, with sizzling chemistry between the characters, great secondary characters, and a love story that won't be soon forgotten. A definite recommend!"
—Love Romances

"A hilarious, romantic read that will have you turning page after page . . . a must-read story."
—Romance Junkies

"Hilariously entertaining."
—Fallen Angel Reviews

"Jack and Stephanie's sizzling chemistry keep the steam rising in this latest 'Wicked Woman' romp. As an added treat, Carr infuses this fun romance with a megadose of sidesplitting humor and irrepressible, eccentric secondary characters."
—*Romantic Times BOOKclub* (4½ stars)

"Witty and sexy."
—Just Erotic Romance Reviews

"Sexy, sassy, delicious fun."
—Shannon McKenna

Pink Ice

SUSANNA CARR

A SIGNET ECLIPSE BOOK

SIGNET ECLIPSE
Published by New American Library, a division of
Penguin Group (USA) Inc., 375 Hudson Street,
New York, New York 10014, USA
Penguin Group (Canada), 90 Eglinton Avenue East, Suite 700, Toronto,
Ontario M4P 2Y3, Canada (a division of Pearson Penguin Canada Inc.)
Penguin Books Ltd., 80 Strand, London WC2R 0RL, England
Penguin Ireland, 25 St. Stephen's Green, Dublin 2,
Ireland (a division of Penguin Books Ltd.)
Penguin Group (Australia), 250 Camberwell Road, Camberwell, Victoria 3124,
Australia (a division of Pearson Australia Group Pty. Ltd.)
Penguin Books India Pvt. Ltd., 11 Community Centre, Panchsheel Park,
New Delhi - 110 017, India
Penguin Group (NZ), cnr Airborne and Rosedale Roads, Albany,
Auckland 1310, New Zealand (a division of Pearson New Zealand Ltd.)
Penguin Books (South Africa) (Pty.) Ltd., 24 Sturdee Avenue,
Rosebank, Johannesburg 2196, South Africa

Penguin Books Ltd., Registered Offices: 80 Strand, London WC2R 0RL, England

First published by Signet Eclipse, an imprint of New American Library,
a division of Penguin Group (USA) Inc.

First Printing, November 2006
10 9 8 7 6 5 4 3 2 1

SIGNET ECLIPSE and logo are trademarks of Penguin Group (USA) Inc.

LIBRARY OF CONGRESS CATALOGING-IN-PUBLICATION DATA:
Carr, Susanna.
  Pink ice / by Susanna Carr.
p. cm.
  ISBN 0-451-21955-4 (trade pbk.)
  I. Title.
  PS3603.A77435P56   2006
813'.6—dc22
                        2006014442

Set in Bembo
Designed by Spring Hoteling

Printed in the United States of America

PUBLISHER'S NOTE
This is a work of fiction. Names, characters, places, and incidents either are the product of the
author's imagination or are used fictitiously, and any resemblance to actual persons, living or
dead, business establishments, events, or locales is entirely coincidental.
    The publisher does not have any control over and does not assume any responsibility for
author or third-party Web sites or their content.

To my sisters, Rebekah, Jennifer, and Rachel

PROLOGUE

"WE ARE AT LIA DASH'S AUCTION!" Nicole's voice trembled with excitement as she squirmed in the gilt-edged chair, taking in everything at the exclusive auction house. "Think about it. We are inches away from the very things she owned!"

"Nicole, keep your hands to yourself and don't make a scene," Lindsay said in a low tone without moving her mouth. "That's all I ask."

" 'Don't make a scene,' " Nicole mimicked. "Oh, please. There aren't that many people here to care."

Sabrina glanced up from the catalog and looked around. What her younger sister said was true. She had expected standing room only for the celebrity auction. After all, Lia Dash had been the epitome of the eighties. She gave rock music a glamorous edge, but her rebellious nature could have taught some MTV darlings a lesson or two.

"That's because of the weather," Lindsay decided, flipping back her hair, which was still wet from the rain. "We nearly got blown away waiting for the doors to open."

Sabrina figured her older sister was right. The storm and wind had knocked out power and phone lines in parts of Seattle. People would probably show up later.

Nicole made a face. "What a bunch of wimps. Nothing could have kept me away." She splayed her hands out in the air. "Nothing!"

Lindsay reached over Sabrina and tapped Nicole's leg with the rolled-up auction catalog. "Behave."

When Nicole started to roll up *her* catalog, Sabrina reached out and grabbed both sisters' wrists. "You guys, please."

She regretted inviting her sisters to the event. She thought they would be thrilled, not to mention act like the adults they were, since this auction celebrated the life of their preteen idol. Lia Dash was more than a fashion designer. She was a legend. An icon. She had lived their dream life.

"Lot number seven," the auctioneer said as an assistant brought out an item. "The mask Lia wore to the launch party of her perfume brand, Masquerade."

Sabrina let go of her sisters and sighed when she saw the masterpiece of rose silk and sequins. She gazed open-mouthed at the accompanying picture that appeared on the overhead screen. Lia's famous features were partially hidden, but the mask couldn't dilute her charisma.

The woman knew how to party. No, it was more than that, Sabrina decided as the auctioneer's voice faded into a low buzz. Lia Dash knew how to be the *life* of the party.

Sabrina wished she had that quality. She winced at the pang of yearning deep in her belly. What was she doing? She could wish all she wanted, but after twenty-six years of coasting through life unnoticed, it wasn't going to happen.

People never remembered her name, let alone that they had met before. Rather than being the belle of the ball, Sabrina was usually roped into helping in the kitchen or taking care of inebriated guests. She never found the opportunity to be the center of attention.

"Oh, the masquerade." Lindsay nudged Sabrina's elbow. "That's when Lia and a certain punk rocker got it on during the party. And then he made the song 'Lia's Masquerade.'"

"Rumors. Unsubstantiated rumors." Nicole ignored Lindsay's scoffs. "How could you believe the guy? I mean, seriously, what kind of man would make a music video based on a one-night stand?"

"Sold!" The auctioneer banged his gavel.

"Now, come on, be quiet," Sabrina pleaded. "I have to concentrate and get some of these dresses for the shop, okay?" The last thing she needed to do was give her boss a legitimate reason to fly into a rage. Not that the woman needed a reason. . . .

"Lot number eight," the auctioneer continued. "A pair of pink diamond earrings."

Nicole sat up straight in her chair. "No. Way."

When she saw the picture on the screen, Sabrina clapped her hand over her mouth. She felt the sting of tears and blinked rapidly. If there was any one thing that represented Lia Dash, it was those earrings.

"Are those . . . ?" Lindsay asked.

"Yes," Sabrina and Nicole said in unison.

"We will start the bidding at fifty thousand dollars," the auctioneer said. His voice sounded slow and disjointed to Sabrina's ears. "Do I hear fifty thousand dollars?"

Sabrina held up her sign. It was an instinctive move. She hadn't thought of bidding. She simply did it.

The man pointed at her. "Fifty thousand dollars. Do I hear fifty-five thousand?"

"Bree!" Lindsay pulled at Sabrina's arm. "What are you doing? You're here for dresses."

"The jewelry is for me." Her heart pounded against her ribs. A sheen of sweat appeared at her hairline. She felt a little bit sick. It was as if she was on a roller coaster ride and praying to get to the end in one piece.

"Fifty-five thousand dollars. Do I hear sixty thousand dollars?"

Her sign went up in a flash.

"Sabrina, stop it," Lindsay's fierce whisper sounded like a hiss. "This is crazy."

"Sixty thousand dollars." The auctioneer nodded at her. "Do I hear sixty-five thousand?"

"I have to have them." Her voice was surprisingly resolute. Those diamonds would change her life. They would make her life more like Lia's. That's what she wanted, no matter what the cost.

"But you can't afford them," Lindsay reminded her.

"Sixty-five thousand dollars. Do I hear seventy thousand?"

Her sister had a point. "Chip in and we'll share," she offered as she bid again. "I get them half of the year, you get them the other."

"Hey!" Nicole protested. "What about me?"

"Okay, we'll all share." She didn't like the idea of having less time with the diamonds, but the price was already way out of her league.

"Eighty thousand dollars. Do I hear eighty thousand dollars?"

Sabrina motioned to the auctioneer.

"No," Lindsay said. "I refuse to share anything with Nicole. Have we forgotten the last time we shared something? The car? The one Nicole totaled?"

Nicole leaned over Sabrina. "I was in high school at the time, it wasn't my fault, and this is different."

"Ninety thousand dollars? Do I hear ninety thousand dollars?"

"Different as in more expensive." Lindsay grabbed Sabrina's outreached arm and held it down. "Would you stop?"

Sabrina turned to her sister and looked her straight in the eye. "Lindsay, if you don't want the earrings, that's fine. Nicole and I will share." Sabrina heard the raised price and she quickly made her bid.

"What makes you think Nicole can afford it?"

"Do I hear one hundred and five thousand dollars? One hundred five thousand dollars?"

She didn't answer. Neither she nor Nicole could afford it, but she couldn't risk losing the earrings. "Are you in or out?"

Lindsay grimaced. "I'm . . ."

"Going . . . going . . ."

Lindsay's shoulders sagged with defeat. "In."

Sabrina's heart jumped at the bang of the gavel. "Sold!" the auctioneer announced. "For one hundred thousand dollars."

One hundred thousand dollars? Sabrina froze. That meant . . .

"Oh. My. God." Nicole turned to face her sisters. "We got the diamonds!"

PINK CHAMPAGNE

CHAPTER ONE

Crashing parties wasn't easy, Sabrina decided as she stood be-hind a row of shrubs. After doing this off and on for almost a year, she discovered one did not easily glide in and grab a champagne flute. It was more about dodging tight security and direct questions.

She took a deep, calming breath, but it didn't work. It never did. She didn't know why she bothered, other than it was a traditional part of her preparty routine. She wasn't about to mess with it.

Sabrina tugged at her halter top before sliding her hands along the slinky fabric. She hadn't been able to wear a bra un-der the couture gown. The lack of lingerie didn't make her feel sexy or scandalous. More like naked and vulnerable.

It might not be the right dress to wear a swanky botanical garden, Sabrina thought as she listened to the clink of glasses and lilting voices. If anything happened to the gown—just one thorn or one smudge of dirt—then her boss would find out she took the dress from the shop.

Sabrina shuddered as she considered the possible consequences. She didn't want to think about it. Her boss wouldn't find out. She hadn't so far.

Enough worrying. It was time to party. Sabrina slid her fingers through her short hair, grateful to find it twig-free. She paused as she brushed her thumb against the pink diamond earrings.

With that touch, confidence flooded through her. The sensations were warm and strong. She knew the earrings would guide her through the night. The idea sounded crazy, but the belief helped every time she crashed a black-tie event.

Sabrina rotated her shoulders back, held her head high and stepped out of the shadows and into the party. It was always at this one moment when her nerves went haywire and her mind screamed for her to run and hide. Her stomach did a free fall, but no one would know that she was freaking out behind the bold smile.

She walked across the lawn, allowing her hips to sway provocatively. She nodded at one cute guy in a tux and smiled broadly at an elderly couple who almost bumped into her. She kept up her pace. Not too slow so that she would look lost, but not too fast that she would raise suspicion.

"Is that a Missoni?"

Sabrina turned to see a young socialite eyeing her gown. The blond woman herself wasn't wearing couture, although her classic gown could be found at the high-end department stores.

"Yes, it is," Sabrina replied with a gracious smile as raw adrenaline pushed through her tight veins.

"Where did you get it?" The young woman asked the question toward the gown's hemline. Sabrina wanted to roll her eyes. She was being upstaged by a dress. Typical.

"There's a vintage dress shop in the historic downtown area. Sloane's. Great selection. Wonderful staff. You should try them out," Sabrina suggested, almost feeling virtuous for giving the shop a referral.

"I definitely will." The woman briefly glanced at Sabrina and strolled off.

It was probably for the best that the dress received more notice, she decided as she watched the woman walk away. If the socialite showed up at the dress shop and recognized the manager, it could prove disastrous. Then again, the shop's most loyal clientele never recognized her around town, so what were the chances?

Sabrina plucked a flute from a waiter passing by and found a spot next to some fragrant, exotic red flowers. She surveyed the crowd as she took a delicate sip of the crisp champagne. Tonight she was going to mix and mingle. She wasn't going to make the mistake of falling into her old habits. Enough of the shyness. She wasn't risking all this to wind up a wallflower!

She wanted her Cinderella moment, but she wasn't going to get that staying on the sidelines. She might even try for a Scarlett O'Hara moment. She wanted to know what it felt like to have beaux fawning over her.

Yeah . . . Sabrina smiled as she conjured the image in her mind. She could have that. Tonight.

She took a step forward and felt a chill sweep down her

exposed spine. It wasn't from the cool summer breeze. It was more like someone was watching her. Staring.

That's what you're here for. Get used to it. Sabrina reached up and fiddled with her earring as if she were touching a talisman. She could do this. For once, all eyes were going to be on her, and she was going to live it up.

Ian West slowly lowered the champagne glass from his mouth when he saw the woman. He swallowed roughly as his chest tightened. The call of the hunt burst through his veins with a sudden violence that left him stunned.

He forced himself to remain still as he watched the woman stroll through the party. He flexed his shoulders, tempted to shed his tuxedo jacket and the gentlemanly guise that went with it.

Narrowing his eyes, Ian let his gaze drift leisurely down her naked back, her pale skin smooth and luminous. His blood heated as he watched the play of muscles. He liked how she moved. Quiet and graceful as the silk clung to her curves as if drenched in liquid.

He couldn't pull his attention away. Ian wanted to caress her back and trap the heat from her skin against his palm. Trace his fingertips down her spine as if it were a priceless string of pearls.

His attention lingered at the flare of her hips. It was obvious that she was wearing nothing under the black silk.

He was ready to pounce.

Ian moved slowly and edged along the crowd, studying the mystery woman. He had yet to see her face, but he already knew she was trouble.

Why would a woman go to great pains to slip into a party

undetected, yet wear a dress that would cause whiplash? And while she wasn't an expert at party-crashing, she knew a few tricks of the trade.

Could she be the thief he was looking for?

Probably not. Ian gritted his teeth at his readiness to discard her as a suspect. Was it instinct or wishful thinking?

There was one piece of evidence that kept him from naming her the prime suspect: Ian hadn't seen her at the other events where the thefts had occurred. He would have noticed every seductive move she had made.

He moved in closer as the woman joined a group of men and introduced herself. She spoke too quietly for him to catch her name. The men gazed adoringly at her, and one was bold enough to place his hand at her waist. Ian locked his jaw, jealous at the sight of the man's fingers spanning the smooth, unblemished skin.

Fighting the urge to pluck the man's hand away, he saw the woman turn her head slightly. Ian's pulse ricocheted as anticipation flooded his chest. He was so intent to see her profile that he almost missed the earrings.

A hot, jagged fire forked through him as he stared at the pink diamonds.

Even from where he stood, he knew they were the real thing. His brain assessed the five-carat earrings, but he smoldered with an old, dangerous fire he thought he had put out years ago.

The cut of the diamond was excellent. The brilliant shape allowed the stone to sparkle and show off the natural hue. He bet the clarity was a VS or higher, but it was difficult to determine with the naked eye. Pink diamonds were unusual. The fact that they were a pale shade, usually classified as pink champagne, was probably the only reason she didn't have a bodyguard trailing her.

But that wouldn't stop a few pros from getting their hands on the earrings. Even as his brain turned to mush, he could list a few thieves who would ignore all the other ice in the room to go for those diamonds.

But would a thief wear the best diamonds in the room?

It would be a good ploy. Ian's mind mulled over the possibility. The puzzle began to take shape as he watched the woman, noticing how she had the group of men's undivided attention. She turned and Ian saw her face.

He took a step back as he stared at her quiet beauty. He felt a shift deep inside him. Something dark and elemental. The force surprised him as it cracked through his hard-earned facade. Ian needed to look away, but he couldn't.

The woman tilted her head back as she laughed, arching her long, slender throat.

She was designed for jewels, Ian decided. He wanted to lay a rope of diamonds along the base of her throat. Shower her with a rainbow of precious stones. He could easily imagine her bathing in baubles.

The woman glanced in his direction and she stilled. Her brown eyes widened a fraction as her lips slowly parted. Ian held her gaze, knowing his eyes glittered with primitive hunger.

She slid her gaze back to the man who was doing his best to charm her. The woman acted as though nothing happened, taking a small sip of champagne, but Ian knew he had rattled her. Her hand trembled slightly against the crystal flute. He knew she wanted to guzzle the glass empty to gain some false courage.

Already her spine straightened defensively. The pulse at

the base of her throat fluttered wildly under her pale skin. Her chest rose and fell.

Ian's mouth went dry as he watched her nipples furl into tight buds and strain against the black silk. Want crashed through him, rocking him off balance.

Whether she liked it or not, her body was responding to the call of the hunt. Would she ignore the warning, or make a run for it?

Either way, he was going to catch her.

CHAPTER TWO

She was in trouble. *Biiig* trouble.

Heat swept across her skin as excitement tugged low in her belly. No man had ever looked at her like that. Like he had to have her. Now.

She always wanted to know how it felt to be desired. Only, she thought she would have handled it differently. She had imagined that she would have welcomed it.

She should have known better. Instinct—or was it habit?—urged her to run. Hide. Disappear. She was good at being invisible.

Sabrina pressed her thighs together as she pretended to listen to the man in front of her. She smiled and nodded slowly as her heart pounded against her ribs.

Who was this guy staring at her? He had to be security. There was a dark edge about him, even though he wore a tuxedo. Putting a tux on this man was like leashing a wild, proud beast. You can wrap a black tie around his neck, but that didn't mean he was civilized.

She wanted to be admired by a bunch of guys with puppy-dog eyes, and she managed to find a lone, hungry wolf.

Trying not to get kicked out of the party suddenly wasn't her top priority. She would find her own way—right now, in fact.

Sabrina's attention slid back to the man with the shadowy, angular features. The truth was that the man fascinated her.

She clenched the champagne glass, somewhat surprised that it didn't snap under her fingers. *Don't look at him. Don't give him eye contact.*

She didn't need to look at him again. One glance was all it took to have every detail burned in her memory. The man was lean and muscular. Everything about him seemed to be strong, sleek male in his prime, from the dark blond hair cropped close to his skull, to his unwavering blue eyes sunk deep in his angular face.

The tuxedo looked custom-made, and it didn't diminish his raw masculinity. He was a couple of inches taller than Sabrina, but his commanding presence made him seem larger than life. She could sense his restrained power from where she stood.

Apprehension curled along her bare shoulders. It was time to go. But no need to make any sudden moves, Sabrina decided. Nothing to make the blond man take action. All she had to do was to oh-so-casually vacate the premises.

"I'm sorry," she interrupted with a look of regret and took a small step back from the circle of men. "I just saw my"— Boss? Mother?—"therapist. I need to speak with her before she leaves."

"Really?" the tall redhead man drawled. He swiveled his head and surveyed the crowd. "Which one is she?"

"Uh . . ." She should have predicted that question. This was what she got for impromptu lying. "Oh, darn. She just turned the corner of the building. If you will excuse me?" She took another step away.

"You can talk to her later." One of the gentlemen wrapped his hand around her arm. The possessive touch irked her, but it didn't rattle her as much as the blond man's hot gaze.

"I'll be right back," she promised with a dazzling smile. Patting the touchy-feely man's forearm, Sabrina was a little surprised by her actions. In real life she would have tripped over the lie and turned bright red.

Sabrina pivoted and with a flirty wave over her shoulder, headed toward the garden's main building. This, unfortunately, was in the opposite direction from where she had snuck in. The security guy was going to descend on her any minute, and she'd rather get far away from the party before he made a scene.

How was she going to get back to the wooded area? She had to skirt around the party and away from the blond man. The trees and bushes would hide her retreat to her less-than-luxurious hatchback parked several blocks away.

Boy, did she blow it this time, Sabrina admitted as she walked along the cobbled garden path. Somehow she had caught security's attention and almost got escorted out of the party. That would have been embarrassing.

Sabrina turned at the corner of the building and looked around. A few feet away she could see elegant couples strolling along the rock garden. Three women and a burly man stood by the parking lot, their evening wear clashing with the clip-boards and walkie-talkies they held.

More important, the blond man with the intense blue eyes wasn't following her. That was strange. She wasn't sure how she had managed to lose him, but she didn't have time to question it.

Placing her champagne glass on the flower box, Sabrina darted down a side path surrounded by tall bushes. She winced as her stiletto heels clattered on the hard path. One of these days she'd figure out how to retreat silently. And while she was at it, she'd learn how to be the belle of the ball without arousing security's suspicions.

No, wrong attitude! She really had to stop doing this. So what if she got a buzz from dressing up and playing Cinderella? Did that compensate for the sheer panic racing along her body right now?

Okay, maybe she was feeling more than panic, Sabrina thought as she veered onto a smaller dirt path. She wasn't sure what she was feeling. One look at that guy and everything around her fell away with a crash. One minute she felt strong and powerful, the next she was free-falling with nothing to grab onto.

As much as she wanted to experience fun and excitement, a larger part of her craved comfort and control. She felt raw and exposed under the man's gaze, as if he knew her deepest, darkest fantasies and would make every one of them come true. Sabrina shivered at the unbidden thought. Some fantasies were too dangerous for her peace of mind to explore.

She halted at the end of the path. *Uh-oh.* This wasn't familiar. The tall trees hid the moon, and the dense foliage looked all the same to her. The footlights didn't offer much help. The sound of the waterfalls seemed amplified in the dusk.

She had to retrace her steps. Great. Just great. Sabrina

whirled around. She yelped and jumped in surprise when she saw the blond man standing in front of her.

He stood in the shadows and she took a cautious step back and brushed up against a bush.

She flinched when he stepped closer. If her heart pounded any harder, it was going to rip out of her chest.

"Leaving already?"

Sabrina's eyelids fluttered and she pressed her lips together. Oh, why did he have to speak? That voice. It was deep and gravelly, like he just woke up.

She gave a sharp nod to his question, her nerves shredding. She didn't think her voice was in working order.

"You just arrived," he pointed out.

She stiffened, her bones ached in protest. How did he know? Had he seen her enter? *How* she entered? A guilty flush seeped along her cheeks, and for one brief moment she was grateful for the shadows.

The man reached out and crooked his finger under her chin. She gasped softly as a jolt rippled straight to her core. His touch was gentle, but she was very aware of the underlying steel.

The man tilted her face to meet his gaze. "Nice diamonds."

"Thank you," she whispered, the words strangling in her tight throat.

The back of his hand trailed down the curve of her throat. Goose bumps dotted her skin, and the silk offered little protection.

He nestled his thumb in the shallow dip under her throat. "No necklace?"

"No," Sabrina answered softly. She swallowed and felt her throat move against his unyielding touch.

"You should be covered in diamonds," the man decided, his gaze never leaving hers. "Along your throat . . ."

She watched his hand drift, narrowly missing the curve of her breast. Her nipples stung as he caressed the length of her bare arm.

"At your hands . . ." He wrapped his fingers around her wrist.

She was entranced by his touch and his smooth tone. Her next breath sputtered in her lungs as he drew her fingers closer.

"Around your finger." He pressed his mouth against the palm of her stiff hand.

Sabrina's eyes widened as her fingers brushed the harsh angle of his cheek. The guy kissed her hand. No one had ever kissed her hand. Which would probably explain why her wrists were fizzing with excitement.

Is this security's way of interrogating? It was very effective. She was about ready to melt into a puddle.

"I'm Ian West." His voice vibrated against her skin.

The name suited him. Sabrina nodded, wondering if this was some protocol for getting kicked out of a party. Not that she needed assistance; she was leaving anyway.

He moved his mouth away from her tingling hand. "And you are?"

Her ribs tightened around her lungs. Should she give him a fake name? Not answer at all? How about a partial name? "Sabrina."

"Sabrina," he repeated as if he were savoring the word against his tongue. "Some advice. The next time you crash a party, don't wear a dress that makes a man want to tear it off you."

She blinked and her mouth fell open. Oh, no, he didn't! He did not say that. "Ex—"

He tugged her closer, the move smooth and almost invisible. Her mouth was now a kiss away from his. She felt her silk gown slap against his leg as her breasts grazed the crisp pleats of his shirt.

"And don't wear jewelry that makes a man wonder what you did to earn it."

Indignation ripped through her and immediately snuffed out when she saw the hungry gleam in his eye. He was going to kiss her.

And she was going to let him. Despite her anger from his comment, she wanted to taste the wildness. Sabrina tipped her head just as a feminine scream splintered the air.

"My bracelet!"

CHAPTER THREE

IAN WEST.

Sabrina leaned against the display counter of beaded hand-bags, her first break of the day. Her feet ached, her body was weary from lack of sleep, but the name kept buzzing in her head. She wished she hadn't known that such a man existed.

Since she'd met him the night before, she'd felt on edge. A restlessness had invaded her body. It poked and itched.

"I'm leaving now," her boss announced as she breezed through the small store. The willowy blonde had no problems walking between the crowded clothing racks. "I have such a headache."

It was probably from all the yelling she did this morning. Sabrina pressed her lips together. She wasn't going to say a thing.

"Don't even think about closing before six," Sloane said. "Do you hear me?"

"Yes," Sabrina answered demurely, although it practically killed her. But after a surprise and random inventory inspection, Sabrina was going to be quiet and agreeable. Basically invisible.

What caused the inspection? Sabrina wondered about that as she watched her boss leave the shop. Sloane had never done that before. Did someone tip her off? Had Sabrina given herself away? Had Sloane been at one of the parties and Sabrina not seen her?

And was she going to test her luck tonight? Sabrina glanced at the ball gowns lining the back wall. There was a grand ball at a downtown hotel. If ever there was an event made for a Cinderella moment, this was it.

Sabrina walked over to the gold taffeta gown. She gathered the puffy skirt in her hands and sighed. Was it worth it?

The bell over the door announced an arrival. Sabrina looked over her shoulder, ready to greet the customer. Her professional smile froze when she saw Ian West in the doorway.

Power shimmered off him. The aggressive lines of his dark gray business suit made him appear more intimidating—more fascinating—than the night before. He should have looked out of place among the chiffons and sequins, but he only made the dress shop feel smaller.

"Sabrina."

The beat of her heart skipped from the simple greeting. She crushed the taffeta in her fists before she realized what she was doing. Ian West was here. In broad daylight. In the store.

She was in big, big trouble.

He walked toward her, maneuvering between the racks with stunning swiftness. He looked at the gown in her hands. "Are you wearing that tonight?"

"What are you doing here?" she asked as she tried to smooth out the fabric. She was so she glad her boss had left. Sabrina glanced at the window, praying that Sloane hadn't forgotten anything and wouldn't come running back inside.

Ian must have caught her guilty look. "I waited for your boss to leave before I entered the store."

How did he know her boss? How did he know she worked here? A billion questions crowded in her mind, but she asked only one. "How did you find me?"

"One of my security guards saw you running to your car. He got the license plate number."

Wow, she didn't see or hear anyone following her. These guys were good. "What is it that you want?"

She couldn't imagine what he could do to her now. There were no repercussions for crashing the party. Were there? Unless . . . Dread lodged against her breastbone. "Do you think I had something to do with the missing bracelet?"

He shrugged, the move drawing her attention to his large shoulders. "You disappeared after the owner noticed it was missing."

Oh, boy. That did make her look bad. She made a run when Ian's back was turned. It wasn't out of guilt, it was out of opportunity! "Coincidence."

"There's no such thing when it comes to jewelry theft," Ian decided.

Anger flashed through her. "I had nothing to do with it, and you know it."

He surprised her by nodding in agreement. "I know you didn't. I had my eyes on you throughout the party."

That fact didn't give her much comfort. She wanted to dodge him and get behind the sales counter. Only, Ian blocked her, and she had a feeling that was by design rather than accident.

"You get your kicks crashing parties, not out of stealing. Why do you do it?" he asked as he pinned her with his intense blue gaze. "For the challenge? The buzz?"

"That's none of your business." She watched him stroke the gold taffeta. Pleasure tripped along her spine. Sabrina hurriedly dropped the ball gown. "If you know I had nothing to do with it, why are you here?"

"Maybe I want to finish what we started."

His smoky voice tugged at her belly. "Too late for that." She didn't sound very convincing, even to her own ears. It didn't help that a vision popped into her head. Both of them naked on a pile of silk and velvet, sinking in the luxurious softness with every move they made.

"Or maybe I'm here to check your diamonds."

The erotic daydream disappeared instantly. Her diamonds? She hadn't expected that. "What about them?" she answered slowly.

"You're not wearing them. Do you still have the earrings?"

"I don't wear them to work."

"Good move." Ian gave a sharp nod. "Your customers would not appreciate the fact that you had better jewelry."

Sabrina glared at him. That had nothing to do with her decision. She had just as much right to own diamonds as her customers. Even if the socialites took the time to notice her, they would assume the earrings were fake.

She felt his gaze flick down her body. She knew what he was thinking. That she intentionally dressed down. He was wrong. The gray dress and discount-store pearls had nothing to do with her customers' feelings. This was the real her.

"Where do you keep your diamonds?" Ian continued. "Do you have a safe?"

A safe? Was this guy for real? Where did he think she lived? "Once again, that is none of your business."

"No safe, huh?" He rubbed his hand against his chin. "I bet they're in your bedroom, tucked away in your jewelry box. From now on, put them either in your garage or laundry room."

"I will do no such thing." Especially since she had neither a garage nor a laundry room.

"Are the diamonds insured?"

She looked at him from the corner of her eye. "Why are you asking these questions?"

"I'll take that as a no."

"I have to ask you to leave." She moved toward the door, praying he would follow. She didn't have the strength to forcibly remove him.

"It's in your best interest to hear me out," he called after her. "I'm an investigator for an insurance company."

"Sure you are."

"I'm investigating a series of jewelry thefts in the Seattle area." His voice sounded closer. He was definitely following her. "The thief will be interested in your diamond earrings."

She didn't know what to say about that and kept walking toward the door.

"Those diamonds are something else." His tone was serious. "No jewel thief could resist them."

"You sound quite sure of that," she said crisply.

"I am."

She rested her hand against the doorknob. "Is this scare tactic some way to sell me a policy? If so, I'm not buying."

One corner of his mouth hitched up. She got the feeling Ian didn't smile very often. "I'm an investigator, not a salesman. I want to use those diamonds as bait."

"Forget it." Sabrina folded her arms across her chest. "I am not handing my jewelry over to you."

"I'm not suggesting that. I want you to wear the earrings at high-profile galas, as a guest, while my security team offers protection. We want to use the diamonds as a lure to grab the jewel thief."

Hold on. He was offering her all-access to the high-society parties, with him as her escort? Uh-huh. Right. It was too good to be true.

Ian leaned closer. "So, what do you say, Sabrina?"

Be strong . . . "No, thank you." She pushed the door open and waited for him to leave.

"Why?" He didn't seem surprised by her refusal.

"I don't trust you." It was way past time to be blunt. "There is no way you are going anywhere near my diamonds. Or me."

Challenge glimmered in his eyes. "We'll see about that. Until tonight," he said in a low voice as he walked past her.

"Good-bye, Mr. West."

"Oh, and Sabrina," Ian looked over his shoulder. "Wear the gold dress."

Ian prowled around the ballroom, glancing at the cracked ceiling mural and heavy chandeliers. How much longer until the party ended? He was bored out of his mind. He was more than ready to take the creaky elevator to his hotel suite and bolt the door shut.

Dodging couples and groups who were intent on upstaging their neighbor, he knew the tarnished elegance of the ballroom was lost on this crowd. The guests were more interested in the newest, biggest, most expensive acquisitions.

That meant the jewels were out in full force tonight. Ian

paused as he saw an elderly woman walk by wearing a tiara. Rubies, emeralds, sapphires competed with the ubiquitous diamonds.

It was a thief's paradise.

He was not going to mess up this time. Last night his attention had been on Sabrina Graham when he should have been on the lookout for other possible suspects.

It was probably a good thing Sabrina rejected his idea. He couldn't think straight around her. She was smart to keep her distance. Now if only he had the same self-discipline and could keep her from invading his mind.

His earpiece crackled. "West?"

"Yeah, Kumar?" Ian asked, turning to see the man's location. He spotted him next to the kitchen double doors.

Kumar motioned for him. "We caught her coming through the service entrance."

Sabrina was here, and Kumar's announcement kick-started his pulse. Ian strode into the loud, bustling kitchen and stopped abruptly.

Standing in the corner, with the security men flanked on either side of her, Sabrina was hard to miss. Her hair looked as soft as feathers. A dusting of gold body glitter clung to her skin. Pink diamonds sparkled at her ears.

He noticed the strapless gown she wore and his cock stirred. The bodice hugged her from her breasts to the swell of her hips, every inch encrusted with crystals. The skirt was nothing more than layers and layers of champagne-colored tulle.

She was bathed in diamonds. It was his fantasy realized.

Sabrina put her hands on her hips. "What is the meaning of this?"

"You didn't wear the gold dress," he answered hoarsely.

Her eyes narrowed into slits. Ian approached her before looking at the security men. "Give us a minute." They nodded and went back to the ballroom.

"Did you have them on the lookout for me?" she asked through clenched teeth.

"Yes. In case you changed your mind."

"Why?" She quickly lowered her voice. "I'm not the one stealing."

He flicked her earlobe with his fingertips. He shouldn't touch her, but he couldn't stop himself. "You are wearing a king's ransom."

Sabrina averted her head and covered her ear with her hand. "They didn't cost *that* much."

Then the woman got the deal of the century. "Since you won't cooperate with me, I need to keep you from these parties. It's for your own protection."

"Oh, please." Sabrina rolled her eyes. "That's a lie and you know it."

Ian felt the corner of his mouth twitch. What happened to the quiet lady he had met last night? Her good manners were slipping, revealing a fiery personality.

"It's not a lie," Ian said, "and I will enforce my decision."

Sabrina stared at him in disbelief. "You're going to bar me from every social event because I won't work with you?"

Ian rocked on his heel as if he gave her words some thought. "Yeah, I'd say that sums it up."

She scowled at him. "Since when has handling party-crashers been a part of your job description? You are looking for jewel thieves. Focus on the real criminals."

"I will once you're gone." He gestured at the service entrance. "Allow me to escort you off the premises."

There was no way she would leave quietly. She was going to negotiate. He could feel it deep in his bones. *One . . . two . . .*

Sabrina tilted her head. "Ian."

Gotcha. Ian dropped his arm. "Yes, Sabrina?"

"I've changed my mind," she said with a sweet smile that turned him inside out. "I would like to hire you as my bodyguard."

He frowned. "Bodyguard?"

She dismissed the word with the wave of her hand. "Bodyguard. Guard. Whatever. Let's work together."

"I'm glad you've come to your senses."

She laced her fingers. "I suggest we go over the rules."

Ian raised an eyebrow. "Rules? What rules?"

"You will get me into these parties, but you will not crowd me. Protect me and the diamonds at a distance. Is that understood?"

"Sabrina," he said in a low growl as he cupped her elbow with his hand. "I will get you into the parties because you will be at my side and clinging to my arm. You will stay there for the duration of the party and never leave my side."

Her arm went rigid. "You're kidding, right?"

"No."

"Come on, Ian." She stomped her foot. "How am I going to have any fun if I'm stuck to you like glue?"

"Fun?" He trailed his fingertips along the inside of her arm and felt her tremor. "Is that what you want? Then your wish is my command."

CHAPTER FOUR

SHE WAS KILLING HIM, IAN DECIDED as he watched Sabrina charm a group of elderly ladies. He stood close enough to catch the faint perfume that roared through his blood. Touching her arm and feeling the soft, warm skin.

There was no way he could last the night.

"Ian, dear," Sabrina drawled, flashing him a sly smile. "Would you fetch me a glass of champagne?"

He lifted an eyebrow. "Excuse me?"

Sabrina batted her eyelashes. He didn't like how his body clenched at her obvious tactics. It shouldn't work.

"I'm positively parched," she told him.

"Darling, you know I can't let you out of my sight for even a minute. You'll have to come with me." He nodded at the women. "Excuse us."

"Aw, Ian," she muttered as they walked away. "You are no fun."

Depends on your definition of fun . . . "I'm not your errand boy."

"How am I supposed to enjoy the party with you breathing down my neck?"

Ian stopped walking and looked down at her. "I'm sorry you can't cruise for guys. But too bad. Get used to it."

"Cruising for guys?" she repeated in disbelief. "Are you out of your mind? Do you think I do all of this to get the attention of a man?"

"Yeah, pretty much," he said as he continued to escort her around the ballroom.

Sabrina shook her head. "If that was my intent, it would be easier to strip naked and stand outside my front door."

Strip naked. Ian winced and swallowed a groan. Why did she have to say that? "Then why do you crash parties?"

Sabrina shrugged. "I like being noticed, being the center of attention, even for a few hours."

She thought she was invisible? He couldn't imagine it. He had noticed Sabrina the moment she appeared on the scene and had been unable to take his eyes off her.

She dipped her head and he knew she was uncomfortable about revealing her motives. "Where to next?" she asked. "We've hit every corner of this crowd."

"Let's dance." He wanted the excuse to touch her and hold her in his arms.

"Dance?" Her eyes widened in horror. "Is that really a good idea? No one is going to make a move while I'm on the dance floor."

"But if they haven't seen the earrings, they will now. Come on." He slipped her arm through his.

Sabrina resisted. "I don't know how to waltz or whatever it is they're doing."

"Follow my lead and you'll be fine." Ian escorted her onto the dance floor. He held her close and silently guided her through the slow, sweet, agonizing dance. Her legs and hips brushed against his. His arm banded around her back and her breasts grazed his chest.

Okay, this might be a bad idea, Ian decided as his cock twitched. He was really getting himself in trouble. He was supposed to protect Sabrina, not proposition her.

Someone tapped his shoulder. It took every ounce of his restraint not to rear back and punch the guy out, because he knew what the man was going to ask.

"May I have this dance?" the stranger asked, his eyes only on Sabrina.

Ian's muscles flexed. He wanted to refuse, but it would benefit his case to draw the thief out. It was required to accept the change of partners.

Ian reluctantly let go and stepped aside. He looked at Sabrina, who flashed a dazzling smile at her next partner. That warm welcome scored him like a knife.

He walked off the dance floor without looking back, his shoes ringing against the parquet floor. He was determined to close this case. The sooner he caught the thief, the sooner he could seduce Sabrina into his bed.

She was the belle of the ball, but somehow it wasn't what she expected. It left her empty and flat, like champagne without the bubbles.

Sabrina glanced over her partner's shoulder, meeting Ian's brooding gaze. What was he angry about? She was dancing, just like he required of her. She kept dancing, continued to accept men's invitations. If he wanted her to stop, he was more than welcome to intrude.

But he seemed perfectly capable of staying in the shadow and sulking. If this was what a bodyguard did, Sabrina might want to reconsider the idea.

"You are the most beautiful woman here," the man holding her declared.

Sabrina glanced up at her dance partner with disbelief. "Thank you." Whether he was sincere or not, it didn't seem to matter. She found herself wishing that Ian thought she was beautiful too.

Sabrina glanced at Ian again and realized that she didn't want to be the center of attention at a party. She wanted to be the sole attention of one man. Ian West.

Having his attention on her meant more than having a group of men bedazzled by her smile. She wanted to dance with him and no one else. Leave the party and take him somewhere private.

Sabrina looked for Ian. Her heart leapt in her throat as she saw him striding toward her, a dark figure cutting through the colorful crowd.

She whirled around faster and faster with her partner. She wanted to spin away, but she wanted Ian to catch her. Once he claimed her, she knew how this night would end.

She wanted it, but she wasn't sure if she was ready. Ian was unlike any man she had ever met. He would change her life, but to him she would simply be one of many forgettable women.

Was it worth it?

Her partner halted although the music swelled. Sabrina

dropped her arms as her partner backed away. Ian said something to the man, but she didn't catch it, her heart thudding in her ears.

Yes, it was worth it. She wouldn't forget this night.

Ian possessively wrapped his arm around her waist before grasping her hand with his. The ferocity in his blue eyes left her speechless.

Every flex of his arm or finger warned her of where he was leading her. He didn't have to say a word. Sabrina wouldn't have argued. He could take her wherever he wished.

He whirled her under a doorway and out of the ballroom. Ian released her from the waist but still held onto her hand. He silently directed her to the banks of elevators and pushed the button.

Sabrina's eyebrow lifted. Presumptuous, wasn't he?

Ian's eyebrow rose in arrogant response. "Don't tell me you don't want this. I know what you've been thinking on the dance floor."

"You're a mind reader? That will come in handy," she said when she finally found her voice. "Don't you think you're rushing it?"

"No."

"You haven't even kissed me." She felt the need to point that out. Hadn't he noticed? She most certainly had.

He cupped the back of her head and pulled her toward him. Sabrina's hands collided against the strong wall of his chest as Ian's mouth claimed hers.

The fierce claim sent sparks zinging through her veins. This guy wanted more than urgent lovemaking. He wanted to take her, bed her, and claim her body and soul.

Ian pulled away, his eyes glittering with desire. Sabrina

sucked on her swollen bottom lip. "So tell me," he said, "am I rushing it?"

The elevator bell chimed and the door drifted open. Now was the time to decide.

"No, you're not rushing," Sabrina said as she hooked her finger underneath his bow tie. "Actually, I've been wondering what's been taking you so long." She walked backward into the elevator and led him in before the doors shut.

The doors closed behind Ian. He pressed the floor button before she grabbed the lapels of his jacket and pulled him closer.

She kissed him hard and inhaled his scent. Her nipples beaded so tight that they stung. She wanted to pull off her dress and rip of his tuxedo. She needed see him naked and press her skin against his.

Sabrina fumbled with his bow tie, each pull and tug mimicking the pull and tug inside her. The black tie hung loose, and she started to work on his white shirt.

Ian's hand dipped under her bodice and his other hand bunched the champagne tulle. They collided against the wall, her mouth bumping and sliding against his.

He cupped her breast. The feel of his hand against her nipple made her shiver with pleasure. Her gasp echoed in the elevator when he pinched her nipple.

She was arching back, desperate for more, for his mouth to latch onto her, when she heard the elevator chime.

Sabrina froze, her muscles locking as Ian flew into action. He yanked her bodice up and pushed off the wall. Grasping her hand, he held her tightly as the door slowly wheezed open.

An older man wearing sweatpants and a wrinkled T-shirt

stepped in. He carried an ice bucket and shuffled barefoot into the elevator. "No ice," he muttered.

Sabrina gave a short nod and tight smile as her pulse screamed inside her. She didn't care about the ice! She wanted to get back to getting naked with Ian.

Her body practically vibrated with need. The elevator creaked and shook as it climbed up. The contraption seemed unusually slow. She had to have Ian. *Now.*

Sabrina fluffed her hair with a shaky hand and brushed her fingertips against the pink earrings. For once, they didn't calm her. They didn't lead the way.

Sabrina felt the old man looking at her. What? *What!* Was her lipstick smeared on her chin? Did she pop out of her dress?

"You dropped your purse."

Sabrina glanced down at the floor and saw the small metal handbag lying on the carpet.

"Oh . . . thank you."

The older man nodded and left the elevator. The moment the door closed, Ian slammed his hand against the stop button.

Sabrina ripped open his shirt, the studs popping. She skimmed her hands against his chest. His flesh was hot and smooth, framing his sculpted muscles. She pressed him against the corner and leaned into him.

As Ian stripped her of her panties, Sabrina went straight for his belt buckle and fumbled it open. She gently revealed his penis and held it in her grasp. He was hot and thick, already slapping against his belly.

Her sex clenched with anticipation as she wrapped her hand around him. She pumped her hand from the base to the tip, watching him harden and swell under her touch.

She watched, her legs wobbling, as Ian grabbed a condom from his wallet and rolled it on with minimum fuss. He backed her against the mirrored walls and wrapped her legs around his waist.

Sabrina skittered up the wall, groaning with pleasure, as Ian slid his finger into her wet, slick entrance. Her hands slid against the mirrors. The only place to hold onto was Ian's shoulders.

His hands burrowed under her puffy skirt. He teased her clit and watched her eyes sparkle with anticipation. She shuddered against his hand as the swift climax stole her breath. She rode it out, then she heard the shower of tinkling crystals.

Sabrina froze when she realized the significance of that sound. "Uh-oh."

Ian paused. "What?"

"My dress is coming apart." She looked down at the floor but couldn't see the crystals.

He closed his eyes. "I can't stop," he whispered, his voice shaking.

She didn't want him to. Looking wildly around the elevator, she saw their mirror image. She appeared flushed and wanton wrapped around Ian.

"Lie down," she told him, pushing insistently at his shoulders.

He reluctantly stepped away from her. As he lay down on the carpet, Sabrina straddled his hips and sank down on him.

Ian reared off the floor as she sheathed him to the hilt. She paused, her mouth sagging open as the wild sensations stormed her body. Her skin felt hot and tight, as if she would explode like confetti.

She glanced at the mirrored walls as Ian grabbed her hips. He rocked her against him, their joining concealed behind her voluminous skirt. The fire flared inside her again as he thrust. She rode him hard, taking him deep, until he bucked wildly. His violent release triggered her own, and she heard her small cries echoing in the elevator.

"Are you sure you don't want to stay in my hotel suite?" Ian asked as he walked her to her apartment.

Sabrina smiled, but it didn't erase the wariness in her eyes. "Thanks, but I need to repair this dress before tomorrow."

Ian tried not to wince. She'd rather spend the night with needle and thread than with him. *Ow.*

He knew she regretted their elevator encounter. He loved every hot, wild, and insane minute of it, but the moment they entered his hotel suite, she got cold feet. It seemed that once was enough for her.

Sabrina shoved the key into the door lock, her haste almost laughable. "Well, good night."

"I want to see you in."

Her gaze flicked over him. "It's not necessary."

"Yes, it is." He didn't want to leave her. He knew the moment she shut that door in his face he was going to have a very lonely night ahead of him.

"Fine, whatever," she muttered and opened the door to her apartment. She flicked on the light and stepped in.

He looked around and was surprised by what he saw. He expected glamorous touches, not the bright and cheerful decor. The studio apartment offered another facet of this woman he already found infinitely intriguing.

"Tomorrow night I have invitations to the philharmonic event. Do you want me to pick you up here or at the store?"

"Here . . ."

She wasn't listening to him. Had she already tuned him out for the night? "Sabrina? Is everything okay?"

"Yeah." She set down her purse and looked at the carpeted floor with a frown. "Yes, everything is fine."

"Cocktails are at seven and the performance is at eight-thirty." His eyes narrowed as he noticed she wasn't listening. "Followed by kinky sex in my suite."

"Okay," she said as she studied the furniture.

"I'll hold you to it." He shoved his hands in his trouser pockets. "You wanna tell me what's going on?"

"This is going to sound strange," she said, walking toward her small entertainment set. "Nothing is out of place, but it feels like someone's been here."

CHAPTER FIVE

SHE WATCHED IAN TENSE. HE WAS like a lazy, sated jungle cat revealing his claws. His face sharpened as he surveyed the small apartment. "Has anything been taken?"

"No." That's what made it so weird. But she couldn't shake it off that someone entered her house and touched her things. Not that she had a great many things someone would want to steal.

She felt stupid and wished she hadn't said anything at all. It wasn't like she wanted to prolong the evening. All she wanted to do was close a very heavy door between Ian and herself and get a grip on what had happened.

She had never acted so wantonly before, and she liked it a little too much. She couldn't imagine having such hot sex with anyone, but with Ian, she had a long list of what she wanted to do next.

Forget closing the door on Ian. She wanted to lure him into her bed and hide away from the world.

Which was so against the plan! The whole point of buying these earrings was to get out of the house, get noticed, and get a social life.

She frowned when she saw Ian crouch to study the front doorknob. "What are you doing?"

"There are scratches. Deep and fresh. Someone picked your lock."

Sabrina's eyes widened and she hurried to the door. Sure enough, there were deep grooves in the metal. "Someone did break in? For what? My TV is still here."

He rose to his full height and glanced at her ears. "For the diamonds."

"But I was wearing these tonight. Your jewel thief wouldn't waste his time." Unless he planned to lie in wait, compromise her security.

Alarm tripped down her spine. She stepped closer to Ian, seeking his strength. Sabrina glanced around her apartment as if someone could spring out like a jack-in-the-box. It was a good thing there weren't that many hiding places.

"Did you stop by here before the party?" he asked as he walked to her miniscule bathroom.

"No, I changed at work and went straight to the ball," she answered as she followed him. "Why do you ask?"

"The thief came here this afternoon." He surveyed the bathroom and stepped back out. "That's when most jewel thieves would strike."

"Are you sure?"

"Definitely." He now made his way to the kitchen area.

"Socialites are known to lay out their gowns and jewels before heading to the salon."

"And the thief thought I would do the same?" Sabrina looked around her apartment. "I don't live like a socialite."

"But you might have laid out your outfit so you could change immediately after work. And this apartment complex would have been empty during the early afternoon."

"You know," she said as he leaned against the kitchen counter, "we're assuming it was your jewel thief. Those scratches look very amateurish. It could be your run-of-the-mill burglar." Hmm . . . that possibility was not making her feel better.

He tested the kitchen window. "Picking a lock is not as easy as it's shown on TV."

A trickle of unease crept down her spine. Forcing her tone to remain light, Sabrina asked, "And how would you know? Picked a few locks in your time?"

He glanced at her. "Yeah, it used to be my specialty."

"Do you mean . . . ?" Nooo, she must have misunderstood.

He double-checked the lock on the window. "Best way to catch a thief is to hire another thief."

She stared at him, her mouth gaping open.

The corner of his lips hitched up with a knowing smile. "Retired thief, that is."

Great. She had just had sex with a thief. Was he staring at her diamonds the entire time? Oh, man. She didn't want to think about it.

Forget that. She agreed for a *thief* to act as her bodyguard? Stupid, stupid, stupid!

"I think we're through here." Ian took her arm and headed for the door.

"We are? Where are *we* going?"

"Back to my hotel room."

Oh, no, no, no. She wasn't going to fall for that. "That's not necessary."

He cast a quick look at her. "Do you really want to stay here?"

"Well . . ." She looked around her studio apartment. She didn't want to be here alone and unprotected.

"You'll be safe at my place," he said as he guided her out the door.

Ha. "How can you say that? You're a thief," she whispered in case the neighbors were listening.

He took the keys from her hands and locked her front door. "Ex-thief."

"Prove it."

"I don't need to." He dropped the keys into her hands.

She gripped the metal with her fist. "You mean you can't. How did you get your job as an insurance investigator?" A thought occurred to her. "You aren't really one, are you?"

"Yeah, I really am," he answered, escorting her back to his car. "And that's how I became one. I know how a thief's mind works."

"This revelation is not endearing me to you," she muttered as she stuffed her key chain back into her purse.

"A jewel thief's mind views a theft like a puzzle. I can usually see how a thief would approach a situation and be there before he does."

"Did you know he was going to break into my apartment?"

He paused as he opened the passenger door and watched her slide in. "No, that's a surprise. It doesn't fit the profile.

This thief works alone, and he doesn't do breaking and entering. Every thief has a specialty, you know."

"What was yours?"

"Doesn't matter." He closed the door and walked around the hood to his side. When he opened the driver door, he continued. "The thief I'm after usually makes the steal at the party. You know, takes pickpocketing to a new level. Very ballsy. B and E wouldn't give him the same thrill."

"Maybe he doesn't think he can get the earrings because you are always hanging around me," Sabrina suggested.

"But he wouldn't change his methods." Ian started the car. "He would stick with what he does best, but find a smarter route."

"Whatever." She pressed her lips together as her mind whirled with all this new information. It wasn't until they were back on the road that it occurred to her. "You know what this means, don't you? You pushed the man too far. I now have a desperate criminal after me. Thanks a lot."

"You're going to be fine." He covered her hand with his. "I'm going to protect you."

She watched him lace their fingers. His strength gave her comfort, and she wanted to believe him. But what did she really know about Ian West? She thought of him as protective and strong, but her instincts also suggested he had a strong code of honor.

"Since we don't know when he will strike," Ian continued, "I'm going to be with you all the time."

"Could you not use the word 'strike'?" Sabrina pulled her hand away.

He put both hands back on the steering wheel. "To be on the safe side, you should wear the earrings constantly."

That she could do, but it would increase the possibility of finding trouble. "How does that make me safe?"

"When the guy makes his move"—his voice turned gruff—"I'm going to be there and take him down."

"You can't watch over me all the time," Sabrina pointed out. "I have to work."

He gave a shrug. "I'll go with you."

"At a dress shop? Think again." She shook her head. "My boss would have a fit."

"We'll figure something out, but right now, you're going to be at my side twenty-four seven."

"Oh, joy."

"Sorry, what?"

"Ian"—she looked straight at him—"what did you steal when you were a thief?"

His gaze flicked over her. "Diamonds."

Sabrina turned and stared out the window. She refused to say anything more. Now if only her earlobes would stop tingling.

Ian leaned against the bedroom door and watched Sabrina toss and turn in his bed. He wanted to join her, but he bet he wouldn't be welcomed. He shouldn't have told her about his past.

But his days as a thief didn't mean he couldn't protect her and her diamonds. He would do everything in his power to keep her safe. Only this thief was confusing the hell out of him.

Or was it that Sabrina was distracting him?

Probably both, he admitted to himself as he entered the room. He had a job, an obligation, and he was sticking to it.

Sabrina was relying on him and he couldn't let her down.

He rubbed his face with his hands and let the tiredness wash over him. Shucking off his tuxedo and allowing it to fall into a heap on the carpet, he quietly slid into bed.

"Uh, what are you doing?" Sabrina sounded wide awake.

"I'm going to sleep." He extinguished the light.

"You can sleep on the sofa."

"You have got to be kidding me." Turning to his side, he curled her back against his chest. She felt good. Warm. His hand spanned along her flat stomach.

"Ian," she murmured.

If she suggested the floor, he was taking her with him. "Mm?"

"Are you out to steal my earrings?"

His heart clenched at her question. Ian glanced at the pink diamonds that caught the moonlight. The heat of interest was dim compared to how he felt about her. That was dangerous.

"No." His voice sounded rough. "I'm not after your diamonds."

She rolled onto her back. "Are you sure? You took your time answering."

"I'm after you."

He saw her smile in the shadows. "You already have me. What more do you want?"

Ian answered by sliding his hand down her naked body. He spanned his fingers over her sex and eased a fingertip into her moist cleft. He loved the sound of her gasp and dipped his finger in farther.

Sabrina silently hooked one leg over his, giving him more access. He toyed with her clit before plunging his finger in deeper. She flexed and bowed against him.

Ian kissed the length of her throat before catching her ear-lobe with his teeth. Her gasp rang out and she tensed before she tugged her way to freedom.

Why did she pull away? Because he hit a sensitive spot? Or because she didn't trust him near the pink ice? No problem, Ian decided as he inched his way down the bed. He'll stay away—far away—from the diamonds.

He reached out and cupped her breast, enjoying the weight and warmth of her. Brushing his thumbs against her nipples, he felt them tighten under his touch.

Sabrina dipped her head, almost shyly, as she arched her back. A fierce, primitive emotion stormed through him. She was offering herself to him. As much as he enjoyed the chase, this moment made it worth it.

Ian's heart hammered against his chest as he bracketed his hands next to her shoulders and hovered above her. His cock twitched. There was nothing more he would like to do than possess Sabrina. Claim her. Drive into her.

It took all of his restraint to lean down and kiss her, drifting down to her throat and capturing the peak of her breast with his mouth. He stayed clear of her diamonds.

He loved how she writhed underneath him, her fingers threading through his hair. He traveled down her ribs, down her stomach. When he dipped his tongue into her navel, she quaked violently.

Ian held her tight, placing gentle kisses against her sweat-slick skin, listening to her whisper incoherently. He kissed along her pelvis bone and felt her muscles tighten with antici-pation. Nudging her knees with his shoulders, he knelt be-tween her legs. He stroked her with his fingers, teasing her clit with his thumb. His fingers glistened with her arousal.

He dipped his head and tasted her. Her muscles contracted, then swelled under his tongue as she flexed her hips. He drove his tongue into her, licking and teasing until a keening cry escaped from her throat.

She collapsed back onto the bed, catching her breath. Ian reached for the bedside table and grabbed the foil packet. After sheathing himself with a condom, he reached for Sabrina again.

Sliding his palms under her hips, Ian drove his cock into her. Sabrina lurched off the mattress, her breath hitching in her throat. Ian remembered that sound. He knew that Sabrina was about to lose all control.

He slowed his pace when all he really wanted to do was plow into her. The slower he went, the wilder Sabrina became. Tossing, rocking underneath him, trying to get him to move faster.

Her fingers dug into his back. His skin was dripped with sweat, his heart pounding fiercely. She looked at him, her brown eyes filled with wonder and awe, and it was enough to drive him over the edge.

Now if only she looked at him like that out of bed. . . .

Chapter Six

IAN SWIRLED HIS DRINK IN THE glass as he sat in the suite's dressing room. He had always wondered why an armchair was provided in what amounted to a large closet. Now he understood how the other half lived.

Sprawling his legs before him, Ian leaned back in the chair and watched Sabrina dress for another night out. Watching her get ready was like seeing her strip in reverse. The highly erotic show was a highlight of his evening.

Wearing nothing but a mint-green silk robe, Sabrina sat in front of the dressing table, dabbing perfume on her skin. It was one of the many gifts he bought for her over the past two weeks. She assumed the purchases were part of the job, but in all honesty, they were for his personal enjoyment.

"I don't know, Ian," Sabrina said as she skimmed the perfume stopper down her throat. "I don't think the jewel thief is going to attend an outdoor concert at a winery. It's not grand enough."

"He'll be there."

"How much do you want to bet that he's not even around?" She dabbed the crook of her elbow and the inside of her wrist. "The thief hasn't struck since the botanical garden party."

That lack of hits worried Ian, but not for the reason Sabrina offered. He knew the thief had been spending all of his energy and time coming up with a plan to get the earrings.

"He's still around."

She glanced up at the mirror and their gaze met in the reflection. He knew what she thought. She didn't like how well he understood the mind of a thief. And there were moments when she questioned if he was truly retired.

How could she think he was after the diamonds? Now that he thought about it, how could this woman share his bed but be incapable of sleeping in front of him? Whenever he woke up, she was already out of bed.

She had trouble trusting him, but that didn't stop her from indulging in mind-boggling sex. She would let him do anything to her—just don't touch the ears. He was beginning to have some amazing, somewhat bizarre fantasies about those ears.

"What's up?" she asked as she put the perfume away. "You look very intent."

"Thinking of strategies," he lied. "The thief is clever."

Sabrina turned around to face him. "I think the thief is a woman."

Ian raised his eyebrow. "Because the thief is clever?"

"Because she can grab a woman's jewelry with a lot less notice than a man could. You know how women do all that leaning in and air-kissing? Or when everyone goes into the ladies' room and refreshes their makeup?"

Sabrina had a point. "A man could do the same," Ian pointed out. "He could meet the woman in a secluded place and grab the jewel while distracting her. The victim would hesitate to tell the authorities what really happened."

She scrunched her nose at his idea. "I like my theory better."

"You know, you're good at this." Her insights and ability at improvisation had come in handy. Not to mention the fact that she was born to wear a party dress. "You should go into this kind of work."

"Thank you," she said as her cheeks turned pink. "But I don't have the nerves."

"Yeah, you do. Anyone who can crash a party and walk around like she's the guest of honor has nerves of steel."

"That's true." She rose from her seat and walked to the closet. "But some of these parties are more fun when you sneak in."

He knew exactly what she meant. There were parties where he entertained himself by thinking of all the different ways he could break in. "You're already becoming jaded," Ian teased her. "Soon you'll want to stay in and have an early night."

"No way. I've spent too many years as a homebody."

"Nothing's wrong with that." He kind of liked the idea of staying home, curled up on the sofa with Sabrina.

"You have no idea how lonely it can be." She shrugged off her robe and let it fall onto the carpet. "I'm the first a friend will call when they need help, but they never seem to remember me when it's a celebration."

"Uh . . ." Whoa. She stood nude before him. The mirrors gave him infinite images of her glorious beauty.

"I spent too many years waiting to get invited to the parties." She grabbed the diaphanous pink dress from the hanger and slipped it over her head. "It's time to play catch-up."

His brain sputtered back to life. Did he black out and miss something? Was that all she planned to wear? "You're—y—"

"What?" She checked her reflection in the mirror.

His black tie suddenly felt too tight. "You're naked under that."

"You noticed. This just came into the store. What do you think?" She whirled around in it, dangerously close to revealing what was underneath.

"The dress is"—he swallowed roughly—"tiny."

"Yeah, that's the point." She twirled again and the hem flirted and teased his imagination.

His cock hardened. "Wow."

"Well, come on." She slipped her feet into a pair of sparkly slides. "Time to party."

Ian took a final gulp of his drink. Knowing that she was completely naked under that slip of a dress was going to drive him insane.

That was one other thing he had noticed since he started escorting Sabrina—the parties were never boring.

During the concert intermission, as they walked along the grounds of the winery to the main building, Sabrina had a hunch she was right. The jewel thief was not going to make his or her presence known tonight. There were not enough big jewels around to tempt him.

The summer night's breeze skipped along her bare arms.

The dress had been a mistake. Although she had received many compliments, she found herself curling into Ian for warmth. The last thing she needed was an excuse to touch him. The smoldering looks he kept giving her were already setting her on edge.

As they stepped into the tasting room, she noticed it was much warmer, thanks in part to the crowd. She slowly circled the room with Ian, but the concertgoers proved to be more interested in music and wine than diamonds. That was fine with her; she wanted to keep Ian's attention all to herself.

With the flex of his fingers that lingered on her hip, she knew Ian was leading her to the wine cellars and then the barrel aging room. The guests milling about grew fewer and fewer.

They stepped into the barrel aging area and Sabrina clenched her teeth when the cold air hit her. As their shoes echoed in the cavernous room, she noticed they were the only ones in there. "Are we allowed to wander around like this?"

"Has that stopped you before?"

Sabrina nudged his arm with her shoulder while they walked down one long row. "I mean it. I have no interest in getting frisked by security tonight."

"Neither do I." Ian's hand drifted to cup her bottom. The possessive touch sent sparks down her pelvis and legs. Throughout the concert, she had been keenly aware of her lack of clothes, especially when Ian placed his hand on her bare thigh. His simple touches teased her senses.

Considering how they were touching and clinging to one another, it's no wonder an attempt hadn't been made on her earrings. She should step away and wander around on her own, for the sake of the case. But she didn't have the willpower. She couldn't remember the last time she had felt this protected and cherished.

Cherished. She wrapped her arms around her, savoring the word. Her handbag slipped from her hands. She bent down to retrieve it, the cold air prickling her skin.

She shot back up to her full height, her purse forgotten, when she heard Ian's groan. "Ian? Are you okay?"

His gaze didn't move away from her hemline. "You shouldn't move like that."

Sabrina tried to hold back her sly smile. "Sorry, I forgot. What if I do this?" She genuflected, touching the floor with one knee. The cold wind traveled up her dress as the hem bunched dangerously high.

A ruddy stain covered his cheeks. "Sabrina."

"Okay, I won't do that," she promised, and got back up.

"If you drop something," he said in a low growl, "I will pick it up for you."

"I can't let you do that," she said as they walked farther down the row. "You're not my errand boy, remember?"

"I'll make the exception for tonight."

She looked around, verifying that they were truly alone. "What if I go like this?" Sabrina reached down and touched her toes. She kept her knees locked and straight.

Yep, that yoga exercise video was finally paying off. She smiled when she felt his hands cup her bare buttocks.

Sabrina slowly straightened, but Ian didn't take his hand away. Instead, he stood directly behind her. "Do that again." His gruff request bordered on a plea.

A hot, naughty thrill zipped low in her belly. She slowly stretched down and touched her toes. She teetered in the slides, but it was the inquisitive caress of Ian's finger that made her knees shake.

"You're already wet for me," he murmured as he stroked his finger along her slit.

Of course she was, Sabrina thought as she bit down on her bottom lip before her moan bounced off the barrels. All Ian had to do was look at her and she was ready.

"I want you." He bucked his pelvis against her bare skin. His trousers felt rough against her skin. "Let's forget the concert and go back to the hotel."

Sabrina rose slightly, grasping her knees with her hands. She looked over her shoulder and offered him what she hoped was a seductive smile. "Take me here," she said in a whisper.

She turned back to face the wall as she heard the metallic rasp of his zipper and then the crinkle of foil. Sabrina nearly jumped when she felt Ian sliding his hand down her spine and guiding her back down.

It was surprising that the barrel aging room didn't feel so cold anymore. As she placed her hands on the floor, her legs felt wobbly and her stretched muscles tingled. Ian rubbed his cock against her wet sex. She parted her legs slightly as the head of his cock nudged her opening.

Ian clasped his hands onto her hips and slowly entered her. She could feel him shake with restraint as his fingers clenched her hips. She drew in a deep breath as he filled her.

He shook with restraint as his pelvis rocked against her slit and teased her clitoris. White-hot pleasure sparkled and rippled under her skin as he pushed and withdrew. She could feel her flesh swell and contract, her legs shaking as his strokes grew faster.

Sabrina moaned as he hit the sweet spot. She flattened her hands on the floor as her world tilted and twirled. Ian's harsh groan of release sounded far away as vibrant colors exploded beneath her closed lids when she came.

She remained in her position, suddenly unsure which way was up. She grabbed her purse with clumsy fingers and Ian assisted her to a standing position. She felt light-headed and dizzy, black dots dancing before her eyes. Her knees threatened to crumple underneath her.

"Are you okay?" he asked, his mouth against her ear.

"Mm-hmm." She pressed a shaky hand against her flushed face. "Just give me a minute."

Leaning against the wall as Ian straightened his clothes, Sabrina took a few deep breaths to compose herself. The world slowly started to right itself, and her body ached with satisfaction and heat.

"Let's go back to the hotel," Ian suggested again as he pulled up his zipper.

Eagerness pulsed through her. She was as insatiable as Ian, Sabrina realized, her lips forming a tired smile. She'd pushed herself off the wall when she noticed the discarded foil wrapper on the floor. "Wait. We should pick this up."

As she bent down to retrieve the wrapper she heard a woman gasp down the row of barrels. "Sabrina?"

She jerked up at the familiar sound. Ignoring the dizzy spell, Sabrina turned around to face her boss's appalled expression.

"Sabrina Graham," Sloane said through clenched teeth as anger pinched her face. "What are you doing in that dress?"

CHAPTER SEVEN

"It's finally hitting me that I got fired," Sabrina told Ian as he opened the door to the hotel suite. "Wow. I've never been fired before. It kind of sucks."

"Yeah, it kind of does." Ian clicked on the lights, wishing he could make things better. He hated feeling powerless. "I'm sorry."

"At least she didn't call the police." She turned and flashed him a wan smile. "Thanks to your fast thinking."

More like his fat wallet, but Sabrina didn't know about that yet. "Not much good it did. You lost your job." This time he couldn't solve the puzzle to make everything work in their favor. Ian felt he'd failed Sabrina.

"It wasn't that fantastic of a career." She tossed the small purse onto the table. She turned suddenly and tipped her forehead against his chest.

Ian froze, holding his arms out, not sure what he should

do. His heart clenched as he slowly wrapped his arms around Sabrina and held her close. From her choppy sigh, it sounded like he had made the right move.

"I don't know how I'm going to keep up with the clothes for the upcoming parties," she said against his shirt.

"Don't worry about it." Ian rubbed gentle circles along her back in an attempt to comfort her.

She sighed deeply. "I shouldn't be so surprised that I got fired. Sloane knew something was up and started doing inspections."

"So what? You were a good walking advertisement for the shop."

Sabrina looked up at him and smiled. "I was, wasn't I? Oh, what am I saying? Everyone saw the diamonds, not the dress."

"That isn't true." Everyone saw a sexy, confident woman. At least, he did. The dress and the earrings added to the exquisite vision.

"Yeah, it is." Tears glistened in her brown eyes.

"Let's look at the bright side. You don't have to deal with Sloane anymore."

That gentle smile was back. "True."

"And you don't have to worry about anyone connecting you with the dress shop."

"That is also true. And I still have my diamonds." Her smile dipped. "But not for much longer."

"What do you mean?"

"I don't know how I'm going to pay these off, now that I don't have a job." She staggered to the nearest chair and sat down with a thump. "It's a good thing Lindsay chipped in."

He tilted his head and stared at her. What did Lindsay have to do with the earrings?

"I don't want to have to tell her that when I give them to her next week. I can already guess what the lecture will be. Older sisters do that."

"What are you talking about?"

"Lindsay," Sabrina said as she fluffed her short hair with her fingers. "She's my older sister."

Ian batted down his annoyance. He knew that. He'd learned everything about Sabrina over the past few weeks. "Why are you giving her the diamonds?"

"You don't know? I didn't tell you?"

A bad feeling pressed against his sternum. "No."

"I got these earrings at an auction." Sabrina jiggled her ear-lobes, and the overhead light hit the diamonds. "But I couldn't afford them on my own. My sisters Lindsay and Nicole share the earrings equally."

He stared at her. Of all the stuff they'd talked about, she didn't think to tell him this important detail?

"Next week my month is up and then I give them to my sister. God knows why." She bumped her head against the high back of the chair. "All she does is put them in her safety deposit box until her month is up."

Ian rubbed his forehead as a headache bloomed. "And then you don't get the earrings again for another month?"

"Two months," she corrected him as she slipped off her shoes. "Nicole gets them after Lindsay."

"So as of next week, we don't have any bait."

Sabrina shrugged and wearily closed her eyes. "I can ask Lindsay if I can keep the earrings for a while longer. But I can't guarantee that she'll agree."

"Tell her the truth." Ian placed his hands on his hips. "She'll be happy to help."

"Think again." Sabrina's eyes opened wide. "You didn't exactly convince me when you told *me* the truth."

"Give it a try." Ian knew Sabrina was right, but he didn't have any alternatives. His only hope was that the jewel thief would make his move soon. He was ready to take on whatever the guy had up his sleeve. Anticipation coiled tight around his chest.

But it also meant he only had one more week with Sabrina.

He wasn't ready for that.

"You lost your job?" Lindsay's voice carried through the shabby hotel bar.

Sabrina winced and motioned for her sister to lower her voice. "Lindsay, please, no lecturing." She wasn't up to it on a good day, and she could barely get through the hour without tearing up.

After all that Sabrina had done to get her Cinderella moment, it didn't last as long as she would have liked. The clock was about to strike twelve and she was going back to the dull, dreary world.

Only this time, she didn't have a job. Or Ian. She glanced at the shadowy corner where Ian was watching over her. Life really wasn't fair.

"And what are you doing wearing those earrings in broad daylight?" Lindsay pointed at the diamonds. "On the streets of Seattle? Have you lost your mind?"

"Can we get back to the matter at hand?" Sabrina motioned for the waitress, but the woman didn't seem to notice. Typical. "You know, there is a jewel thief after these earrings. . . ."

"All the more reason to lock them up tight." Lindsay

grabbed her black purse and opened it. "Give them to me and I will put them in my safety deposit box right now."

"I can't do that." If she quit now, Ian would never catch the thief. He wouldn't track down his client's jewels. All of the time they'd spent together would have been in vain. She didn't want to be a regret.

"Is this because you have the hots for your bodyguard?" She glanced out of the corner of her eye and studied Ian.

"He's more than a bodyguard."

"Oh, no." Lindsay drew the word out. "Oh, please, no."

Sabrina hunched her shoulders. "What?"

"You're falling for him!" She clasped the side of her head as if she'd suddenly developed a migraine. "Don't do that! Get a grip!"

Too late. "Why can't I do that?"

"Okay, look." She flattened her hands on the table and leaned forward. "I understand he's sexy, he has that tough, craggy look going for him, and it's obvious that he's totally into you."

Sabrina perked up with that last insight. "It is?"

"But he's dangling you like bait. Do you think he cares what happens to your diamonds? No, he doesn't." Lindsay shook her head in case Sabrina wasn't getting the message. "And do you know why? Because protecting your diamonds isn't his job."

Lindsay made a very good point, but Sabrina knew Ian cared. It was more than instinct or wishful thinking. Or was it? "I volunteered to be the bait."

Her older sister rolled her eyes. "Because he looks good in a tuxedo, right?"

"Because I wanted to have the time of my life," Sabrina admitted. "And guess what? I am."

"I'm sure you are, but wait until you wake up with a handful of bills and a broken heart."

"It's not because I have a gorgeous guy at my side, or because I get to dress up and drink champagne every night," Sabrina insisted. "It's because for once I'm not standing on the sidelines waiting for life to happen. I'm not keeping quiet. I'm not keeping my head down waiting to get noticed."

"And look where it got you." Lindsay made a flourishing move with her wrist. "Unemployed."

"I lost my job because I took dresses from the shop without permission."

"Why did you do that in the first place? That is so unlike you." Lindsay's jaw shifted to the side. "Did he put you up to it?"

"No! This was all my doing. I knew there was a possibility that I would get caught, but I did it anyway." Sabrina tried to flag down the waitress one more time, waving her arms as if she were directing air traffic. "And you know what? It was worth it."

Her sister looked at her as if she had sprouted another head. "Why would you do something so stupid?"

"Lindsay, I was stuck in that job for years, always listening to these women brag or complain about a life I never got a glimpse of. But once I saw those diamonds, I knew life could be different. *I* could be different."

"Great." Lindsay leaned back in her chair. "You're pretending to be Lia Dash. It's time for you to seek counseling."

"I'm not being Lia," Sabrina said as she gritted her teeth. "I'm being me. It just took Lia's earrings to give me the courage."

"I don't understand," Lindsay said, shaking her head. "They are diamonds; they aren't magic."

"I'm aware of that." An edge crept into Sabrina's voice and she did nothing to soften it. "The earrings make me feel special. That's all that matters."

"Don't get used to it," Lindsay warned. "Those earrings are mine in two days."

"I know." So much for convincing Lindsay to let her hold onto them for a little longer. She had a feeling it wouldn't work.

"And then what are you going to do?"

"Learn how to have the time of my life without them," she answered with a brave smile.

But she wasn't so certain. Forget about the parties or the fancy hotel. What about Ian? Would he find her so special without the diamonds?

CHAPTER EIGHT

SABRINA SAT IN FRONT OF THE dressing table, listlessly sweeping the perfume stopper against her throat. She stared blankly at her reflection. The sparkling earrings, the silver Grecian gown, the professional coiffed hair were perfect for a fairy-tale night at the charity ball.

But she didn't want to go. She wished she could stay in the hotel suite with Ian. This would be their final night together. The last thing she wanted to do was share him with a hundred other people.

The past couple of days had been tense. She probably shouldn't have told Ian that someone had made a grab for her earrings when she was in the hotel spa. At least, she thought someone had yanked her ears while her body was wrapped up like a mummy. She couldn't say for sure, since her eyes were covered with cucumbers.

It didn't help with Ian prowling around the suite, trying to

figure out how the thief's mind worked. He had been so focused on the puzzle that there were times he hadn't noticed
her walk into the room.

That shouldn't have bothered her, but it was a clear sign
that the end was near. He was already pulling away. She
couldn't believe how much she missed being the center of his
attention.

Now it was the last night, Sabrina thought as she slipped
on a pair of heels. As of tomorrow, Lindsay got the diamonds.
She didn't seem to care that she was taking away Sabrina's fantasy life with the pink ice. Older sisters were unsympathetic
creatures.

"Remember, Sabrina," Ian said as he strode into the suite's
dressing room, putting on his tuxedo jacket. "Stay close to me
at all times. Do not accept any dances, do not—you know
what? Just don't let go of my arm."

Sabrina nodded silently. They'd already been through this
a thousand times.

"The thief might not even be there tonight. I hope he is,"
Ian said. "This is our last opportunity."

Sabrina kept nodding while she collected her purse.

"He's going to do what he does best: grab the jewels at the
party. We've made it virtually impossible for him to get the
diamonds, so he's going to raise it to the next level."

If this was Ian's pep talk, she didn't want to hear his
gloom-and-doom speech. "Okay."

He stood in front of her and grasped her shoulders. "You
have nothing to worry about, Sabrina. I'm going to take care
of you."

"You mean the diamonds."

His eyes narrowed. "I mean you."

"I'm going to be fine." A small smile danced on her mouth as she patted his shoulder. "I've seen to it."

Suspicion crept into his harsh face. "What are you talking about?"

Sabrina's smile brightened. Her plan was working. She just might pull this off!

"What?" His fingers flexed and bit into her shoulders. "What's going on?"

"You didn't notice."

"Notice what?" Impatience burred his voice.

"I'm not wearing the diamonds," she announced softly.

He glanced at her ears. "What are you talking about? You—" His eyes widened.

"Lindsay sent a copy of the diamonds to the hotel. They're costume jewelry. You wouldn't know it unless you got very close."

Worry clouded his eyes. "That's not going to fool the thief."

"You didn't notice," she pointed out and leaned against his chest.

"I'm not willing to take this risk."

"I am." She slipped something into his inside jacket pocket. Ian immediately covered her hand with his.

"What was that?" His sharp tone clipped his words.

"The real earrings."

His hand gripped hers. "You're giving me your earrings?"

Sabrina straightened the lapel of his jacket. "For the night. I want them somewhere safe."

She watched the play of muscles in the strong column of his throat. "You trust me?" he finally asked.

"Yes." It took her a while to figure it out. Ian was an

ex-thief, but then, so was she. Whether it was diamonds or dresses, they both had made their mistakes.

He turned abruptly. "I'm going to put them in the hotel safe."

"No good. This thief would have paid a hotel staff member to keep an eye out for anything like that."

Ian growled in the back of his throat.

"You know I'm right."

Ian stopped and dipped his head. "This is a bad idea."

She took his hand in hers. "No, it's going to work."

"These earrings are not in the safest place." He tapped the pocket. "The guy has taken pickpocketing to a new level. You don't want your diamonds on me."

"Yes, I do." She knew Ian West was the kind of man who would protect her and take care of what was important. It wasn't some sort of test. She knew it and wasn't going to second-guess herself.

"And if the real diamonds get stolen?"

She knew what he was really asking. She stood on her tiptoes and kissed him softly on the cheek. "Then I won't blame you."

Ian closed his eyes as if he were in pain. "Sabrina . . ."

"Come on, Ian." She tugged him to the door. "We don't want to be late. It's time to catch a thief."

Ian held Sabrina's hand firmly in his grip. He wasn't letting her out of his reach, let alone out of his sight.

He was constantly aware of the diamonds in his pocket. They weren't that big, yet he could feel them poking. Prodding. Scoring his skin.

He was really losing it.

"Ian," Sabrina said, leaning against his arm. "You are going to have to let go of me sometime."

Pain ripped a jagged hole through his chest. He wasn't ready to let her go. He didn't want this to be their last night.

"Ian?"

"If the thief makes his move tonight, you could be in danger," he said as he scanned the room again.

"You knew that the minute I was involved in this sting," she reminded him lightly.

Ian closed his eyes with regret. The idea had seemed idiotically simple: Catch the thief and get the girl.

He hadn't expected to put Sabrina in danger. He didn't predict that he would fall this hard for her and muddle his strategic thinking. So much for being an expert on investigation and deduction.

That didn't matter right now. He wanted to hide her and keep her safe. Even if it meant letting the thief get away.

"It's going to be okay."

"I don't want anything to happen to you."

"That's the problem, Ian," she said with a soft sigh. "I'm twenty-seven years old and nothing has happened to me."

"You know what I mean."

Sabrina pouted her lips, wet and rosy from the champagne. The small, manipulative move was enough to make his pulse race as he imagined those plump lips encircling his cock.

"Sabrina . . ." He meant it as a warning, but it came out as a groan.

She leaned into him, her breasts pressing against his arm as she whispered in his ear. "I promise I'll be good."

He didn't want *that* necessarily.

"I'll do a quick circle around the room," she bargained. The eagerness in her voice was crystal clear. "Say hello to a few people, ask that woman if that's a Versace she's wearing, and I'll be back before you know it."

He shouldn't refuse.

"And if someone looks remotely suspicious, you can tackle him," Sabrina tossed in the bargain.

"Okay."

"Okay? Really?" She studied his tight expression. "It was the promise of violence that tipped you over, huh?"

"But you are going to owe me for this."

She flashed him a look of amused disbelief. "Says who?"

"Says me." He tightened his grasp on her hand and brushed his thumb against hers. "And I'll decide on my payment when you get back."

Sabrina waggled her eyebrows. "Can't wait to hear what you have in mind."

"Then I suggest you hurry back." He released her, his heart caught in his throat. He hadn't felt this afraid since the first time he had been caught stealing. And then he had been surrounded by trigger-happy guards.

Sabrina slowly walked the perimeter of the hall and schmoozed. It was as if she drew in the energy from the room and let it radiate from her, more powerful and brilliant than before.

He watched her turn and make her way to the back of the room, his stomach already in knots. She should stay away from the French doors and move to the center of the room. Ian wanted to call her over and haul her against his side.

She glided from one corner to the next, and Ian felt the

shift in his chest. He loved this woman but he couldn't stay. His next case was already waiting. Would Sabrina be interested in joining him? Permanently?

What was stopping him from asking, besides the fact that he had no idea what her answer would be? He would ask her. Tonight. Here and now, he decided as he watched her stroll back to him, the sway of her hips matching the ache in his groin.

When was the stupid party going to end? There was nothing he wanted more than to take Sabrina back to the hotel suite and throw her onto the bed.

There must have been something in his expression. A blush suffused her cheeks and her lips held a wicked tilt. Hot desire kicked in his veins. He stood still, waiting for Sabina to come to him. Enjoying her full attention as she came closer . . . closer . . .

The chandeliers flickered. Ian blinked, and the room plunged into darkness.

CHAPTER NINE

A SUDDEN HUSH SWEPT ACROSS THE room. "Sabrina?" Ian called out, shattering the eerie silence.

He moved through the sea of people who stood like statues. His heart missed a beat when she didn't reply. He pushed and shoved to the spot he last saw her. "Sabrina!"

His foot bumped something soft and he felt it skitter on the smooth floor. Ian reached down to retrieve it as the generator kicked on, flooding the room with lights.

He was holding Sabrina's handbag.

Ian surveyed the crowd, his heart pounding hard. He saw the doors leading to the grounds and ran outside, hearing his security men run behind him.

"Sabrina?" he yelled. A flash of silver peeked along the stone balustrade. He heard grunts and a muffled scream and ran to the railing.

He came to an abrupt standstill when he saw two women

in evening gowns wrestling in the dirt. Sabrina was much smaller than the other woman, but she didn't let that stop her as she yanked the long blond hair of her opponent.

The other woman was dressed in a strapless black gown, looking less than elegant as she kicked the feet out from under Sabrina. Sabrina yelped and made a grab for the thin, tanned woman, pulling her down along with her. The silver and black dresses flipped and twisted over each other.

Ian had put his foot on the rail and was ready to jump over when Sabrina got the edge of the struggle. With a loud, satisfied grunt, she pinned her opponent to the dirt.

"Sabrina, are you okay?"

She looked up, her smiling face streaked with dirt. "Of course. I grew up with two sisters and one bathroom. I know how to fight."

He jumped over the railing and landed in a crouch beside the women.

"Show-off," Sabrina muttered.

"How else—" He caught a glimpse of the vicious tear in her gown. "Never mind."

"I think I found your jewel thief," she said proudly.

"Jewel thief?" the blond woman shrieked. "Are you crazy?"

"What makes you so sure?" Ian asked.

"The way she keeps grabbing for my ears is a pretty good indication."

He nodded. "I would say so."

"I did no such thing!" the woman said, her eyes wide with indignation. "The lights go out and suddenly this woman attacks me."

"You are so full of it," Sabrina said.

"Sabrina," Ian said, "you can get off her now."

"Oh, right." She jumped up and watched him yank the thief up by her arm. "I told you it was a woman."

"Yes, you did." He looked at Sabrina just when a glimmer of recognition brightened her eyes.

"Hey, it's the Missoni girl!" Sabrina announced, pointing her finger at the thief.

"What?"

"The botanical garden party. She knew my dress was a Missoni and asked where I got it. She showed more interest in the dress than in my earrings." Sabrina pointed her finger at the blond woman. "That was sneaky of you."

The thief rolled her eyes. "I don't know what you're talking about. I happen to be married to a very wealthy man, and he is going to sue you."

"Oooh, I'm scared." Sarcasm dripped from Sabrina's words.

Ian sensed his coworker walking beside him, having prudently taken the stairs. "Kumar, watch over her as we wait for the police."

"Sure thing, West." He grabbed hold of the woman's arms and held them behind her back.

"Excuse me, but do you know who I am?" the woman asked in a haughty tone. When no one responded, she flipped back her long hair and announced: "I am Mercer Whitley-Cooke. My husband is—"

"Going to have to call a lawyer for you," Kumar finished for her as he took her away.

"Come here, Sabrina," Ian said as he shrugged off his jacket and draped it on her shoulders. "I think you need to sit down."

"I'm fine. Never better. That was—whoa!" She grabbed onto him as her knees caved in. "Ian?"

"I'm right here." And if he had anything to say about it, he always would be.

"Well, we did it!" Sabrina announced as they enter the hotel suite. Her blood was fizzing like champagne.

"Yes, we did," Ian replied as he closed the door behind them. "We make a good team."

"That was kind of fun." Minus that one moment of complete terror when she was grabbed from behind and dragged out of the ball.

"No, it wasn't. I couldn't find you."

"But you did." She knew he would.

"Almost too late."

"I flipped Mercer Whitley-Whatever over my back! I had her in a headlock! I still have what it takes. What is too late about that?"

He looked at her with a knee-knocking intensity. Sabrina tried not to get too excited. From the way he was acting, he was probably checking for scrapes and cuts.

"You ruined your dress," he finally said.

Sabrina held the dirt-streaked skirt away from her leg and clucked her tongue. "Yeah, this definitely can't be repaired."

Ian reached for the inside pocket of his jacket and took out the diamonds. He looked at the jewels for a moment before handing them to her. "Here are your earrings."

"Thanks." She didn't glance at the earrings as she set them down on the end table.

"You still need to be careful with those. We might have caught Mercer, but she didn't know anything about the break-in at your apartment. I'm inclined to believe her, since it deviates from her methods. But that means another jewel thief is after the diamonds."

"I'll let my sisters know."

"You know, Mercer did try to grab for the earrings when you were in the spa."

"I'm glad she confessed to that. For a minute there I thought I had been getting paranoid. But you know what? It makes sense. She's a woman who knows her way around a spa."

"A little too much."

"Okay, so she had one too many nips and tucks. And she has that pampered trophy wife look about her."

"No, I meant she was so bored with her life that she went back to her pickpocketing ways."

"I think she never gave it up, and that her husband was her invitation to get to the good stuff." She couldn't imagine any woman getting bored of the good life.

"According to her husband," Ian continued, "he met Mercer when she picked his pocket. At the time, he thought it was a refreshing method of getting picked up."

Sabrina rolled her eyes. The guy probably wouldn't have thought it was cute if Mercer had been an average-looking woman. "Little did he know that once they got married, she would spend her time stealing millions of dollars from his friends."

"As if she didn't have enough money already."

"I bet her prenup sucked, and this was her way of building a nest egg." Sabrina gave a tired sigh. "Hopefully she'll cough up the rest of the jewelry she stole and then your case will be solved."

Ian was silent for a moment before he thrust his hands into his trouser pockets. "When you were missing, a lot of thoughts ran through my head. I didn't know if you were okay."

"I did surprisingly well, don't you think?" She felt pretty good about how she had handled it.

He removed his hands and folded his arms across his chest. "You didn't know if I would come after you, since I had the earrings."

The thought had never occurred to her. Was that what he was worried about? "I knew you would."

"You didn't know how much you mean to me."

She stilled, afraid to move in case it shattered the moment. "Ian?"

"Since you've stayed with me in this suite, I've been having this fantasy," Ian confessed, rubbing the back of his neck with his hand. "It's you and me as a team, circling the globe together and hunting down jewel thieves."

"Really?" A ray of hope filled her. She was probably glowing from it.

Ian held his hands up. "But after tonight, we can forget it."

"What?" Sabrina's mouth dropped open. "Come on, Ian. Why not?"

"I am not putting my wife in danger."

"Wife?" The hope burned so bright it hurt.

Ian scrunched up his face. "I'm messing this up." He crouched down next to her. "Sabrina, I can't walk away from you. I want to stay. Have you by my side. In my bed. Protect you, love you, marry you."

She leaned forward. "I accept."

"I'm not done."

"Sorry." She leaned back.

"I know that my being a thief—"

"Ex-thief."

"Is a problem for you. Even though I work on the other side, I have never been ashamed of my past. That is, until I saw that look in your eyes."

Sabrina caught her bottom lip with the edge of her teeth. She wasn't ashamed of his past, but it did bother her. That was before she knew what kind of man he really was, someone she could trust and rely on.

Ian looked away. "I wanted to be the man of your dreams, and it hurt knowing there was no chance of reaching that goal."

What? Here she thought she wasn't exciting enough, glamorous enough to capture Ian's heart, and he was worried about not being good enough for her? He had it all wrong! Sabrina opened her mouth, but Ian stopped her with the press of his fingers against her lips.

"I can't change the past, but I can promise you this," he solemnly vowed, his eyes intense on her face. "I'm going to strive to be the man you're proud to have as a husband."

"You're already there," she said against his fingers. "And I still accept."

Ian cradled her face in his hands and kissed her breathless. She was ready to deepen the kiss when he pulled away.

"We should celebrate." He rose and helped Sabrina out of the chair. "Where should we go? Name it and I'll take you there."

Hmm . . . Where did she want him to take her? Her face lit up when an idea struck and Sabrina walked over to the door. "Anywhere?"

"Anywhere," he promised. "The sky is the limit."

She opened the door and placed the DO NOT DISTURB sign on the handle.

"What's going on?"

Sabrina turned around and smiled. "We're staying in tonight," she said as she kicked the door shut.

He frowned. "You don't want to celebrate?"

"Don't worry, Ian, we are." She pulled him closer and brushed her lips against his. "Only this time, dressing up is strictly prohibited."

A TOUCH OF PINK

CHAPTER ONE

DOMINIC STARK WOKE UP WHEN HE heard the sliding glass door open. He didn't move, sensing her gaze on him. He waited until the door closed before he opened his eyes.

Peeking under his lashes, he watched Lindsay Graham stride onto the balcony. Swaddled in a white terry-cloth bathrobe provided by the hotel, Lindsay walked to the rail and stared out onto the ocean. Storm clouds were rolling in, the fierce wind pulling at her long brown hair.

This was it, Dominic realized as he propped up on one elbow. Lindsay would be returning to Seattle that morning. That fact gave him a pang, swift and sharp. He sleepily rubbed his chest, but the ache wouldn't disappear.

If he was going to make his move, it had to be now. This was his last chance. He had to get these diamonds.

He should have gotten them his first day here. How difficult should it have been? Granted, he was not a professional thief, but considering how he crisscrossed the country and spent a small fortune in pursuing the earrings, he shouldn't have been distracted.

Then Lindsay stepped out of the hotel pool wearing a tiny pink bikini and those earrings. Dominic had been rooted on the spot as he had watched the water streak down her toned, sun-kissed body. His mouth had gone dry and he had acquired the fierce desire to lick every drop off Lindsay Graham.

And then she had paused in front of him and smiled before she strolled away. Dominic had to follow, knowing his wish would be granted.

His self-imposed one-night deadline extended to another night and another. A week had passed and he had made no serious attempt to take them.

It was now or never. He had to get them. Even though it meant he could never see Lindsay again.

But they had had no future from the start. She came to the island looking for a fling. As far as she was concerned, he wasn't the kind of guy you introduce to your mother. Yeah, he knew a lot about the woman, down to the fact that she wore those earrings only on vacation.

That was the weirdest thing of all. Seeing those diamonds should have turned him off. But he usually didn't notice the earrings when he looked at her.

That should have been his first warning. Lindsay Graham was deceptively dangerous. He wasn't prepared for her brand of seduction.

He strode to the sliding glass door, the plush carpeting masking his footsteps. He knew he had to make a decision. Either get the earrings or get the girl. He wanted both, but it had to be one or the other.

Dominic opened the door and Lindsay gave a start. She turned slightly. "Did I wake you?" she asked.

He couldn't answer. He could only stare at her ear. No diamond. For the first time this week. She wore them to bed last night.

"Why are you standing out in the rain?" he asked, his voice gruff with sleep, as his mind whirled. Where were the earrings? Probably in her purse, nestled safely in the original white velvet box.

She lifted her hand and felt the sparse raindrops as if she hadn't realized. "I wanted to get one last look at Hawaii," she said, turning her attention back onto the beach and the crashing ocean waves.

Dominic flexed his fingers and looked back toward the chair where her purse sat. All he had to do was slip his hands in the black leather and palm the diamonds.

So why was he stepping onto the balcony and closing the door behind him? Why was he going after Lindsay?

Later . . . Dominic decided as he stood behind Lindsay and cupped her shoulders. He would get the earrings later.

The white terry cloth felt soft under his hands and Lindsay relaxed against his chest. Dominic's chest squeezed hard. Lindsay wasn't one who trusted easily. He hadn't needed to read an in-depth report to find that out.

He gathered her long hair and scooped it to the side, revealing the elegant slope of her neck. He lowered his mouth against her throat, placing a kiss on her pulse point.

The heat and taste of her skin whetted his appetite. He curled his arm around her waist and held her tight. He wasn't ready to let her go.

He trailed his fingertips along the opening of her bathrobe

and dipped his hand in. Dominic captured her breast and thumbed her nipple, listening to Lindsay's sharp intake of breath. He growled with satisfaction as her nipple hardened.

"Dominic!" Lindsay belatedly gathered the robe with her hand, but he wasn't going to let go. "We're outside."

"So?" he asked as he pushed the bathrobe off her shoulder with his other hand.

"Someone will see us."

"So?" he asked with a smile. That was something about Lindsay he didn't get. She could be adventurous behind closed doors, yet the minute they were out of the room, no touching. Hot, sizzling looks that made him want to act on it no matter where they were, but no public displays of affection out of Lindsay.

That didn't stop him from trying. He considered it a mission. He would love to see her ignore their surroundings and claim him. That way he would know that he wasn't the only one caught in the spell.

He tugged at her belt and felt the bathrobe give way. She gasped and whirled around. "Dom—" Her eyes widened when she noticed he was standing naked beside her. She looked frantically around to make sure no one saw them. "Dominic!"

He tipped his head back and laughed when she opened her robe only in an attempt to cover him up. "Lindsay, no one is going to be around in this weather."

"You never know." She looked behind her at the beach to see if there was anyone walking in the rain.

He grabbed the edges of the robe and drew her closer. His cock pressed against her belly and her breasts brushed against his skin. It still wasn't close enough for his liking.

"We can't do this," she murmured. "I have to get ready for my flight home."

"All the more reason why we should." He walked her toward the patio chaise.

She glanced at the hotel room and back at him. "Uh . . ." She grabbed onto him, her nails scraping his shoulders, as he lowered her onto the padded cushion.

He covered her body with his. The rain spattered against his skin as a gust of wind buffeted his back. Dominic bracketed her face with his arms. He tenderly brushed Lindsay's hair from her face before he kissed her gently.

His hand wandered down the curves, slowly parting the bathrobe, before he cupped her sex. Lindsay gasped against his mouth as his hand met her wet heat.

Dominic rose and knelt between her legs. He looked down at her, loving the sight of Lindsay sprawled underneath him. Her face was flushed and her brown eyes were half-mast and glittery.

Her hair was tangled and the bathrobe slid down her arms and hung open, brushing against the floor. Lindsay's breath grew choppy as he drew tiny, insistent circles against her clit. She looked pagan and untamed, igniting a wicked fire through his blood.

"Play with your breasts," he told her as he slid his finger into her. He locked his jaw, trembling with need, as her flesh greedily clamped against him.

"I—" She spared a look at the balcony railing.

"Come on, Lindsay." He pressed his thumb against her clit. "Do it for me."

She shyly cupped her breasts. As she stroked and fondled, he noticed that her pale skin still held the whisker marks from last night. Dominic liked seeing his brand on her. Too bad it would disappear by the time she returned home.

Lindsay tweaked her nipples and shivered. "Harder," he urged her.

She obeyed, pinching the peaks of her breasts as he trapped her clit between his fingers and squeezed. Lindsay arched back and whimpered as pleasure rippled through her body, the drops of rain slithering down her flushed face.

"Now offer them to me," Dominic said, his voice raspy.

She did so proudly. He leaned down and took one rosy crest in his mouth. He drew her in, nipping her with the edge of his teeth. He found her taste addicting.

Lindsay moaned softly, grabbing the back of his head when Dominic pulled back. "Put your legs around me."

He lifted her hips off the chaise and she hooked her knees around his waist. His jaw clicked with barely restrained need as he drove inside her. A high mewl ripped from Lindsay's throat as she grabbed onto the chaise.

"Touch yourself," he said between clenched teeth.

She let go and rubbed her nipple with one hand. Her other hand reached between them. She teased her clit as he pumped into her, hard and fast.

The sight drove him to the edge. He felt the tingle at the bottom of his feet and in his chest. The white-hot needles kicked in his lower back. He tried to hold it off, his sweat mingling with the raindrops. Watching the pleasure build in her, Dominic was desperate to make this moment last.

This was exactly how he wanted to remember Lindsay Graham. Naked and wild underneath him.

Because he would never see her like this again.

★   ★   ★

Lindsay leaned back in her plane seat and looked out onto the clouds. *Good-bye, Hawaii. Good-bye, Dominic.*

No, no, no. Lindsay pressed her lips together and blinked back the tears. She wasn't going to think about that. What happened in Hawaii stayed in Hawaii.

That was the point. The whole motive of her weekend getaways and short holidays. There she could let loose and there would be no consequences. Then she came back home, where order and method ruled the day.

It wasn't as if she threw caution to the wind and indulged in a three-day bender. For the past year, her trips were marked off her calendar with military precision. She only went when her workload allowed it and when she had the pink diamond earrings.

Glancing at her purse resting by her feet, she smiled at the thought of the earrings, once owned by a woman famous for her passion. There was no doubt in Lindsay's mind that Lia Dash wore the diamonds when she seduced legendary lovers. And if the diamonds assisted Lia through her grand passions, who's to say the earrings couldn't help her?

Okay, so maybe she was being superstitious, Lindsay decided with a wry smile. She usually placed her beliefs in facts and figures. It's what made her successful managing retirement portfolios.

But she was inching close to thirty, and until this week she hadn't experienced soulful ecstasy or red-hot desire. She found a few sparks, a bit of fun, and some comfortable companionship, but that was it. No all-consuming, gut-wrenching passion.

Except in Hawaii. She had worn the earrings on previous trips, but she hadn't found anything close to what she found with Dominic. Lindsay shifted in her seat as her body tingled from the memories. Dominic could have been her grand passion. When she was with him, everything disappeared. She felt alive. Beautiful. And for once, out of control.

It was a good thing she nipped it in the bud when she did. One week was all she allowed. Sure, she would have loved to have stayed for another week—another day even—but that wild chaos would have spilled into her everyday life.

And that could never happen. She was successful because of her routine. It could be tedious—and downright boring—but the advantages far outweighed the problems.

Still, she wasn't ready to go back home. She wanted to stay in Dominic's arms, enjoy the wantonness he uncovered in her.

Maybe she'd feel that way again when she wore the earrings. She doubted it. Lindsay had a feeling that when she saw the diamonds again, all she would remember would be Dominic.

Lindsay gnawed at her bottom lip as she stared at her purse. No time like the present to test it out. She bent down and retrieved her purse, realizing for the first time how the bag clashed with her resort wardrobe.

She didn't think to change purses, since it always met her needs. Just opening the bag and looking at the ruthless organization brought her peace of mind. Everything from her cell phone to her day planner had a designated area. Even the earrings.

She retrieved the white velvet jewelry box and flipped open the lid. Her breath snagged in her chest. She blinked and opened her eyes wide until they burned, but the vision remained the same.

There was only one earring in the box.

CHAPTER TWO

"ONE OF THE DIAMONDS IS MISSING," Lindsay said in a horrified whisper. She lay down on her sofa and covered her eyes with her arm. "How could this have happened?"

She really didn't want to believe it, but there was no denying the fact. After searching her luggage and exhausting every avenue to locate the jewel, she called her sisters over to her place and broke the news.

"Are you sure?" Sabrina asked, holding the white velvet box.

"Positive." She wouldn't have said anything otherwise. Saying it out loud only intensified the pain. The earring really was gone. Lindsay flattened her hand against her churning stomach. She was going to be sick.

"You *lost* the other earring?" Nicole asked as she held the remaining pink diamond to the light, inspecting it closely. "Just when it's my turn again?"

Sabrina swiveled to glare at their youngest sister. "Nicole!"

"I'll find it," Lindsay swore.

"Oh, yeah, right." Nicole turned and glared at Lindsay. "You couldn't lose them the day your turn starts? Nope. You got to enjoy them the whole month."

Hardly. She had left them in her safety deposit box until she went to Hawaii. She wished she had kept them locked up.

Okay, that was a lie, Lindsay acknowledged as she rubbed her eyes with the heels of her hands. Now that they're gone, she wished she had worn them all the time. She wished she hadn't been so afraid to enjoy them.

"I need those earrings now!" Nicole wailed. "You guys got more turns than me. This is so unfair."

"Nothing can be done about it," Sabrina said with a warning edge in her tone. "Lindsay, call the hotel immediately."

"I already did." Oh, what she wouldn't do to curl up and throw a blanket over her. Anything to blot out what was happening.

She did everything she could, but there were no signs of the earring. She knew there wouldn't be. Her suspicions were deepening.

Lindsay slowly sat up and wrapped her arms around her stomach. It hurt to breathe. It didn't matter how much she hated to consider the possibility; she had to face the facts. And do something about it.

Nicole cleared her throat. "I'd like to point out that after all the warnings you gave me to be careful, who lost one of the diamonds?"

Lindsay rolled her eyes. Trust her little sister to focus on the important things in life. "It's not my fault."

Nicole scoffed at the statement. "Are you kidding me?"

"Someone took it." She rose from the sofa and started to pace. Lindsay felt disloyal suggesting it. She had no proof, just a hunch.

"Anyone in mind?" Sabrina asked, her gaze sharpening on Lindsay.

Lindsay closed her eyes as she felt the sting of tears. "Dominic Stark."

"Who's Dominic?" Sabrina asked gently.

"A man I met." The pain clawed at her and she struggled to get the words out.

Nicole held up her hands. "Wait a second, wait a second. You hooked up with a guy in Hawaii?" She pointed at Lindsay. "*You?*"

Her sister's disbelief only brought home the truth Lindsay was trying to avoid. That Dominic probably hadn't been interested in her. That she was wild and free in front of someone who seduced her only for the earring.

Lindsay fought the urge to crumple onto the floor in a heap. Embarrassment and anger scorched through her, leaving her skin hot and blotchy.

Hell hath no fury like a woman scorned. She understood each nuance of that quote. And she was going to teach it to Dominic Stark.

Lindsay exhaled slowly and rolled her shoulders back. "Bree, let's find out how useful that fiancé of yours can be. See what information he can get on Dominic Stark."

"Okay." Concern clouded Sabrina's eyes. "What are you going to do with the information?"

"I'm going to get the earring back." Her spine straightened with resolve. Saying those words did something to her.

She latched onto the wispy tendrils of control for the first time since had she made the discovery.

"Get it back?" Sabrina asked. "How?"

"Fight fire with fire." How else would she get close enough to him? Search his place? Wrap her hands around his throat . . .

"You're going to try and seduce a master seducer?" Nicole's voice rose with every word. "The guy who just scammed you?"

Lindsay flinched. She wanted to lash out, but her sister spoke the truth. "That's right."

Nicole looked at Sabrina. "Well, that settles it. We're never getting it back."

"Yes, we will," Lindsay said, jutting her chin. "Count on it."

Dominic sat in the hotel bar, oblivious to the tourists and honeymoon couples around him. He set his glass down on the table and rolled the pink diamond in his other palm.

After all these years, the earrings were finally in his possession. Well, one of them. Dominic shook his head in self-disgust. He blamed that decision on a moment of weakness.

It didn't matter. One earring was enough to serve his purpose. Dominic clenched the piece of jewelry in his fist, the diamond and gold scratching his skin.

The question now was when he would fulfill this mission. It had been two days since he'd stolen the diamond, and he'd done nothing. He hadn't even left the hotel.

He thought he would have moved faster, accomplish his mission and return to normal life. But something was holding him back. What happened to the fire that used to burn in him? The one that forged this quest from the beginning?

Dominic leaned back in his seat and stared at his empty glass. No, a refill wasn't going to give him the answers. He had gotten this far based on patience and restraint. He wasn't going to deviate now.

A laugh from the lobby pierced his troubled thoughts. The feminine sound warmed him deep inside. He glanced up, the familiarity tugging at his memory.

He watched the woman smiling at the doorman as she entered the hotel. There was something—Lindsay? Dominic's world tilted for one infinitesimal moment.

She came back?

He slipped the earring into his shirt pocket as he stared at Lindsay. His mind filtered her progress in slow motion as the luxurious surroundings' noises faded into the background.

Lindsay's long brown hair streamed behind her as the short pink dress lovingly hugged every curve. The crinkly fabric tugged at every sway her hips made, inching up her thigh. There was a lot of leg between the flirty hem and her pink stiletto heels.

Dominic felt his jaw drop as he watched her head to the registration desk. If it weren't for the familiar black purse, he would have thought it was a different woman. This woman walked like a warrior. It was a confident, take-no-prisoners stride. It was the sexiest, most alluring sight he had ever seen.

He rose from his seat without realizing it, and made his way to Lindsay. He couldn't believe she came back. Returning would have messed up her precious schedule, and he had bet she would have filled out a police report and that would have been it. Was his mind—his guilt—playing tricks? He had to find out.

She didn't see him approaching, her hair a soft, silky curtain concealing her face. His senses were reigniting as he got closer.

He stood beside her and she didn't notice. That bothered him, almost as much as her scent. The smoky spice perfume lingered in the air, conjuring images of the exotic and the forbidden.

"Lindsay?"

She turned around. Something flashed in her eyes. An emotion he couldn't define.

"Dominic!" She smiled and placed a chaste kiss on his cheek. "What are still doing here? I thought you had to leave for some business thing?"

That was a kiss? What kind of welcome was that? He wanted to sweep her into his arms and kiss her senseless, but he held back. Lindsay didn't do public displays of affection. He needed to remember that. Dominic placed his hand on her waist and placed a kiss next to her mouth.

She stepped back, breaking contact. "Well?" she asked.

Well, what? He belatedly remembered what she had said. "I have a few business meetings on the island. What about you?"

She sighed and grimaced. "I lost one of my earrings."

"Earrings?" Regret crashed through him. He wanted to freeze and rewind before he took the jewel. Bring back the moment when it was just him and a fascinating woman.

"Oh, right. I forgot that men don't notice these things." She spared a glance at the woman behind the desk and they shared a long-suffering look. "I wore these pink diamond earrings. They're the real thing. But I lost one of them."

"Uh-huh." Did she suspect him? Had she figured out the

time line right down to the only opportunity he had to get them? He doubted it. The police would be interrogating him if that had been the case.

"It has to be somewhere around here, so I decided to look for it myself."

It felt like the earring was burning a hole in his shirt pocket.

"Okay, that's not the whole truth." Lindsay leaned in closer. "I could have had the police do their work, but I had so much fun here. This gives me the perfect excuse to extend my holiday."

"True." His eyes were riveted on the bra strap peeking from underneath her collar. He wanted to slowly peel off her pink dress and reveal the antique ivory lace. It was the kind of feminine frothiness that made his mind buzz.

She hadn't worn that kind of stuff before. Dominic would have remembered. Most of what Lindsay wore—and didn't wear—teased his imagination and stole into his dreams.

"By the way," she continued brightly, oblivious to his carnal thoughts, "have you seen the earring?" she asked him as she signed a hotel form.

"No." Dominic frowned. He didn't like how easily the lie fell from his lips. What kind of man was he turning into?

His grimness faded as he looked into her face, experiencing the full effect of her quiet beauty. Her features were carefully made up, but she didn't attempt to hide the sprinkle of freckles on her nose. He liked those freckles almost as much as he liked her eyes.

When his gaze collided with hers, Dominic's breath caught tightly in his chest. He stared into the brown depths, fascinated by the mix of interest, uncertainty, and bravado.

It was the bravado that gave him pause. "How long are you staying?" he asked.

She nervously cleared her throat. "I don't know."

"In that case, let me take you to dinner." The shake of her head surprised him. "Dancing?" He wanted those legs entwined with his. Or wrapped around his hips. Curled around his shoulders.

"I'm sorry, Dominic. Considering how jammed my schedule is, I probably shouldn't make any arrangements."

"I beg your pardon?" She wasn't going to have time for him? Last week she couldn't get enough!

"Oh, I hope you don't take this the wrong way," she said as she received her card key. "It's not like I don't *want* to spend time with you, but I'm going to be busy."

He felt as if he had been kicked in the stomach. He stared deep into her eyes, trying to uncover what was really going on. If she didn't think he took the earring, why was she keeping her distance?

The attraction was there, no doubt about it. He was familiar with the heightened color staining her pale face. Her breath puffed unevenly from her parted lips.

Her gaze skittered away, but his rib cage still felt tight. Dominic gritted his teeth before he did something stupid like steal another touch.

He shouldn't pursue her. Lindsay Graham was turning into a weakness of his. It would be best if he stayed away. Keep all contact to a minimum.

But he wanted to make one thing clear. "I don't understand. Are you here for business or pleasure?"

"How can I put it?" She gnawed her bottom lip. "Dominic, what we had was great, but it was meant to be short-term."

He stared at her as his ribs squeezed his lungs. Was she giving him the shaft?

She placed her palm against her as if she were making a pledge. "I wouldn't dream of placing any expectations on you just because we're staying in the hotel."

He couldn't stop staring. His blood roared in his ears. Didn't their time together mean anything to her?

Lindsay reached for his hand and gave a firm shake. Dominic was too dumbfounded to trap her hand in his. To draw her closer.

She briskly dropped her hand. "Good luck in all your endeavors, okay?" She walked around him. "See you around!" She tossed the comment over her shoulder.

Dominic turned and watched her walk to the bank of elevators. She just blew him off. She was here to have more fun—more flings—without him?

He would see about that!

CHAPTER THREE

THE MOMENT LINDSAY CLOSED THE DOOR to her hotel room, she locked it with one hand and grabbed her cell phone with the other. Punching in her sister's number, she waited until she heard Sabrina's voice before she sagged against the door.

"This is the stupidest idea I've ever had," Lindsay announced.

"Is Dominic still at the hotel?" her sister asked.

"Yes, your information was right. I saw him."

"Already? Did you talk?"

"Yeah." Her reaction scared her. She expected to feel anger, but not the rush of heat pouring over her at the sight of his gorgeous face. The mysterious glitter in his eyes made her feel infinitely vulnerable.

The guy oozed sexuality. It was potent stuff, coming at her in waves. And she was supposed to harness it for her own use? Uh-uh. No way.

Her legs started to wobble as she remembered his pleasure in seeing her. His gentle touch. She could still feel the heat of his fingerprint branding her hip.

Okay, she had to sit down. Lindsay made a cautious bee-line for the bed. "I have no idea what I'm doing."

"Does he suspect anything?"

"No." Lindsay's heel snagged against the carpeting and she stumbled to a stop. How was she supposed to seduce the guy when she couldn't even walk? Or put two words together?

"What's wrong?"

"Bree, I have to flirt my way into Dominic's bedroom and see if he has the diamond, and you're asking me what's wrong?" She could probably seduce him if she was wearing the earrings. She couldn't rely on her own devices.

"You can do it."

"I'm not so sure." Lindsay chewed the corner of her lip. The articles she found on the web gave her some basics. "Top Ten Ways of Getting Him in Bed." "Feng Shui of Flirting." But what if they don't work?

"Did you give him the brush-off?" Sabrina asked.

"Yeah, you were right." Lindsay sank onto the bed. "I think I offended him."

"It's going to be okay," Sabrina said. "Assuming he has the diamond, he's going to avoid you. If you had shown that you wanted to pick up where you left off, his next move would be to check out of the hotel. But if you're avoiding him, he won't be able to resist you."

"I'll take your word for it." She lay down on the bed.

"And you're dressed to kill, right?"

Lindsay looked down at the dress she'd borrowed from Nicole. Even though her sisters had "borrowed" clothes from her closet in the past, Lindsay never reciprocated. It didn't matter if they were the same size—Lindsay never liked her sisters' sense of style.

Now if only her little sister didn't add to that sin by dressing so provocatively. Lindsay raised her leg and stared at the pink stilettos. They served her purpose, but she would never wear these come-and-get-me shoes in her real life.

But she was wearing them now. She was on a mission. Lindsay's mouth set into a firm line as anger churned in her stomach. She had to get what was hers, even if it meant playing Dominic's game when she didn't know all the tricks or rules.

She was in a situation where she had no idea what to expect and couldn't predict the outcome. It had been a long time since she'd allowed herself to be in a situation where she didn't have a backup plan, an emergency plan, and a safety net.

She was past scared. Her skin threatened to break out into hives. Her stomach was tied in knots. Every nerve screamed for her to reconsider.

Lindsay couldn't think about that. She had to focus on what she could do and ignore what she couldn't control. "Have you found out anything else about Dominic?"

"His name really is Dominic Stark and he really is a venture capitalist from Los Angeles."

Lindsay closed her eyes with relief. He didn't lie about that. Something as essential as his name. His identity. Why did that make her feel better?

"He has no police record and no ties to criminal activity," Sabrina continued. "Oh, and he's filthy rich."

She hadn't thought about that, but it didn't surprise her. "I wonder why he felt the need to steal the earring? Maybe he didn't steal it."

"We've been through this already," Sabrina said. "You had the earrings that morning. You put them in your purse. No one was near that purse except for Dominic."

"But maybe I dropped it. Maybe I-I . . ."

"You know you put both earrings in the purse."

"Yes." There was no doubt.

"The three of us went through that purse of yours to see if it was still in there. There is no way a five-carat diamond could have fallen out of the jewelry case, through a zippered compartment, pass another zippered compartment and escape from the clasp without a little help."

"Okay, fine. It was taken."

"And that purse wasn't out of your sight once you left the hotel room."

"Okay, okay. It's likely that Dominic took the earring."

"And why only one? That is what bugs me," Sabrina confided. "Do you think you interrupted him during the theft?"

"No, it shouldn't have taken more time to swipe the other earring." Why *did* he take one earring? To make her think she dropped the other one? Probably.

"Hmm. Okay, I'll keep digging and see if there's anything else in this guy's past."

Lindsay sat up as a thought occurred to her. "Maybe we should learn more about the earrings while we're at it."

"I'll have Nicole research the earrings while I learn more about Dominic Stark. If there's a connection, we'll find it."

The sooner, the better. She didn't have that much vacation time left, nor did she have money to burn on an impromptu tropical getaway.

"So what are you going to do now?"

Hide in my bedroom until the earring pops up. "I am going to wear Nicole's sexiest outfit and prowl the hotel's nightclub," she answered in a monotone voice.

"Atta girl!"

Lindsay shuffled to a stop at the entrance of the hotel's nightclub. Her determination wavered. There was nothing she would like more to do than run back to her room and bolt the door. She would kick off the ankle-wrap sandals—what was her sister doing with these impractical four-inch heels?—and peel off the barely-there black dress.

But that wasn't going to get her the earring.

Hooking the spaghetti-strap back onto her shoulder, Lindsay slowly made her way through the crowd and found the bar. She leaned her forearms on the smooth counter and felt her hemline go up. Lindsay discreetly tugged at the short dress before cautiously looking around the room.

The club was busy, the loud music throbbing through the walls and floor. How was she supposed to catch the attention of men when she could barely think?

Smile. Every article mentioned that. Even though Lindsay would rather be scowling, she smiled. Big.

No, that can't be right. There had to be more than that to picking up men. If all it took was a smile, she would have men trailing her along the streets of Seattle.

What was it that she did differently when she went on vacation? Well, for one, she wore Lia Dash's diamonds. But men never notice things like earrings. The jewelry was meant to boost her confidence, not necessarily attract men.

What did she do during trips that she didn't do at home? Wear something more revealing? Check. Wait for some guy to make the first move? Double check.

Hmm, she did that back home with varying levels of success. She wasn't aggressive and never made the first move.

Project. That was it! She could project sexual allure. It was all about attitude. She always made it clear that she was available when on vacation.

Only sometimes it took men a few days to figure it out. She didn't have that kind of luxury this time.

"Think sexy," she muttered softly to herself. "Shoulders back, chin up, stomach in, weight distributed on one foot (not easy to do on four-inch heels), place one hand on hip, jut other hip out."

Now . . . wait.

The music echoed in her ears. A dull ache in the base of her spine spread to her hip bone. Cool air swirled around her as she stood by herself in the crowded room. Even the bartender didn't notice her.

Lindsay looked at her feet. *I feel like a loser. Why is nothing happening?*

She frowned as tension increased. *Dominic.* Her body went on full alert. She sensed him. He was somewhere in the club, watching her.

Lindsay scanned the room, found him, and reluctantly met his gaze head-on. Her heart skipped a beat and she saw Dominic Stark leaning against the wall with a crystal tumbler in his hands. His stance said it all—he was proud and arrogant.

Although he didn't have the physique of a bodybuilder, he had an aura of physical strength. The burgundy shirt he wore fell down his defined abdomen. His black trousers hung low on his flat stomach and showcased his lean thighs. Her gaze traveled back to Dominic's face. That was where the real power was conveyed. Thick, dark hair framed the tanned face. Lines fanned from the corners of his arctic brown eyes.

Lindsay's ribs felt like they would crumble under the tension. She wanted to look away—needed to—but Dominic's gaze held her fast. She knew he would let her go when he was good and ready.

A tremor swept across her shoulders and down her spine. Oh, what had she seen in this guy? She didn't like the man being in complete charge. Especially when the man was someone like Dominic. Someone whom she couldn't predict, couldn't control.

Someone tapped her on the shoulder. Lindsay jumped and whirled around. The man standing next to her was about the same height as she. He was handsome in a pretty-boy kind of way. Undemanding and nonthreatening.

"Dance?" he asked over the music.

Lindsay flashed him her most confident smile. This was a man she could flirt with. She could hold her own. She could control the situation. "Sure."

He lead her to the dance floor, twirled her, and gathered her in his arms. Lindsay's laugh died in her throat when she realized Dominic was directly in her line of vision.

He nodded his head in a sort of mock bow, like he knew what she was up to. Lindsay looked away and stared deep into her dance partner's eyes.

The guy took this as a sign to hold her closer. He pressed his hand against the small of her back and pressed her against his groin.

Lindsay quelled the instinct to pull back. This was part of the plan. Make Dominic think that she was moving and looking for more conquests.

The strategy made her uneasy. Even now, she couldn't

look at Dominic. She could feel the heat of his gaze on her. She sensed the smirk playing on his lips.

Okay, Dominic wasn't buying this ploy. She had to look more convincing. What could she do? Give this stranger a deep-throated kiss?

No, she couldn't. She just couldn't.

Her dance partner thrust his knee between her thighs. She grabbed his shoulders and straddled him. His pants scratched her soft skin as the man pressed his leg against her cleft.

She rode the stranger's leg, sliding up and down. Colorful lights swirled around her like a kaleidoscope. She dropped her hands from the man's shoulders as he arched her back, his hips pumping to the music.

Lindsay felt Dominic's gaze commanding her to turn and face him. She battled against the insistent demand.

The strap to her dress slid down her shoulder. Sweat glimmered off her skin. She could feel the excitement thrumming under her dance partner's skin, but she had no idea what the man looked like. All she could think about was Dominic.

She could no longer resist, and took a peek at Dominic. His expression was grim as his eyes glittered with frank need.

Lindsay gasped softly as her body felt like it was plunging into boiling water. A hot, liquid sensation flooded her womb. She craved Dominic's touch.

She stopped abruptly and pulled away from her dance partner. She didn't know how much more she could handle. Bestowing a distracted smile by way of thanks, Lindsay walked away and headed for the center of the dance floor, hopefully away from Dominic's watchful gaze.

She wished Dominic would leave. No, she wished he would stay. Would carry her to his room and claim her. Drive his cock into her so that the tight coil inside her would spring free.

He was the only man who could do that. The only one she wanted. She swallowed awkwardly as reality doused her prickly flushed skin. How could she have fallen for Dominic, yearn for him, when he stole and lied to her?

She didn't trust her instincts or feelings right now. She needed to find more men. More dance partners. The only thing she could do was follow this plan to the end—and pray that Dominic didn't catch her.

CHAPTER FOUR

THE PRIMITIVE ROAR ECHOED DEEP INSIDE him. Her words reverberated in his mind. She wanted to extend her holiday, but not
with him.

Anger and jealousy stirred his blood. He couldn't remember the last time he had felt this way. It had to be the pink
diamond's doing. He should have known that earring was
cursed.

Lindsay was his, and she needed to remember that. Her
dance ignited a need for retribution. He pushed away from the
wall and slammed his glass onto the table.

There was no way she could have heard his pursuit, but
her head jerked up. It was as if she had caught a scent of trouble. When her gaze met his, she withdrew; her body shimmered with tension. She was poised for flight.

It was time for him to hunt.

How much of a head start would Lindsay get? Not much

with those shoes designed to be caught in hot pursuit. A head start wouldn't do her any good even if she wore running shoes. He would catch her.

She could try to take him on a wild chase. He knew he would get her in the end. Dominic hoped she gave him somewhat of a challenge. It made the capture sweeter.

Pride deserted her. She turned and fled, using the crowd as camouflage. It was a weak response, Dominic decided as he closed the distance with determined strides.

His muscles were on full alert and his gaze tapered in on Lindsay like the point of an arrow. The dancers around him evaporated into a curl of smoke.

Hmm . . . Maybe she wasn't as brazen as she acted, Dominic decided as he watched her dart around tables. She didn't look back, but he knew she was aware of him. She scurried in those killer heels and her spine was ramrod straight. Dominic bet her focus never wavered from the exit.

But did she really think she could get away? She obviously didn't think Dominic was a worthy foe. He couldn't wait to show her otherwise.

How could someone so clever underestimate him?

He had always thought she was smart and sexy. Dominic found Lindsay exotic, but her intelligence was a big part of her beauty. The confident energy brought color to her pale face and gave her jaw a rakish tilt. Her slender body hummed with a passion for whatever she had been discussing.

But all that had changed when she returned to Hawaii. What was going on? He intended to find out.

Lindsay left the club and veered right. She passed the crowded bank of phones and bolted into the women's room.

Her heels skidded on the slick tiled floor and she disappeared with an ungainly slide.

Classic retreat. Dominic rolled his eyes. He expected something different from Lindsay.

He followed her, holding the door to let a tipsy woman leave. Dominic allowed the door to swing shut. He looked around the room, which turned out to be a lounge leading into the bathroom.

Lindsay was the only woman in the room. Her hands gripped the makeup table and her head hung. She glanced out of the corner of her eye and jerked straight up when she spotted him.

Their eyes clung as he strode toward her. Her brown eyes cast a mysterious spell over him. He felt controlled and in control. The heady mix fizzed inside him, ready to explode.

Lindsay didn't break eye contact. She stood next to the dressing table as he approached her. She seethed with attitude, her arms folded tightly across her chest. He would bet she was ready to gouge him with her stiletto.

"What?" Her eyes flashed with defiant anger. "Can't I get a moment to myself without being hassled?"

"Need a break from seducing every man on your radar?" He leaned against the table, barring her path to the door. "That must be wearing."

"I don't know what you're talking about." Haughtiness shone in each word as she stepped around him.

"Yes, you do."

She turned to inspect her reflection in the mirror. "Jealous?"

"Yes, but that's what you wanted." Dominic caught her by the wrist and drew her hand to his face. "I can't help but wonder why you're doing it," he said softly.

Her hand curled into a fist. "I'm here to have fun. Try not to ruin it for me."

"Fun . . . but not with me." He brushed his lips against each knuckle. The sweet smoky perfume whetted his appetite.

"That's right." The pulse in her throat jumped wildly.

"What's really going on?"

"Nothing." She yanked her hand away from his grasp and took a step back.

Dominic matched her retreat with a step forward.

"You need to leave."

"Not without you." Lindsay Graham was different from any other woman he knew. The guy who won her heart would truly be lucky. That guy would find passion, loyalty, and strength in his mate. He would have a woman who would protect him as much as he protected her.

But he wouldn't be that guy. It didn't matter that he fell for her—and fell hard. He was the man who stole something special from her, and there was no forgiving that sin.

"Enough with the games, Lindsay." He was tired and driven half mad with need. If he saw her in another man's arms one more time, he could not be held accountable for his actions.

"Once again, I don't know what you're talking about."

"Let me make it clear." He closed in on her with his last step. Her heel clinked against the table. "I want you naked, in my bed, tonight."

★   ★   ★

His raw statement aroused her. Okay, that wasn't true. Watching Dominic follow her with that intense expression was all it took to make her wet.

Her nipples poked against her dress, ready to be plucked and squeezed. She covered the evidence with her arms, but she couldn't hide the truth. She wanted Dominic to catch her. Why was she so powerless against Dominic's brand of sex appeal?

Dominic reached out and cradled her face with both hands. His skin was warm and rough. He swooped down, and her eyelashes fluttered closed.

He tasted just as she remembered. One hundred percent pure male. Hard and on the edge of primitive. His mouth invaded hers and demanded surrender. And Lindsay wanted to do just that.

Her fingers bit into the corner of the table. Dominic's hands skimmed down to her breasts and sides. His hands were large and territorial as they roamed her curves. She felt vulnerable and open for his next invasion. She felt free and uninhibited. Uncontained.

And that freaked her out. She felt wet and swollen. Every nerve ending was ready to burst out of her skin.

Dominic boldly cupped her breast, and Lindsay's knees began to wobble. She swore an orgasm was brewing in the backs of her knees. His mouth slipped from hers and sloped down to her jaw before burrowing into her neck.

She curled into him, her cheek grazed against his lustrous black hair. He was too close. But not close enough, and wouldn't be until his naked body joined hers.

Lindsay's pelvis collided with his groin. His cock felt hard and powerful. Thick and heavy. As she struggled with the need for having him drive in, stretch and fill her to the hilt, Dominic hooked her legs around his waist.

Her heels grazed his dark pants. The scent of sex assailed her. He tilted her back, the table's edge digging into the back of her legs.

She was as off-balance as she felt. Her eyes widened as the knowledge filtered her sluggish mind. She was at his mercy.

The idea excited her. It shouldn't have. She should leave. Right here and now, before she regretted it. But she couldn't. That would be the ultimate regret. She did the complete opposite and rooted for his mouth with hungry desperation.

Dominic shoved her skirt up. With one hand pressing against her bottom, he slid his other hand along her legs until he pressed against her hot mound.

He pushed aside the scrap of satin and stroked her clit. She gasped as pleasure coiled her womb. Lindsay gripped the table's edge until her palms burned.

He dipped his blunt finger into her wetness. Her flesh gripped onto Dominic. Ensnaring him, drawing him in.

Oh—my . . . Her muscles trembled and couldn't stop. Sparks danced through her body.

Her hands slid across the tabletop. She grappled for balance and tumbled against the mirror. Lindsay's breath hitched in her throat as her back hit the metal beam. The resulting distant ache felt good.

Dominic devoured her with another toe-curling openmouthed kiss as he pumped her with his finger. She tore her mouth away, inhaling raggedly when he moved his other hand against her swollen clit.

Lindsay moaned as savage need clawed to another level. Dominic's teeth grazed her neck and she arched to accommodate him. He suckled her pulse point, drawing it deep in his hot mouth as her lower body mimicked the sensation.

Her climax happened with sudden violence. White-hot energy exploded from her center and whooshed through her stomach and legs. She buckled under the force as it scorched her breasts and neck before tearing through her mind. Lindsay clutched onto Dominic until he drew out the last wrenching shudder.

He held her tight. So tight it was difficult to fill her lungs with air. He paused and tilted his head back.

"Lindsay?" The glitter of desire faded into concern. He brushed his knuckle as gently as a feather under her eye. "Lindsay, don't cry."

She batted his hand away and frantically dabbed her fingertips under her eyelashes, trying to hide the fact that tears staining her skin. Why did he have to notice?

Linsday dropped one leg shakily from his hip. She had to get out of here. She wasn't a crier. She wasn't even a screamer. Maybe—maybe!—a soft moaner. She . . . she didn't do these things. Showing her reaction meant offering a glimpse of your soul.

And she did it all in front of Dominic.

Lindsay pushed him with all her might and ran for the door. Ran for cover. And prayed that Dominic wouldn't follow her this time.

Lindsay swiped the steam off her bathroom mirror with a shaky hand. She pulled the thin towel tighter across her breasts and wondered why the hot shower didn't erase all the tension from her body. She had stayed under the scalding spray until the water stabbed her skin like needles.

She now stared at her reflection, but she felt as if she was looking at someone else. Her slicked hair was already twisting into wet ropes. Her pale, unmade face was familiar, but something was different.

She was different.

Lindsay stared blindly into the porcelain sink. What was she doing? Her flirtation and seduction had gotten out of hand. Why? It never did with any man other than Dominic.

Lindsay rubbed her bare arms as goose bumps blanketed her flesh. Dominic knew what her body craved. Knew how to pleasure her before she could ask. Before she could understand what she wanted.

Her forehead puckered with a frown. Lindsay had to admit the obvious. She was in way over her head. With Dominic.

She raised her head and peered into the mirror again. She unflinchingly took it all in: the passion glowing from her eyes, the sensuality burgeoning underneath her skin.

All along she had been hiding from this side of her, and Dominic managed to uncover it with his touch. It was like an uncivilized creature lurking underneath the mild-mannered woman. And she didn't think the woman had the power over the creature.

The ultimate question was, did Dominic?

CHAPTER FIVE

HER CELL PHONE RANG VERY EARLY in the morning. Lindsay whimpered as she batted her hand along the bedside table, blindly searching for the small electronic device. She had barely had any sleep, spending most of the night pacing her hotel room. She seriously needed a vacation after this vacation.

Lindsay flipped open the phone and heard her little sister's voice. "Nicole, do you know what time it is?"

"We've got a problem."

"I'm aware of that," she said and yawned.

"No, I mean we've been handling this the wrong way." Urgency vibrated through Nicole's voice. "These earrings are tainted!"

Lindsay cracked one eye open. "Say what?"

"They were the center of a scandal thirty years ago."

"Nicole, I know you like to read the tabloids and tell-alls, but—"

"I'm serious! These earrings were a part of a love triangle. The mob. Sex. Grand theft. Did I mention sex?"

She opened the other eye. "Just give me the facts."

"Herbert Wendell was the jeweler who designed the earrings," Nicole began, as if narrating a true-crime episode on TV.

"Never heard of him."

"He was a big name for his time. Wined and dined the Hollywood circuit. He got commissions from celebrities, royalty, senators. Even the mob."

"Quite a clientele." Lindsay cracked another yawn.

"But no one knew that he didn't design the jewelry. A young, beautiful artist in the back room was the true creative force."

Suspicion pricked at her sleepy mind. "What was her name?"

"Cleo Stark."

Lindsay sagged deeper into the pillow. "Oh, no."

"But wait, there's more."

"Now you're sounding like an infomercial. Is Herbert Dominic's father?"

"Yes," Nicole said, annoyed at the interruption, "but they were not married. Herb played the eligible bachelor image to the hilt."

"Herbert sounds like a real charmer."

"But it all went downhill when some bigwig commissioned dear old Herb to design a pair of earrings for his daughter using some heirloom diamonds."

"What happened?"

"Once the earrings were made, they went missing. Herb blamed Cleo and kicked her out, along with Dominic. Cleo blamed Herbert. She says he gave them to the other woman in his life."

"Oooh. There was a girlfriend?"

"Yeah, but no one knew who it was. Herb denied her existence all the way through. I think it was probably some Hollywood starlet who needed bus money back home."

"And the bigwig?" Lindsay asked.

"Ruined Herbert. I'm trying to find out who he was, but I keep winding up at dead ends. No one names him, so my guess is that's it's the mob."

Lindsay rolled her eyes. "Why do I feel a conspiracy theory brewing?"

"Well, I question if dear old Herb's death was really an accident."

Lindsay grimaced. "Herbert died?"

"About a year after all of this happened, so roughly thirty years ago."

"So the earrings were never recovered?"

"That's right."

"And twenty years ago, the earrings resurfaced when Lia Dash made a splash on the fashion scene."

"By that time the scandal had died down, and no one put those earrings together with the mobster's heirloom diamonds."

"Hmm . . ." That didn't explain why Dominic was after the earrings now. "What happened to Cleo?"

"I don't think she ever had the earrings. She couldn't get another job in the jewelry business thanks to Herb, and she struggled to make ends meet until Dominic made his fortune. She died about two years ago."

"The same year of Lia's auction." Now the pieces were

connecting. "Dominic sees those earrings and he wants them."

"It's all about going full circle."

"Why would he want them? They brought his family nothing but grief and destruction."

"Forget about that. Focus on the fact that we went the wrong way in getting them back!"

"How is the seduction plan the wrong way to go?"

"The scandal was all about a love triangle, and you're down there trying to get him jealous!"

Lindsay jackknifed up. "Oh, my God. You're right." If she was trying to make him jealous, would he think the diamond brought bad luck?

She gasped when she realized how Dominic would achieve full circle. He would destroy the diamond earring because it destroyed his family. "What am I going to do?"

"I say abandon the strategy," Nicole advised.

She kicked off her bedcovers. "I have to go find Dominic."

"Oh, yeah. Good luck on that. We'll see if he wants to have anything to do with you now."

Lindsay found Dominic by the pool. A patio umbrella shielded him from the hot morning sun as he sat next to a table covered in financial newspapers. He talked on his cell phone in hushed tones.

She took a deep breath and walked toward Dominic. Her heart slammed against her ribs. Lindsay felt she was going to capture a dangerous beast with her bare hands. She might win, but not without getting a few scratches.

The new plan was . . . Well, she didn't have one. She was winging it. Yesterday she had tried to get into his room when the maids did their rounds. Either these maids were really smart cookies, or sneaking into another person's hotel room was a lot harder than the movies made it appear.

That meant the only way she could get into his room was by invitation. He had made it clear that he wanted her, but that was last night.

As her heel clicked against the concrete, she slowly made her way to his table. Approaching him was a form of surrender, and that bothered her. She was showing that she was willing to put aside her pride because she wanted to be with him.

And the problem was, she wasn't pretending. She wanted him, wanted to be with him, and stay. Getting the diamond earring was making her act on it.

Worse, she wanted more than a night or a fling. She felt like there were many layers to Dominic Stark and it could take her an eternity to learn them all. Yet once she got the earring back, she couldn't hang around and wait for him to steal it again.

Of course, first she had to get invited into Dominic's room.

That meant she had to proposition him. She would risk rejection. No, Lindsay corrected her thought. She would risk Dominic accepting the challenge.

Dominic didn't salute her approach with a smile or a nod. His dark, hooded eyes met hers. The muscles under his T-shirt tightened.

Was he ready to pounce? She wobbled a bit under his watchful gaze. She silently stood in front of him, unsure of what to do or say. She knew one thing for certain: She shouldn't have worn the bright orange bandeau or the orange and yellow sarong. They were much too skimpy and flimsy to handle Dominic's direct gaze.

Her leg brushed against his, but he didn't nudge her away. Instead he sprawled his legs out until his feet blocked hers. Was it a challenge to move closer? She could easily get trapped between his long, muscular legs. He could imprison her until he was ready to let her go.

The idea excited her. Longing flooded her breasts, making them feel heavy and full. The sensation traveled to her abdomen and even farther down. The immediate response alarmed Lindsay and she kept her guard up.

"Dominic." The tension made her voice hoarse.

"Lindsay."

"Can I buy you another drink?" She motioned at the almost empty glass next to his newspaper. "How about a mimosa?"

"Why?" His eyes glittered with suspicion. He tilted his head. "What's in it for you?"

She pressed her lips together for a moment. "Whatever you want." There. She had said it. So why couldn't she breathe? Why was her body shivering with anticipation?

His eyebrow raised a notch and he swung his arm over the back of his chair. "You better be careful. You don't know what I want."

Her breath puffed out raggedly through her lips. She knew what *she* wanted. She wanted to bolt. Give up this sham, go back to her safe home and hide.

Dominic's casual, open gestures were warnings. He was going to lure her into a sensual, mind-boggling trap. One she wasn't ready for.

At least she was aware of this. That gave her the edge. She was not going to let this man's sex appeal intimidate her. Lindsay could have him on her terms.

All she had to do was keep her wits about her and not get cornered. With that in mind, she dragged over the neighboring patio chair and perched on the edge. She sat directly in front of him, meeting his gaze as her legs bumped against his. He didn't move his knee away from hers. She decided she wouldn't move either.

"You know, you're right," Lindsay agreed and leaned closer to him. She wanted to draw him in quick before she got caught. "I don't know what you want. Maybe you should tell me."

His stony expression didn't change, but the bronze weathered skin tightened against his harsh features. "Maybe I will. One day."

Panic bubbled up her throat until she could taste it. She didn't have much time. Why was Dominic playing hard to get now?

What was she doing wrong? Lindsay tried to remember the flirting checklist. Smile . . . attitude . . . body language! She forgot body language.

She leaned back and mimicked his casual stance, tossing her arm over the back of her chair. When she felt her bandeau slip, she realized it wasn't the brightest move. "I'll wait."

His eyes flickered across her body. His gaze rested several times on her breasts. She shifted uncomfortably as her nipples hardened against the lightweight material. She hoped the wait wouldn't be long.

"Why do you want to buy me a drink?"

"Maybe I want to get you drunk and have my way with you." Her smile was positively mischievous at the idea. "Or maybe I decided that I misjudged you."

"Uh-huh." From the skeptical tilt of his eyebrows, Dominic was obviously not buying either scenario. He was intrigued, maybe, but not convinced. "What makes you think I'm interested anymore?"

She flinched inwardly as insecurity stabbed her. She wanted to run for sure. "A hunch." She swallowed awkwardly and looked down at their touching legs. Realizing the loss of eye contact made her vulnerable, she determinedly looked back at him.

Dominic watched her closely. The aggressive gleam in his eye began to fade. "You could do better than that."

She didn't think she could. She really didn't. "Maybe I want to reciprocate," she replied softly.

Dominic leaned forward. His eyes burrowed in on her, piercing her seductive image, right past her good girl layer and straight to the woman she concealed. "Reciprocate what?"

He wanted her to spell it out? Lindsay instinctively drew back. Wasn't flirting and seduction all about innuendos and suggestion?

Body language. She kept forgetting about the body language. A person could lie, twist the truth, or evade it altogether with the right moves. She leaned forward until she could inhale his clean scent. Every instinct screamed to keep a safe distance.

But a safe distance wouldn't get her what she wanted. Playing it safe wasn't going to get her into Dominic's bed. She reached out and cupped his knee. The heat rippled through her palm and pooled in her wrist until it coursed down her arm.

"What we were doing last night. Only this time it's your turn," Lindsay promised. "We can do whatever you want."

His knee tensed under her touch. "Are we negotiating now?"

Something inside her relaxed. He wasn't fighting this.

They were on the same wavelength. "Yeah," Lindsay said, her voice filling with excitement. "We're negotiating."

His hand closed over hers. Lindsay was caught between his solid knee and his big, heavy hand. She tried to pull away, but it was too late. Dominic wasn't ready to let her go. She was trapped.

The knowledge made her tug harder. Dominic responded by circling his callused finger and thumb around her wrist, chaining her down with a simple, deft move.

"Let's cut to the chase," Dominic said in a sensuous drawl. "What is it that you really want?"

CHAPTER SIX

DOMINIC WATCHED LINDSAY'S EYES WIDEN WITH caution. A little too late for that, he decided as he felt her hand curl into a protective fist.

Had she been so certain that he was an easy target because of what happened between them? What was he thinking? Of course he was.

Well, he would have been more agreeable had she approached him honestly. Lindsay was after something, and it wasn't his body. He had a very good idea what she really wanted.

Lindsay wetted her mouth with an anxious dart of her tongue. "I'm not sure—"

"I'll tell you what I want." Dominic rubbed his thumb against her wrist. Her pulse skittered under his touch. "And you tell me what you want. Let's start with you first."

"I don't . . ." She slowly shook her head.

"You know, Lindsay, I've always thought you were a straightforward kind of woman, but I never thought of you as a coward."

"Excuse me?" Her voice rose with outrage. She tried to yank from his grasp again, but he wouldn't let her break free. Not just yet.

"You act like you don't want me and then you're all over me like a rash." And it was a rash he wasn't trying to get rid of. Fake or not, when she approached him with her come-hither attitude, he about swallowed his tongue.

She glared at him. "A simple 'no' would have sufficed," she said in a snippy tone that made him laugh.

"And when you're feeling real vulnerable, you start using words like 'sufficed.'" Dominic smiled knowingly.

"Okay, enough. You're not interested." Her mouth drew into a tight, straight line. "I got it. You can let go of me now." She pulled again.

"No, because you *don't* get it."

"What don't I get?" she asked through clenched teeth.

"I want you." He felt no weakness in stating the truth. Maybe he should. His feelings for Lindsay were a liability.

She looked as if she didn't know if his wanting was a good thing. He was willing to prove otherwise with a hands-on presentation.

"If I want you and you want me, why are we still sitting here?" She tilted her head, indicating the patio.

"Because you're playing games with me, sweetheart. Tell me what you really want."

He watched the slender column of her throat work as she swallowed nervously. The love bite he gave her peeked from under her long hair. His chest swelled at the sight of his branding. He probably shouldn't feel that way. He shouldn't like seeing his mark, his bold claim on her.

"I know you took my earring," she said in a low, fierce tone, "and I came back to get it."

Dominic blinked, but not out of surprise. He saw the passion glittering in her eyes and tightening her features. It was probably not a good time to tell her she was beautiful when she was angry.

"Lindsay! I'm deeply offended." He ignored her sizzling glare. "What makes you think I have it?"

"Who is playing games now? I know all about the scandal those earrings caused your parents."

Hmm . . . She worked faster than he had anticipated. He would do well not to underestimate her. "What if I offer you money for the earrings?"

Her eyes narrowed into slits. "It's a little too late for that, and they are not for sale."

Dominic casually reached for his glass of orange juice, the glass slick with condensation. "I can double the amount you paid for them."

"Who cares? I've had better offers for those earrings."

The corner of his mouth twitched. "I know."

That gave her pause. "You were the anonymous offer?" she guessed. "Why didn't you buy the earrings at the auction? It would have been a lot cheaper for you."

And a lot less hassle, but then he would never have met Lindsay. "There had been a problem with the telecommunication system at the auction house. Didn't you notice that no one on the phones made a bid?"

She frowned, trying to remember. "I wasn't paying attention."

He set the glass back down on the table with a decisive clink. "So you're willing to do anything to get your earring back. Did I understand that?"

Her jaw clenched. "Within reason."

"That doesn't make it nearly as much fun." He took a sip of the orange juice, hoping she didn't notice the tremor in his hand.

"In case you haven't noticed," she said as she folded her arms, "I'm not having fun."

"Yes, you are." He looked at her and rested his forearms on his knees. "Let's make a deal."

"You can do that when you ask for a plea bargain," she said with a saccharine-sweet smile. "I want my earring now."

He wasn't too worried about that possibility. Lindsay would have called the cops by now. "I tell you what . . ."

"I'm not making a deal," she said, raising her voice. "You are not in a position to negotiate."

"If you spend one night in my bed, I'll give the earring to you."

Her lips parted in surprise and she blinked. "What?"

"See, I can be reasonable," Dominic said proudly.

Lindsay's mouth opened and closed. "Reasonable? You want me to sleep with you in exchange for an earring? An earring that you stole from me?"

He reviewed the deal in his mind. "That sounds right. What part is confusing you?"

"We've already slept together." A blush crept up her neck and flooded her cheeks.

"The deal isn't retroactive."

"I don't believe this," she muttered to herself. Her forehead crinkled with a frown and she rubbed the furrows with her fingertips. Dominic fought the urge to erase the worried lines with his lips.

He knew what Lindsay thought of him and he couldn't change that. This was his last chance of having her in his bed, and he would get her any way he wanted. He'd take it, even if it meant it could only last one night.

And he was willing to abandoning his quest for the one night. After all, he had already given up one of the earrings for her.

"What's your answer, Lindsay? Do I get you in my bed any way I want in exchange for the earring?"

Her hand stopped and she looked up. "What kind of woman do you think I am?"

Was this a trick question? "Mine."

Her glare gave him the answer. Disappointment flooded his chest. He'd lost his chance. "Hey, I'm not going to change my mind. I know what I want and I told you."

"And let me guess"—she rose from her seat, the chair legs scraping against the concrete—"once I walk away from the table, the offer is no longer available."

"You have until the end of the day." It was a risk extending the deadline. She might call the cops, but they wouldn't find any incriminating evidence on him.

"Thanks for the warning. Now here's one for you. I'm not giving up, so you'd better watch your back. I'll be sure to watch mine." She moved to leave and paused uncertainly as she caught a glimpse of his feral smile.

"You do that," Dominic said as a primal response licked his blood. "But it won't do you much good while you're underneath me."

★   ★   ★

It was hopeless. Lindsay stepped into the elevator that would whisk her to the safety of her hotel room. As the doors closed, she rested her head against the wall and groaned. Okay, maybe not hopeless. All she had to do was take Dominic up on his offer.

Not in a million years!

She looked at her hazy reflection in the elevator door as she zipped up each floor. What possessed her to wear Nicole's clothes? She looked like . . . well, like a good girl trying to be bad.

Now she knew what happened to bad girls.

The doors slid open and she stepped into the hallway, deep in thought. One night for the diamond . . . She shivered and rubbed her arms. It scared her, and yet a strange, unfamiliar excitement bubbled underneath.

She paused when she got to her door, wondering if she had it in her to take Dominic up on his offer. It could be the most amazing experience.

She was his for one night . . . any way he wanted.

Lindsay held her breath in anticipation as she imagined Dominic having his way with her. He would have all the power and control. She would accept whatever he gave her.

Her stomach clenched with panic. No. No way.

She shook her head, her caution outmatching the buzz she felt when considering all the possibilities. She knew better than to agree to this devil's bargain. If she accepted, it wasn't something she could just keep in the past. It would tear apart her orderly existence, leaving her with wild and chaotic memories.

She couldn't risk that . . . could she?

CHAPTER SEVEN

LINDSAY RAISED HER FIST AND HESITATED at the last minute. She smoothed her slicked-back chignon with shaky fingers as she stared at Dominic's hotel door.

"I can't believe I'm doing this," she muttered aloud. But she committed herself. She had already left Dominic a terse message saying she would be at his hotel room at seven.

There was no going back, she realized as she tapped her knuckles on the door. He knew that she had agreed to the deal. It was up to her to follow through.

She stood there for an eternity, clenching her purse with stiff fingers. The metallic sound of the latch irritated her already frayed nerves. She was amazed that she was still standing by the time Dominic opened the door.

The first thing Lindsay noticed was that he was barefoot. Her gaze slid up his dark trousers to his unbuttoned white dress shirt. She couldn't quite manage to look him in the eye, so she kept her attention level to his darkly tanned chest. His hard, smooth chest . . .

Maybe she should look somewhere else.

"Lindsay." He moved to the side to let her in. "I thought you wouldn't show up."

She cleared her throat. "Well, you were wrong." She stepped inside the room. It looked exactly like hers, but it seemed colder. She shivered. Maybe she shouldn't have worn the black dress.

"You look beautiful," he said standing by her shoulder. "May I take your purse?"

"Sure." She unclenched her fingers from the leather and passed it to him. She folded her arms across her chest to ward off the cold and stared at the drawn curtains on the other side of the room.

"Is the color of your dress supposed to symbolize something?" His voice was right behind her.

Her lips twitched with a small smile. "No." She chose the dress because it was neither formal nor casual. She had no idea what a one-night sex slave wore.

Dominic stood beside her, gently cupping her elbow. "Would you like a drink?"

Lindsay glanced out the corner of her eye. Dominic was acting like a . . . a gentleman. Very suspicious.

She should be relieved. She'd had hazy visions of him jumping her the minute she arrived and tearing her clothes off before tossing her onto the bed.

She wasn't sure if the courtly behavior was any less dangerous.

"Lindsay?"

"Hmm?" Oh, right. He asked her about a drink. "Yes, thank you. Whatever you're having."

Her throat was dry and tight, but she couldn't think about choking back a drink. The only reason she agreed was to keep him occupied and move his attention elsewhere. If ever she had a chance to find the earring in his room, now was the time.

Walking slowly through the sitting area, Lindsay glided her hand along the back of the chair before reaching the small desk. She opened the drawer with feigned nonchalance, but it didn't slide easily. She winced when the wood squeaked. How does one rifle through papers without being heard?

Lindsay shoved the drawer closed. The desk was too obvious. Too easy. Dominic probably hid the earring in the closet or the bathroom. Most likely under the bed.

Her stomach flipped. *The bed*. She had tried her best not to look in that direction. And maybe Dominic had predicted that, making the bed the best hiding place.

She slowly turned and faced the bed. *See, not so bad*. It looked like any normal queen-sized bed. Same mocha-colored bedspread as hers. Lots of big pillows and—

Lindsay blinked and looked again. Her lungs seemed to shrivel as her last breath escaped her throat. There really were thin black restraints attached to the center of the bed and dangling to the floor.

"What are those?" She couldn't take her eyes off them.

"Restraints you can connect under the mattress," Dominic said as he approached her. "The bed doesn't have a headboard, so I went out and bought these."

Her heart pounded against her ribs. "You want to be tied down?" she asked hopefully as she accepted the glass of red wine.

"No," he replied with a slanted smile. "They're for you."

Her finger pressed tight against the glass stem. "I—you—"

"I get you for one night—any way I want," he reminded her and took a sip of his wine.

"B-but I . . ."

He looked over the rim of the wineglass. "That was the deal."

Yeah, but he didn't mention anything about tying her up! During the week they had shared, not once did he show an interest in using restraints.

"Lindsay?"

She turned to him, her chest rising and falling rapidly. She forced herself to look into his brown eyes.

"We won't do anything you can't handle."

He would be surprised at how little she could handle. He'd only seen her in vacation mode, when she was eager to try something new and different. That was the kind of woman she wanted to be, not the kind that she was.

"You can walk out of here at any time."

And walk away from the earring, Lindsay silently added as her lips straightened into a grim line. She knew the gentlemanly behavior was a trick.

But she wasn't going to walk away or give up. She would handle this. She'd taken control of Dominic in bed before and she would do it again.

Anyway, the earring was hers. Lindsay set her glass down on the bedside table and kicked off her black heels. She wasn't going to let him have it. "Let's get started."

His eyes gleamed. With amusement? Excitement? She couldn't tell. "What's the rush? We have all night."

"I'm aware of that." Boy, was she ever. She pulled at the pins that held up her hair. Her fingers stilled when Dominic placed his hands on hers.

"Don't I get the honors?" he asked softly.

She shrugged and reluctantly dropped her hands. "Yeah, sure. Why not? It's your night."

He set his glass down and moved in front of her. Lindsay looked at the floor, masking her nervousness. Dominic removed the pins one by one, and she stood motionless. She found his raised arms like an intimate prison.

She closed her eyes as her hair fell past her shoulders in waves. Dominic tossed the pins on the table with a clatter before spearing his hands into the soft, thick mass. Lindsay's scalp tingled with pleasure as he played with her hair.

Dominic drifted his hands down until he brushed his thumbs along her jaw. He tipped her head back, but Lindsay still didn't open her eyes. She parted her lips, waiting for his mouth to press against hers.

A wicked thrill skittered through her body when Dominic kissed her. His touch was soft but insistent. He slowly invaded her mouth before gently slipping his tongue past her lips.

Lindsay flattened her hands against his chest. She slid her fingers underneath the unbuttoned shirt, seeking the warmth of his skin. She explored the slopes and planes of his chest as he deepened his kiss, stealing her breath away.

She didn't notice how her dress sagged and gaped until she heard the drag of the zipper. Lindsay opened her eyes just as the black dress slid down her breasts.

Before it could fall completely, she clasped the material to her chest and looked up into Dominic's face. Lust sharpened his features as a dull flush stained his high cheekbones. The glitter in his dark, smoky eyes gave her a heavy sensation deep in her belly.

"Let go." Dominic's voice was quiet but rough.

Lindsay tightened her hold. She couldn't do this. No, she could. So why wasn't she? What was her problem? She wanted this.

She glanced at the bed. *That* was the problem. She wanted this. She wanted him. It wasn't about the earring.

Let go. Lindsay's breath caught in her throat as she released the dress. It fell past her hips before landing in a puddle at her bare feet. Lindsay instinctively covered her breasts with her arms. Shyness and uncertainty overwhelmed her as she stood before Dominic wearing only black panties.

The silence electrified the room. Lindsay trembled as she waited for Dominic's next move. She heard the rustling of his shirt before it hit the ground.

"Take everything off," he told her as he pulled down the bedcovers with an urgent yank, "and then lie down in the center of the bed."

Lindsay hooked her finger under the waistband of her panties and shucked them off. Her moves were fast and clumsy, her awkwardness intensifying as she crawled onto the bed. She concentrated on keeping her hands to her sides. It proved more difficult than she expected.

Dominic picked up one of the restraints and reached for her hand. No matter how hard she tried to be calm, her muscles tightened. She bunched her hands into fists, her nails digging into her palms.

After he bound her wrist, he moved down the bed. She jerked when he grasped her leg.

"My legs?" she said hoarsely as he wrapped the soft cuff around her ankle. "There's no need."

"Yes, there is," he said as he bound her ankle before he went around the bed to take care of the other arm and leg. "It's my night."

"It's my earring to begin with," she muttered under her breath.

Okay, she could handle this. Lindsay breathed in and out as her pulse raced. It was no big deal. Dominic wouldn't hurt her. She knew that fact deep in her bones.

Yet that didn't stop her from testing the resistance of the black straps. They didn't let her move very much at all. A touch of anxiety curled through her limbs.

She tensed as Dominic stood by the foot of the bed. She was sprawled naked before him. Exposed. Vulnerable. His for the taking.

She tensed when he crawled between her parted legs. He skimmed his hands over her body. Her stomach clenched as he flattened his hand possessively on her abdomen.

His hands and mouth were everywhere. On her breasts, her stomach, the curve of her hip. His touch was unpredictable. He could tickle the spot behind her knee or graze her hard nipple with his tooth. He could cup her mound, lick her ear, or suckle her toe as she squeaked out her protest.

She couldn't touch him. Couldn't turn away. Couldn't move closer. And she definitely couldn't hide how aroused she had become. All she could do was watch him sheath his penis with a condom.

She felt a quaver ripple along her pelvis as he raised her bottom from the wrinkled sheets. Dominic surged into her with one thrust. She groaned, arching back as he filled and stretched her to the hilt.

Lindsay hated the restraints. She wanted them off. Her

conviction deepened with every move he made. The cuffs chafed and bit her skin. She wanted to touch him. Wrap her legs around him. Grab his face and kiss him.

Dominic's strokes grew quick and fierce. An unbearable heat pushed under her skin. She bucked wildly, crying out, as the jolt ripped through her. The cuffs yanked her and she boomeranged back onto the mattress as she rocked against Dominic.

Lindsay's head collapsed onto pillows that were slipping off the bed. She weakly closed her eyes and gasped for her next breath as Dominic continued to thrust. She wanted to wipe the sheen of sweat off her flushed skin. Her arms and legs trembled as her core throbbed.

Her pulse quickened as the heat flickered deep in her belly. A ghost of a smile swept along her swollen lips. The night was far from over.

CHAPTER EIGHT

THE RAIN WAS GETTING TO HER, Lindsay decided as she walked briskly down the Seattle sidewalk. They must be having worse weather than usual. She couldn't remember the last time clouds had spit cold, sharp raindrops at her.

At least she'd had a break from the dull winter thanks to her two trips to Hawaii. Lindsay shuffled to a standstill. *Hawaii . . .*

No, no, no. She pulled her shoulders back and forged on. It was time to get back to work. To her life. To reality.

She was already behind schedule thanks to her impromptu trip to retrieve the earring. Now she had to cram more work into an already packed workday. But first she had to hand over the remaining earring.

Lindsay wondered how she was doing on time and glanced down at her watch. She made note of the time before her gaze slid to the faint pink mark under the gold band.

The mark on her wrist taunted her. It was a souvenir from that night Dominic had tied her up. It was as if the real her was erupting out of the good-girl shell. Even though the mark would disappear, the night would linger with her forever.

She was already feeling different. The coiled hair at the back of her head seemed too severe now. Her suits were color-less. The efficiency of her apartment used to bring her peace; now it made her feel antsy.

What she needed was the hotel room with the mocha-colored sheets. The black restraints. Dominic . . .

She vividly remembered how she had felt when she left Dominic sleeping that morning. She hadn't wanted to leave, but at the same time, she wanted to get away and regain her composure. It turned out she didn't have to worry about see-ing him again: When she opened her purse to get her card key, the pink diamond earring was lying safely inside.

He had snuck the earring there when she first arrived. She would have never thought to look there. And then it had hit her on the way back to her room; she could have walked out at any time that night and would have had the earring.

Just went to prove she had been in way over her head when she got involved with the likes of Dominic Stark.

Lindsay stopped walking when she realized she had missed the coffeehouse. She retraced her steps and entered the estab-lishment, immediately finding her sisters.

Nicole was sprawled on the overstuffed orange sofa, while Sabrina sat in a wide brown chair, her jeans-clad legs tucked underneath her.

"Lindsay! About time!" Nicole held out her hand. "Give me the other earring."

"Sheesh, Nicole. May I sit down first?" She shook her

head as she maneuvered around the coffee table and perched onto a straight-back chair.

"I already lost a week of the earrings," Nicole pointed out.

"Lindsay already promised that we will make it up to you," Sabrina said, "so what's the rush?"

Nicole's expression brightened. "There's this guy."

Lindsay shot a look at Sabrina. "Why am I not surprised?" she muttered.

"I met him at the museum. His name is Alex and he's in charge of a traveling exhibit. I've seen him off and on for about a year as we negotiated the terms of the exhibit."

"So?" Lindsay asked.

"Alex is hot. And sophisticated." Nicole flopped back into the sofa with a groan. "And he probably thinks that I'm a flake."

Lindsay flashed another look at Sabrina.

"Don't even say it," Nicole warned them. "I know I can be flaky at times. But the earrings will make me look more sophisticated, give me some class."

"Yeah, okay, whatever," Lindsay muttered just as the barista approached. She ordered a black coffee, watching Nicole tap her foot impatiently.

"Enough stalling," Nicole said as she inched toward the purse. "Don't make me come after it."

"Stay away from my purse. You know the rules." Lindsay opened the black handbag and took out the earring as Nicole pounced.

"Believe me," Nicole said as she stared at the pink diamond in her hand, "I don't want to borrow anything in there other than this earring."

"You guys, don't cause a scene," Sabrina warned them. "So, Lindsay, how did you manage to get the earrings? Did you act like Tom Cruise in *Mission: Impossible*? Or was it more like Pierce in *The Thomas Crown Affair*?"

"Nothing like that," Lindsay said, the blush crawling up her neck. "He gave it back to me."

Sabrina frowned. "How did you convince him?"

"I just . . . did."

"Uh-huh." Sabrina acquired a speculative gleam in her brown eyes.

Lindsay needed to fake it. "What?" she asked innocently, preoccupied by blowing on her hot coffee before taking a tentative sip.

Sabrina leaned back in her chair and smiled wide. "He was waiting to give it back to you."

Lindsay gagged on the brew. "Are you crazy?"

"He could have taken both earrings, but he didn't. Did you ever ask him why?"

Lindsay shook her head.

"Maybe you should."

"I'm not in contact with him anymore," Lindsay softly pointed out. She blinked hard as unexpected tears stung her eyes. "I got the earring back."

"You need to stay away from that guy," Nicole said as she put the earring on. "He did you wrong."

Yeah, he took the earring. That overshadowed the good times, the pleasure, and the excitement he'd shown her. That should cancel out what she felt about him.

In time she'd laugh over the fact that she had fallen in love with him. Or worse, that she fell for him the second time she went to Hawaii. Lindsay hastily took a sip of the coffee, letting it burn her tongue.

But no one needed to know about that lapse of judgment. In time, what she felt would fade away. She would make sure of it.

"He didn't have to leave an earring behind," Sabrina said. "And he didn't need to give the other one back."

"Why are you defending him?" Lindsay set the mug down hard on the table. "He used me."

"You're assuming things."

"No, she's not," Nicole argued. "Stop putting romantic thoughts in her head." She turned to Lindsay. "I still think you should have called the cops."

Lindsay was somewhat surprised that she hadn't. She would have in any other situation. Had she always believed Dominic would return the diamond? Or had it been wishful thinking that became true by accident?

"Nicole, for all you know Dominic could have made a great sacrifice for Lindsay in the name of love."

Nicole scoffed at the idea. "More like in the name of I-don't-need-a-prison-record. I don't know why we're arguing about this. There's only one way Lindsay would know for sure, and that's not going to happen."

"Why can't it happen?" Sabrina asked.

"What? You want her to track him down?" Nicole asked, her voice rising in disbelief.

Track him down . . .

Sabrina shrugged. "Sure, why not?"

"For what?" Nicole splayed her arms out wide. "He gave the earring back."

"You're right." Lindsay rose from her seat and tucked her purse under her arm.

Sabrina and Nicole shared a confused glance. "Who's right?" Nicole asked.

"There's only one way to find out, and I'm going to take it."

Dominic stepped into his home and dumped his bags in the entry hall, but the heavy shroud of weariness didn't lift. He didn't know what the problem was. He was used to the plane ride from Honolulu to Los Angeles. It was not a big deal.

If anything, he should have felt lighter. He had managed to discard a thirty-year-old quest. He was no longer hunting for the diamonds that had once cast a shadow on his life.

He didn't destroy the diamonds like he had planned. The destruction wouldn't have broken the cycle. It would have only pulled him down, continued to haunt him. He could see that now.

Dominic should feel good that he had given the diamond back to Lindsay. His mother's creation lived on. It would be adored by the woman he loved and cherished.

But he had lost that woman. Dominic sagged against the wall. Sure, he got one night of fantasy with the woman of his dreams, but that only pushed her farther away. He had made one mistake after the next, and he couldn't fix them.

With some effort, Dominic pushed away from the wall and walked to the back of the house. The walls were closing in on him. He needed to go outside and clear his head.

Dominic strode to the expanse of windows overlooking his backyard. The sun was beginning to set, washing the sky with pastels. His pool beckoned.

What was that pink? Dominic's eyes widened as he watched Lindsay Graham emerge from the water.

Okay, he was hallucinating. That had to be it. Jet lag or something. But those reasons didn't stop his heart from rising to his throat.

She wore a tiny pink bikini—the same one she had worn when they first met. He remembered how the flimsy scraps of fabric tormented his imagination. Only this time her skin was golden brown and her eyes held a confident, sassy gleam.

He was at the back door before he realized it. Dominic wanted to rush onto the patio before the mirage evaporated. Instead he strolled over to Lindsay, grabbing a towel on the way and hoping she didn't notice how his hand shook.

"Lindsay," he said by way of greeting as his pulse skipped fast in his veins. "Breaking and entering?"

"I thought I would repay the favor," she said. She twisted her long hair in a rope and squeezed the water out of it. "Since you broke into my sister's apartment almost two months ago."

Dominic jerked his head back in surprise. How did she know about that? He had been careful. "When did you figure it out?"

She shrugged and took the towel he offered. "I knew you were on the earrings' trail for a while, and I wouldn't put it past you."

So much for his short-lived career in crime. "I guess we're even now." He kept his arms at his sides, but couldn't stop flexing his hands.

Lindsay wrapped the towel around her. "Yep, we're even."

He couldn't hold back anymore. Dominic grabbed the ends of the towel and hauled her against his chest. Her wet body left an imprint on his clothes.

"Why are you here?" he asked in a low, fierce tone. "You have both earrings."

She tilted her chin to look up into his face. She was not in any way intimidated by his mood. "Why did you only take one earring in the first place?"

She hadn't figured that out? That guilt had swamped him when he took the pink ice. It was the first time he hesitated, and the first time he questioned what he was doing. At the last moment he only took one.

That compromise ate away at him. It made him all too aware of his weakness. At first he thought the weakness was that he didn't take both earrings. That Lindsay was his weakness, his Achilles' heel.

But that turned out to be the opposite. His weakness was grabbing the diamonds in the first place. He bent and broke his own principles to finish something that had already been laid to rest. "Does it matter?" he finally answered Lindsay.

"Not really." She gave him a sly look, as if she had known what his answer would be. "Not when you think about how you stole from me, seduced me, gave me an offer I couldn't refuse . . ."

"I gave the earring back."

She nodded in acknowledgment. "True."

He bunched more of the towel into his hand. The feel of her body against his made it difficult to think. "And what about you?"

"What about me?"

"You drove me crazy and turned me inside out to the point that I couldn't see straight."

Her smile was slow and breathtaking. "Really?"

Dominic scowled back at her. "This isn't something to be proud of."

"Don't be too sure."

What was she doing here? There was something going on that he couldn't see. "Shouldn't you be in Seattle? Working?"

She nodded. "My bosses are getting fed up with the time off I've taken."

"So why are you doing it?"

"I have something important to do." Her mood grew serious as she stared into his eyes. "Like wiping the slate clean between you and me. It's time to start over."

Hope swelled in his chest until it pinched. "Just like that?"

"Yes." She shyly ducked her head. "For you I can."

Dominic swallowed roughly. "And my past sins won't ever be mentioned again?"

"Well, I can't promise you that," she said, a teasing gleam entering her eyes as she pulled back. "But I won't make you pay for it over and over."

He dropped his hold on the towel. "What's this plan of yours? How does it work?"

"We go back to the time when I met you at the hotel swimming pool." She moved away. "I walked by and you followed."

Dominic stepped into her path and cupped her face with his hands. He claimed her mouth with his, the impact shaking him. He wanted to savor this touch. He had once thought that he would never have this privilege again.

Lindsay pulled away, breathless. She swiped her tongue seductively over her lips. "You didn't do *that* the last time," she reminded him.

"And that was my first mistake," he said and lowered his head for another kiss.

PINK POSITIVE

CHAPTER ONE

"WHY DO YOU READ THAT KIND of trash?"

Nicole Graham glanced up from the tabloid and looked at her coworker. "Because I have an inquiring mind and I want to know what's going on in the world."

"It's filled with gossip, rumors, and lies," Andrea declared as she finished the last drops from her soda can. "I heard that all the tabloid editors come up with story ideas by getting drunk together at a local bar."

"You can't prove that." A smile tugged on Nicole's mouth. "Does that mean you're spreading gossip, rumors, and lies?"

Andrea's eyes narrowed when she realized she'd got caught in her own accusation. She stuck out her tongue.

"Good comeback," Nicole said with a laugh. "You shouldn't knock these tabloids. They uncover a lot of stories before mainstream newspapers even start looking."

"Sure they do."

"There are some very good articles in here. Like this one about Lia Dash." She tapped the newsprint. "It says that she helped capture a spy in 1980."

That she could believe, Nicole decided as she studied a photo of the celebrity, who had died two years ago. Lia had been her childhood idol. Nothing stopped the woman. She was brave and modest. She wore an air of elegant mystery with style and panache.

"Now there's a change of pace," Andrea said. "That trash usually talks about sex, drugs, and rock 'n' roll. Who was the spy Lia supposedly caught?"

"It doesn't say."

"Mm-hmm. Who's the source? A 'close insider'?" Andrea curled her finger into quotation marks.

"A high-ranking official who worked on the case," Nicole defended haughtily. "His name is not allowed to be divulged or it will compromise national security."

"Riiiight." Andrea rolled her eyes.

Okay, maybe she wanted to believe that Lia Dash fought for truth, justice, and the American way. A superhero, but with better fashion sense. Someone who didn't need bizarre mutations to find the courage inside her—and do something about it.

"Nicole, I hate to say this, but you are so gullible," Andrea said as she rose from the couch. "You believe every story that is fed to you."

"Not *every* story." She happened to like the ones about the rich, famous, and scandalous. The juicier the better.

Her co-worker glanced at the wall clock. "Lunch time is over."

"I'll be right there." She buried her nose back in the tabloid.

"Don't let the director catch you up here," Andrea warned as she tossed her soda can into the trash.

"Mm-hmm." She and Andrea usually snuck into the donors' lounge to eat lunch. The beautifully decorated room should have been on the cover of a magazine, but it was rarely used. Only donors who contributed a small fortune were invited into the lounge, and they were usually too busy making money to visit.

"It's days like these when I want to quit my job," Andrea said as she checked her appearance in the chrome refrigerator. "Why is the woman a director when she can't handle stressful situations? I mean, it's only a meeting."

Nicole glanced up. "What meeting?"

Andrea looked over her shoulder. "You mean you don't know? You're not up on the office gossip, but you know every salacious bit of trivia on some dead celebrity."

"Andrea."

"Alex Rafferty is dropping by today."

Nicole's feet slipped off the coffee table and hit the floor with a thud. "What? Why didn't anyone tell me? I'm working on that collection!"

"You have to check your e-mails more often."

She stood up and marched over to Andrea. "He's supposed to show up next week."

"Tell him that."

Nicole clenched the newspaper in her hand. "I'm not ready!"

"Yeah." Andrea gave Nicole's clothes the once-over and tsked. "Don't you wish you hadn't worn that outfit today?"

"That's because I let my sister borrow all of my new clothes." She should have known that impetuous generosity would turn around and slap her upside the head.

"Why'd you do that?"

"It was an emergency." Nicole twisted the newspaper into a rope. "She doesn't have anything that shows cleavage."

"And now you don't," Andrea pointed out.

Nicole looked at her reflection in the coffee service and combed her shoulder-length hair with her fingers. "Oh, not good. Not good at all."

The chunky green sweater dwarfed her. Not one bump showed where her breasts or hips were located. The A-line khaki skirt did nothing for her legs, and the flat shoes were comfortable but dowdy.

"Of course he *would* show up on laundry day," Nicole muttered as she stretched the sweater down her hips. It only made her look worse. "What am I going to do?"

"It's not that bad." Andrea failed at sounding convincing.

"No, it is. Fate is wrecking my plans." She stomped her foot in frustration. "All I wanted to do was make him forget his first impression of me."

"What was that?"

"At the donors' party last year. I borrowed one of Sabrina's cocktail dresses." She cringed in memory. She and her sisters had always been the same size. When had that changed? "And I accidentally flashed him."

"Oh, I remember that." Andrea leaned against the refrigerator. "Don't worry, Nicole. It doesn't count as flashing if you were wearing a bra."

"Then the next time he showed up I had a cold and looked horrible." She was surprised that her hacking up a lung and runny nose didn't make Alex run for cover. Then again, she didn't remember much of what happened that day thanks to her cough medicine. For all she knew, she had blabbed out all of the museum's secrets.

"Everyone looks horrible when they're sick," Andrea decided. "No big."

"What about that time I was flirting with him and found out my skirt was caught in my pantyhose?"

Andrea shrugged one shoulder. "So he knows you wear sexy underwear. I would see that as a plus."

"And do you know that all the times I've seen him, I wasn't wearing the earrings?"

"Oh, here we go again." She pushed off the refrigerator and walked to the door.

Nicole followed her into the hallway. "I'm serious, Andrea. I need those earrings." It was just her luck that Lindsay had lost them.

"Guys don't notice earrings," her coworker said with great authority. "If they do, then they're gay."

Nicole scoffed at that sweeping statement. "No they aren't."

Andrea grabbed the banister as she headed down the winding spiral staircase. "How many guys have you dated who've said something about your earrings?"

She thought about it. "One. And he's the reason I don't wear dangling earrings anymore."

"Really? What did he say?"

"Something along the lines of 'Get it off! Get it off!'" Nicole's voice bounced off the white marble walls.

Andrea glanced over at her, giving her a strange look.

"My earring got caught in his pubic hair when I gave him a blow j—"

She crashed into a couple walking up the steps. "Sorry, I didn't . . ." Nicole forgot what she was saying as she saw Alex and the museum director standing before her.

Amusement gleamed in his green eyes as the dull red crept up her neck and face. It was creeping elsewhere too, not that anyone could tell thanks to her voluminous sweater and skirt.

"Nicole." The museum director's eyes were wide with horror, but her voice was edged with frost. "You remember Alex Rafferty? He's supervising the traveling collection of royal jewels?"

"Yes, of course. Hello, Alex." She reluctantly offered her hand, when she really wanted to slink away just like Andrea was doing.

"It's good to see you again, Nicole." His hand enveloped hers. She flinched when she felt the jolt of his touch, but she didn't pull away.

She pressed her lips together and waited for him to make some sort of comment. None came. Of course not, Nicole realized with relief. Alex Rafferty was a true gentleman. A sexy, sophisticated man who invaded her dreams and made her wake up hot and sweaty, but he was still a gentleman.

"Since you are the curator for the exhibit"—the director sounded like she was already regretting that decision—"would you please show Mr. Rafferty the publicity plans we've made."

"Of course." Nicole's smile was tight and hurting her cheeks. She didn't know how much longer she could keep it up.

"Do I need to come with you?"

Nicole's jaw stiffened. The last thing she needed was for her boss to act as her chaperone. "Not at all. I can handle this."

The director gave one final, not-too-sure-she-should-leave look before she turned in the other direction and walked down the steps.

Why did these things happen to her? Because she didn't have the earrings, that's why! Her sister had better find that other diamond fast.

She looked back at Alex, her eyes level with his since she was on the top step. She could get lost in those green eyes.

Alex stepped to the side and gestured for her to walk past him. "After you."

"Thanks." *Keep it professional, girl. If you throw yourself at him, you're going to fall onto the ground with a big splat.*

And with that reminder, Nicole discreetly smoothed her hands along her skirt, making sure it wasn't caught in any pantyhose, before she continued walking down the stairs.

Alex forced his muscles to relax when Nicole stepped in front and guided him to her office. He was still tense and stiff, but at least she was in front of him.

That was a good thing, since he couldn't stop staring at her mouth. The wide smile and full lips. He wondered what she would taste like.

He wasn't getting any better at this. Every time they met, he found himself wanting to get closer to this woman. If he wasn't craving to hold her and comfort her while she was battling a cold, he was fantasizing about the glimpses of sexy lingerie she wore.

But today he barely said hello and he started to imagine what it would be like if she bestowed the same favor she gave her ex-boyfriend. He could clearly see Nicole kneeling before him. Her hands would grip the base of his cock and cradle his balls. He wouldn't care if she wore dangling, sharp earrings.

And then she would twirl her tongue along the tip of his cock before she closed those pink lips over him. He would cup his hands behind her head, splaying his fingers into her soft, silky hair. At first he would pump gently into her mouth, but as she sucked him in deeper, her cheeks concaving with every draw, he would thrust harder, faster, until he—

"You came earlier than I expected."

Nicole's voice sharply yanked him out of his daydream. "I beg your pardon?"

"I thought you were arriving next week."

"Right. That had been my intentions, but I found myself ahead of schedule." He also found it extremely difficult to walk with a hard-on. "I hope it's not inconvenient for you."

Nicole looked over her shoulder and flashed him a sunny smile that made his heart twist. "Not at all."

"Good." Alex smiled back. *Found himself ahead of schedule?* More like he moved mountains around the clock so he could get to Seattle as soon as possible. His reasons had nothing to do with ambition—the sole purpose was to see Nicole again.

He couldn't remember the last time a woman had driven him to this level of distraction—and he hadn't even gone on a date with her!

This attraction could not have come at a worse time. Supervising the royal family's personal collection of jewels required more than minute planning and top-of-the-line security. He had to employ all of his skills of diplomacy and illusion. A kingdom whose influence and power reached back centuries depended on him to keep its secrets. He wouldn't fail—as long as he kept his head straight and focused on anything but Nicole's mouth.

"Here we are." Nicole ushered him into her compact and colorful office. He looked around, noting the framed diplomas, awards, and thank-you notes written by children dotting the dark purple walls. A Mardi Gras bead necklace was tangled in a lovingly cared-for plant. The wooden bookcase held old museum catalogs and files.

"I think the publicity folder is here on my desk," Nicole said as she walked over to the piece of furniture that took up most of the room. "Take a seat."

His choices were a furry red beanbag chair or a battered plastic lawn chair that had seen better days. He went for the plastic.

"Ah, found it!" She handed him a slim folder.

"Thanks." Alex carefully avoided brushing his fingers along hers. He opened the folder and glanced at the first page. *Uh-oh.*

Alex's heart pounded in his ears. His mind had already pinpointed twenty-seven diplomatic and constitutional nightmares by the time he looked up at Nicole's expectant face.

"You plan to emphasize the role of the princesses?" In all of their negotiations and planning, this was not mentioned. It could be the deal-breaker.

"Yes!" She radiated excitement. It was clear that Nicole was passionate about the subject. "Since the majority of the jewels are worn by them, it only makes sense."

"I see." He reached for his shirt pocket and extracted his carbon-steel fountain pen. He saw her eyebrows rise before she looked at her jar of disposable ballpoint pens.

He looked down at the folder again, giving himself time to organize his thoughts. "The slant you want to put on the publicity materials is different from that of the other museums that have had this collection. I'd like to hear your mission statement."

"Well"—she gave a shrug—"I think it's self-explanatory. This is a museum that celebrates women."

Alex nodded and slowly uncapped his pen. He was well aware of the museum's focus. It was the reason they didn't elect to show the jewels at a bigger museum.

The royal family allowed the collection out of the country in order to attract a specific tourist, namely the affluent older woman. But the royal family didn't want to compromise its privacy. That was Alex's mission throughout this project.

"So," Nicole continued, "I thought while we're displaying the jewels, we should really showcase the women who wear the jewelry. I've been gathering old pictures of princesses at official events as they wore some of the specific pieces. Those are very rare."

His gut clenched.

"I'm also having a difficult time putting together the family tree. How many wives and children can a king possibly have?"

"Quite a few."

"Which led me to consider highlighting key princesses." Nicole's chair squeaked as she leaned back. "Those who fall in the same age-group as our target audience."

"I see."

"We should humanize these names." She moved her hands in the air. "Share anecdotes, casual snapshots, stuff like that. Give the viewer a story so they can relate to the princesses."

"Uh-huh." *Anecdotes? Casual snapshots?* The royal family never released these. Didn't Nicole know that?

"Every girl at one point of her life dreams of being a princess. This collection will remind them of that."

Alex caught Nicole's wistful look. "Did you want to be a princess?"

"I still do," she said with a deprecating smile.

Alex nodded and leafed through the plan. It was a good thing he came early. He needed all the time he could get to balance the royal family's needs with the museum's.

"What do you think?" Nicole finally asked.

"These are good ideas, but we won't be able to use all of them." *Or any of them.* "The royal family is very strict about the public viewing of its women."

Her eyebrows rose higher. "Are you kidding me?"

"It's their way of protecting them."

Her jaw shifted to one side. "Uh-huh."

Alex knew Nicole was trying hard not to offer her opinion. Despite his years of training and experience, he found himself wanting to tell her that he agreed with her. But that went against everything he was taught on the job. He would not rip the veil of secrecy to please this woman.

Alex looked down and crossed out one bulleted idea in the publicity plan that would enrage the royal family. "I'm sure we can find a way to celebrate the princesses while meeting the royal family's needs for privacy."

"Mm-hmm."

That suspicious murmur said it all. She obviously was fluent in double-talk and vague promises. Nicole Graham was going to keep him on his toes for the next two weeks.

"Perhaps we can work on this together." He raised his hand as Nicole opened her mouth. "I promise that I want this event to be successful for everyone involved."

"Your collection is a priority of mine." Nicole folded her hands and placed them on the desktop. "When the jewelry arrives, I will be doing intensive prepping on it for four months."

"And I'm looking forward to joining you during the initial phase." Almost too much. "Now for us to keep on schedule, I suggest we work on this publicity plan during the next two weeks."

"I'm in the middle of handling the temporary exhibit that is holding the space for your collection." Her tight smile looked like it was about to crack. "That's what I'm working on for the next two weeks."

"Then that means working together after hours." He saw a glimmer in her eyes, but it disappeared before he could determine what it meant.

"After hours?" she repeated in a squeak. "Here at the museum?"

"Would that be a problem?"

Her smile was almost predatory, and a streak of excitement zipped up his spine. "Not at all."

CHAPTER TWO

ALEX COULDN'T BELIEVE IT. IT HAD been two weeks of working after hours with Nicole Graham and he was ready to go insane. The woman exasperated, beguiled, confused, and surprised him every time he turned around.

He knew what the problem was. It wasn't that her ideas were diametrically opposed to his; it was that he had been working up close and personal with the woman and hadn't given in to his wildest fantasies.

One kiss was all he needed and he would work all night until he got the publicity plans together. Okay, maybe he would need a little more than one kiss. Of course, that would cause major problems at work, but he was willing to risk it. In fact, if he could tug Nicole onto his lap, he would be the most agreeable man at work. He needed to be agreeable considering some of Nicole's crazy ideas.

"Throne?" Alex raised his head and stared at Nicole as they

shuffled through the paperwork. It was his last night there and he was still learning about some of Nicole's plans. "What do you mean you're going to use the throne?"

"Don't worry." She waved the concern away with the flick of her hand. "It's not a real one. The carpenters made one for us years ago for a different exhibit."

"A throne?"

"I think the carpenters used an empress throne as a guideline. The back is very low and the seat is wide to accommodate the gowns and capes."

A nagging suspicion curled in his gut. "What do you plan to do with it?"

"Replace one of the benches with it. That way visitors can know what it's like to sit on a throne."

Alex couldn't hide his look of horror.

"Oh, come on," Nicole said impatiently. "You worry too much. The idea is to make the visitors feel closer to the subject."

"Not *that* close." Why was Nicole determined to make this a hands-on project? The exhibit needed to be hands-off if they were to maintain decorum and dignity.

She put her hands on her hips, the move hitching up her short navy blue skirt and pulling at her white blouse. The promise of a glimpse of her curves momentarily distracted Alex.

"Why not?" she asked. "What's wrong with doing something fun like that?"

"The royal family relies on pomp and pageantry." How many times did he have to tell her this? "Maybe a touch of mystery and fantasy. When the viewer gets too close, the royals lose one of their most important traits."

"Oh, please." Nicole rolled her eyes. "That is so not true. You just don't want to use the throne because you're afraid it might be tacky."

"Might?" he muttered and immediately stiffened when he realized his slip. He would never mutter anything when handling negotiations. He won every point because he kept his cool.

How did Nicole get under his skin like this? He quickly suppressed the confusion welling up inside him. He was always forgetting to keep his guard up, that's all. It might not be easy, but he could do it.

"Would you like to see the throne?"

"Now?" Might as well. A change of scenery might clear his head.

"It's in the storeroom. We save all of our props," Nicole explained as she opened her office door and stepped out into the hallway. "You never know when you might need something again."

He followed her. "How many times have you needed a throne?"

"The occasion hasn't come up too often," Nicole admitted. "But this is not your typical throne."

"Of course."

They walked to the main floor of the dark museum. It was like a different place when everyone had gone home. A few security guards wandered along the rooms, but the quiet atmosphere only made Alex more aware of how alone he was with Nicole.

Work together after hours . . . What had he been thinking?

The building itself was dramatic. Gigantic stone lions rested outside the front doors, and once inside, visitors were greeted by a tall, sleek entry. He wasn't sure how someone like Nicole could work in a place filled with cold stone and marble, but he bet she was comfortable in the labyrinthine floor plan that encouraged slow exploration.

She took him through the maze of rooms, the light fixtures casting spotlights on random artwork and artifacts.

Alex stopped and took a step back when he saw a waist-down mannequin wearing an iron contraption. He resisted the urge to touch the metal. "What is this?" he asked Nicole, his voice echoing.

She walked back to where he stood. "It's a chastity belt, probably made around the sixteenth century. Note the padlock."

The belt looked heavy and painful. "What's it doing at the museum?"

"It's part of the Female Sexuality Through the Ages collection."

"Are you kidding me?" He looked around the room. The artifacts looked more like torture devices.

"Don't worry, your collection is on the other side of the building," Nicole assured him; yet strangely that was the last thing on his mind. "No one will group the royal family's jewelry with this collection."

"Female Sexuality Through the Ages?" he repeated, feeling a little stunned and off-balance.

"From Mesopotamia to the sexual myths still held today." She pointed at the words painted on the wall as she walked through the room.

He swallowed roughly. "I see."

She walked to the next room. "Here we are at the fertility and contraception display." She motioned at an artifact like a game-show model. "Did you know that animal dung was commonly used as a spermicide?"

And did she know that that tidbit of information did nothing to stop his cock from stirring? It should have. He wished it had.

Alex stared at the oversized fertility goddesses lined up against the walls. Some of the sculptures had several pairs of naked breasts. Call him conservative, but he felt two was plenty.

"Is this your most popular exhibit?" he asked in a strangled voice.

"It doesn't get the same buzz as our traveling limited-time-only collections," Nicole answered, and Alex had to smile at her careful answer. "But our visitors always make a point of dropping in."

"I bet." He walked behind her as they went through the hall of hetaeras, courtesans, prostitutes, and madams. The lights were low, the silence grating on his nerves. He could hear the swish of her skirt and the rasp of her nylons. His own breathing grew harsh.

"We're almost there," Nicole promised as they cut through the next room filled with sex toys.

Alex shuffled to a stop when an ancient bronze dildo captured his attention. His eyes widened at the size and girth of the toy. A quick glance at the information explained that it was found in a tomb in China. The experts guessed that it was made by artisans who specialized in creating dildo casts.

What a job. Alex closed his eyes. He needed to get out of here. There was no way he could spend another minute in Nicole's company without tossing her onto one of the display cases and sinking into her.

Maybe not in this room, he decided as he noticed some of the extra-large dildos. He could do without the comparison.

He heard the clip of her heels on the hard floor. "Alex? There you are." She stepped into one of the spotlights. "I wondered where I lost you."

He made a conscientious effort to ignore the toys on display and looked up high at the walls. He frowned at the artwork. It didn't make sense, but then heat invading his blood probably fried his brain in the process. "What's with the temple theme?"

"There were lots of cults in ancient times that encouraged female masturbation. Some ceremonies at the temple required it."

He was going to lose it. Right here. Right now.

"The storeroom is right outside," she said as she stepped out of the light and walked deeper into the shadows. "You're going to love the throne."

Throne? Oh, yeah. Right. They were going to the storeroom to look at the throne.

Alex automatically followed her. "I noticed the sex collection didn't offer anything hands-on."

Nicole's laugh bounced off the walls as they found their way into the darkened hallway. "I didn't work on the exhibit. If I had, I would have installed a pole and tossed in a box of fans in the exotic dancer area."

Lust, hot and wild, clamped down on his body. He couldn't move as his mind conjured up an image of Nicole sliding and swinging on a silver pole.

"Hold on," she said, and he heard the jingle of keys. "I can't find the one for the storeroom."

Alex took a step back. Nicole's citrus perfume hit him in

the back of his throat and he wanted to taste her scented skin. But first he would want to touch her hair and see if it was as soft as it looked. He wanted to sink his fingers in. Just once.

"Here we are. Got it." She slid the key into the lock and pulled the door open. Nicole hit the switch, flooding the room with lights.

Alex blinked and hesitated to step inside. As long as all the phalluses and breast-baring goddesses were outside the store-room, he would be able to keep his hands off Nicole.

Nicole couldn't believe she had done something so incredibly *stupid*! She hurried down one row of props, not really looking at items around her. How was she going to recover from this gaffe? She wasn't, plain and simple.

What had she been doing walking him through the exhibit? She could have gone the long way. But no, she went right through and gave him the grand tour!

Nicole cringed and felt her face go hot. She should have answered his questions and just kept walking. Definitely should have kept her mouth shut about female masturbation ceremonies.

The look in his eye could have been either shock or interest. It was hard to tell with the dim lighting. Considering how her life was going, she was going to choose shock.

Why did she have to do that? If she wanted to gain Alex's attention—and in a good way—she needed to act like a lady. Sophisticated men like him only dated women of class.

She needed those earrings. That would give her some ready-made class. In the meantime, she would have to think like Lia. What would Lia Dash do in this situation?

She would definitely not have talked about animal dung contraception.

Nicole could really, really use Lia's pink diamond earrings right about now. A couple more days without them and she would have Alex Rafferty running away.

"Ah, here we are," Nicole said when she spotted the empress throne. She slapped her hand on the carved armrest. "What do you think?"

He pulled it away from the wall to get a better look, and Nicole was glad he had folded up the sleeves of his dress shirt. She had no idea how lean and muscular his arms were. The man shouldn't hide his body in business suits.

She watched Alex walk around the throne, his hands on his lean hips. Her eyes were drawn to his loosened tie and the unbuttoned collar. She wanted to see more of him, but what were the chances?

"What's your verdict?" she asked, and he circled the chair again.

"It's a bench," he said without looking up.

"It's an empress throne," she corrected. "Sit down and see for yourself."

He followed her suggestion and sat down on the plush purple cushion. "It's wide. You could fit about one and a half people on this."

Okay, that conjured some images she shouldn't consider. "What do you think about it?"

He settled back into it, the throne squeaking with every move. "It's not comfortable."

She wasn't worried about that. It was all about the look. "That's fine. I don't expect visitors to sit there for hours."

"They aren't going to last more than a few minutes." He

put his elbow on one of the armrests, but didn't quite reach the other side. "This has the shape of a *U*."

"Not really. The actual seat is a flat surface. I admit this throne is untraditional—most thrones have straight lines and high backs."

"It feels like I'm sitting in a bowl." He surprised her by shifting in the chair and putting his legs over one of the armrests. "A half a bowl. Maybe a scoop."

"You don't want it in the exhibit." She got the message loud and clear. She shouldn't have told him the idea. From now on, she would do whatever she felt was necessary. More time would be saved if she said sorry rather than asked for permission.

"I'm undecided," Alex said and shifted his shoulders against the carved armrest.

"Alex, you haven't liked any of my ideas since you got here." She folded her arms across her chest. "Believe it or not, I know my job. I know how to create buzz and I know what the public wants to see."

He tilted his head back and looked up at her. "I never questioned that."

"I can showcase this collection. Give it some pizzazz, some mystery. Tell them what I want to tell them. Create an illusion."

"Your job is a lot like mine."

"But I don't tell you how to do your job."

Alex's green eyes shuttered. "And I'm not telling you, either. I'm carrying out the royal family's wishes."

Nicole sighed with frustration and ruffled her hair with her fingers. "This isn't going to work," she decided as she perched herself on the throne's cushion.

"Sure it is." He scooted over to accommodate her.

"Really?" Disbelief dripped from her voice. "Name one decision I made that you agreed to. No, no." She held up her hand. "Let's make it easier for you. Name one decision I made today that you approved."

He paused, and Nicole's spirits started to sink. She wasn't too sure if proving her point was a good thing.

Alex studied her face. "I approve of your perfume."

She blinked. "My . . . perfume?"

He leaned toward her. "I highly approve of it."

Her skin tingled. What did he mean by that? Was he really struggling to prove his point? Was he making a prelude to nuzzling her neck? Nicole tilted her head, hoping it was the latter. "I meant about the exhibit."

"You didn't say." His voice was soft and smoky. "What's the name of your perfume?"

Her mind went blank. "I—I can't remember."

"Hmm." A faint smile played on his mouth.

"Alex"—she tried to sound firm but had a feeling she failed miserably—"are you trying to distract me from this argument?"

"What argument?" His gaze was cloudy as it fastened on the beating pulse at her throat.

That didn't answer her question. Okay, what would Lia do in *this* situation? Kiss him? Accuse him of being improper and knee him to get the point across?

She wasn't sure, but Nicole knew what she would like to do, and kissing him was only the beginning.

Nicole was very aware of him. The rise and fall of his chest. The scent of his soap. Alex's hip pressed against hers. No matter where she moved, she would touch him. It was too tempting. . . .

Do it.

She leaned forward and pressed her mouth against his. She gasped as the spark pricked her lips. Closing her eyes, she savored the feel of his soft, firm touch.

Nicole slowly explored his mouth, moving from one side to the other. She pressed kisses along his mouth and then outlined his lips with the tip of her tongue.

He parted his lips and she darted her tongue inside his mouth. She licked the inside of his lip before nipping it with her teeth. She cupped the sides of his face with her hands as he deepened the kiss.

Nicole raised her head, slightly breathless, and looked into Alex's face. She licked her swollen lips when she saw the fierce glow in his green eyes. Excitement swirled around her chest and coiled low in her hips, pressing down.

Alex reached out and grasped her waist with large, commanding hands. Her eyes widened and she let out a squeak as loud as the protesting wooden throne when he lifted her up. Her knees knocked against his legs as she awkwardly straddled him.

"Alex, this isn't a good idea." It was a snug fit. Her knees and shoes pressed against the sides. Her legs clamped around his, and her sex clenched as she felt every hard muscle underneath her.

"Yes, it is." His hands roamed along her sides, and she couldn't stop the shiver of pleasure.

She bit her lip and smiled. "There you go disagreeing with me again."

He cupped the back of her head and brought her lips down on his. His kisses quickly grew hard and fierce. She surrendered to the sucking, biting, and licking.

She slid her hands down his shirt. The crisply laundered fabric trapped his body heat. Nicole wanted to feel all of it without barriers.

She tugged at his uncooperative tie and quickly abandoned it. Tossing it over his shoulder, she fumbled with his buttons until she could slide her hands against his bare chest.

The heat from his skin curled along her arms. She skimmed her fingers against the defined muscles of his chest. Her nails grazed his flat nipples before getting caught in the whorls of dark hair.

Nicole's breath hitched in her throat when she felt Alex's hands slip under her blouse. Her chest tightened as his hands swept along her ribs before he flicked open her bra. She groaned against his mouth when he cupped her breasts.

Nicole tore her mouth away from his, arching into his hands. The throne creaked loudly underneath them as he cradled her breasts and teased her nipples.

Alex leaned forward and captured the tip of her breast in his mouth. Nicole gasped, clenching his hair with her hands as he sucked hard. She felt the pull down to her core. She rocked against his penis, bearing down hard as wild need clawed at her.

He bucked against her as he drew her nipple deeper into her mouth. Nicole rode his penis, desperately trying to hold back her moans, and wishing they weren't wearing so many clothes.

Alex bunched her skirt up with one hand. He moved his hand to where they touched and sought her clit. Rubbing her through her damp panties, he pulled on her nipple with his mouth and pressed her clit with his fingers.

Nicole stiffened as the lightning struck through her. She heard the keening cry and a loud crack before she tumbled. Her mind did a free fall and she held tightly onto Alex. Her fingers dug into his shoulders when her knees hit something hard.

Ow. That jolted her out of the blissful sensations. She blinked dazedly as her eyes slowly focused on her surroundings. She was tangled with Alex on the floor, the throne underneath them in pieces.

She gasped in concern when she saw Alex rubbing the back of his head. "Are you okay?" She touched his head to make sure there weren't any cuts or swelling.

"Yeah." His voice was low and husky. "You?"

"Yeah." Now probably wasn't the time to say, *G-r-r-reat! Never better!* Especially when she probably gave the guy a concussion.

Alex propped himself up on his elbows and surveyed the damage. "I don't think it's salvageable."

"Guess we won't be using it for the exhibit," she said shakily as she disentangled her legs from his.

"Now see," he said with a slanted smile, "there's another decision of yours I agree with."

Nicole considered pushing him, but decided against it. It wasn't a classy thing to do . . . and she needed to lean on him until her legs stopped trembling.

CHAPTER THREE

Nicole felt the spring in her walk as she hurried to the museum. Alex would be back today. Her stomach jittered with nerves. She hadn't seen him since that night on the throne—bad timing on her part—and with the exception of e-mails and unfulfilling phone calls, she hadn't had any contact with him.

But that was going to change today. She was on a mission to seduce the man of her dreams, and her plans were indestructible. *Watch out, Alex.*

Nicole was prepared. She'd had two months to work on this special project. Everything was in place. New outfit? Check. Perfume he liked? Double check.

Hooking her hair behind her ears, Nicole's fingers collided with the pink diamonds. Both of them.

She sighed with satisfaction as she climbed the steps. Granted, the diamonds were heavy, but the weight gave her peace instead of discomfort. She was finally going to wear the earrings around Alex.

Her friend was probably right that he wouldn't notice or care about the earrings. That wasn't the point. The earrings were for her. They reminded her to stand tall and walk proudly. Take charge and stake her claim. Okay, maybe not that far, but she did act dignified and regal when she wore the pink diamonds.

She strode into her office with her head held high, nodding at Andrea as they passed in the hallway.

"You've got the earrings back!" her coworker said by way of greeting.

"Just in the nick of time." It was a good thing she could guilt Lindsay into using her time with the diamonds. It took some doing, but after growing up with the woman, she knew how to work it.

She didn't feel the least bit bad about it either. Lindsay had lost the diamonds in the first place and was required to make it up to her. Anyway, Nicole needed them as much as possible for the next few months.

Andrea leaned against the office door as she watched Nicole settle in. "I thought you didn't need them anymore now that you have Alex wrapped around your finger."

"Hardly!" It was more like the other way around.

"I saw the way he acted around you." Andrea shook her finger at Nicole. "He couldn't take his eyes off you. Put the guy out of his misery and have some hot and sweaty sex with him. Only this time, stay away from creaky chairs."

"Andrea! I shouldn't have told you about that." Nicole sat down at her desk, looking busy as she mulled over what her friend said. Alex watched her all the time? She had no idea. What inelegant things had she done in front of him?

Never mind, she had the earrings now. They just happened to be more necessary than she thought.

"Puhleeze. You tell me everything. You can't help yourself." Andrea flopped in the beanbag chair. "But why the throne, of all things? There's plenty of kinky stuff to use in the storeroom."

Nicole glanced up from her calendar. "How would you know?"

Andrea shrugged. "Everyone has sex in there."

"I dare to be different."

"You can always do it on the lion statues outside on the front steps. But if you think whisker burns are bad, imagine what the stone will do to your thighs." Andrea hissed in her breath and shuddered.

Her coworker sounded a bit too knowledgeable about that. Nicole raised her hand in protest. "Too much information."

Andrea wasn't listening. She stared at the ceiling as she considered the unlimited possibilities the museum had to offer. "But most people around here prefer the donors' lounge because there aren't any security cameras."

"I don't want to know about the sexual practices of the volunteers." And she wanted even less to discuss her plans for Alex—which was so unlike her!

What was wrong with her? "Too much information" was not in her vocabulary! And the museum gossip? She was always ready to hear the dirt.

But these days she regretted telling Andrea what had happened between her and Alex. Now she wanted to guard every cherished moment she had with him. Keep it safe and not have her relationship, or lack thereof, prodded and poked, dissected and analyzed.

She didn't know why she felt that way. Was it because she didn't want anyone messing with something that was special to her? Or was it because she knew she stood on shaky ground when it came to Alex?

Alex Rafferty was the sexiest and most sophisticated man she'd ever met. In fact, she hadn't met a man like him before. She had no idea how to get close and reach him. She was definitely hands-on, and he was more restrained.

In all of her dating experience, she had never been with a gentleman. The lack of practice was giving her trouble now. She dreamed of meeting someone like Alex, but she didn't know how to hold onto the dream.

Her phone rang, startling her. She quickly picked it up, knocking over the jar of pens in the process. "Nicole Graham speaking."

"Nicole, where are you?" the director said in a well-modulated tone that sent a chill down Nicole's spine. Her boss only used it when she was really in trouble. "Mr. Rafferty has arrived with the jewelry collection."

"I'll be right there." She hung up the phone and took a deep breath. So much for being in take-charge mode where nothing could go wrong. "Alex is here with the jewels."

"Look at you. Your face just lit up." Andrea's voice went high and squeaky. "That's so cute."

"No, it didn't." She opened one of her desk drawers, her haste making her clumsy. She pulled out her compact mirror and checked her reflection. No lighting up as far as she could tell.

"You haven't seen the dude for two months and you have the glow." Andrea shook her head. "You have it bad."

"I'm not listening to you." She checked her makeup but only noticed how her earrings sparkled. "How do I look?"

Andrea gave her a thumbs-up. "Remind him what he's been missing."

Nicole hurried out of her office and went to the archives on the third floor. She chose the workroom that included the in-house vault. The jewels would stay in the room until the exhibit was ready.

She first noticed the security detail outside the door. She nodded at the men wearing earpieces and stopped at the threshold. Alex and the museum director stood inside the workroom, deep in discussion.

Her heart skipped a beat. She bet her face was glowing as she watched Alex. He was more than a gorgeous guy who knew how to wear a suit. His commanding presence and charisma made her weak at the knees.

Alex turned and she looked into his green eyes. Nicole didn't realize she was holding her breath until a slow, sexy smile spread across his face. Her heart swelled until it hurt as she exhaled with something close to relief.

She walked toward him, but it felt like she was floating. She felt graceful. Beautiful. Was it because of the way he was looking at her, or because the earrings made her that way?

Nicole decided she wasn't going to question her luck and just run with it.

If the museum director hadn't been in the room, he would have marched over and swept Nicole into his arms. After he'd kissed her long and hard, he would have cornered her against the wall, torn off that flirty dress, and acted out every fantasy he'd had about her for the past two months.

"Hi, Alex," she said with a smile that turned his mind into mush, and offered her hand.

Her hand? He wanted more than her hand.

But he would take what he was offered. He slid his hand against hers and caressed his thumb along her knuckles before he reluctantly let go.

She stood close to him as she listened to her boss say something. He would have liked to curl his arm around her waist and hold her tight against his side, embrace her and erase all those lonely nights he had suffered.

"Any problems during the transport?" she asked as she looked at all the locked metal cases.

"None at—" He caught a glimpse of her earrings. Pink diamond earrings. Blood roared through his ears.

What was going on? He'd only seen that kind of flawless pink champagne diamond in one place—and Nicole would never be allowed in there.

His heart pounded so hard against his chest he was surprised his ribs didn't crack. He blinked in confusion before looking at the metal boxes. He shook the vision from his mind and looked at her ears again.

Where did she get those earrings? A million other questions bombarded his mind. Did she know the history of those diamonds? The significance?

He flinched when she placed her hand on his forearm. She frowned and let go. "Are you okay?"

"Yes." He cleared his throat. "Yes, I'm fine." Alex slid his finger behind his collar. His shirt suddenly felt too tight. The walls of his throat constricted, making it difficult to breathe.

She said something to her boss, the voices morphing into a low buzz as he continued to stare at her. In all his years on the job, nothing had prepared him for this. One false move, one question that accidentally revealed too much, and the results could be cataclysmic.

He wanted to drag her away, find a secluded spot, and get the truth. Alex pulled at his tie, dislodging the perfect knot. Should he do that now? Or should he wait? Would it be best to leave his discovery well alone?

"May we see the jewelry now?" she asked, the gleam in her eyes dancing with barely suppressed excitement.

He wanted to say no. His instincts screamed for him to block her view of the jewels. But that would raise suspicions, the one thing he couldn't have.

Alex silently keyed in the password codes and flipped open the first case lid. He watched Nicole, his eyes stinging from the intensity, as he revealed the jewels one by one.

She gasped with pleasure and the sound reverberated inside him. It reminded him of that night in the storeroom. His body tightened as his cocked twitched.

She clapped her hands together and held them close to her chest. "They are beautiful," she declared in an awed whisper.

He didn't say anything. Alex bit down on his tongue, his jaw locked, as he watched Nicole go down the line of cases. He kept his hands behind his back unless he was entering the passwords.

Nicole and her boss oohed over the sapphires and ahhed at the emeralds. Her hands trembled as she smoothed a finger along a pearl ring, and shook when she hesitated to touch the large cameo brooch. Her eyes widened at the bracelets and anklets, but she practically had an orgasm when she saw the coronets, diadems, and tiaras.

When she walked toward the wedding jewelry sets, panic started to claw at him. *Don't make the connection . . .* he prayed as she studied the set. She spoke to her boss, pointing out something about the design. *Do not make the connection. . . .*

She glanced up at him and he forced himself to remain still and keep his expression blank.

"This is going to be a great exhibit," Nicole said with a wide smile. "I've got a bunch of ideas already."

He heard what she said, but he didn't catch it. All he knew was that she didn't make the connection. Alex wanted to sag with relief, but the panic still coursed through his veins.

"We should put these in the vault now," the museum director decided as she cast one more lingering look at the tiaras.

Alex gritted his teeth until they threatened to shatter. Itemizing the jewelry before it went into the vault was a long, drawn-out process.

He suffered through each piece of jewelry, answering questions when asked, signing forms when they were put in front of him. The minutes stretched to hours, but the sense of urgency pounding inside him was unwavering.

"Could you excuse me for a moment?" Alex asked as he signed the last dotted line. "I . . . need to check in with my superiors."

The excuse must have been credible. Nicole offered a quick, searching glance, but didn't say anything. Her boss waved him off before she went over the paperwork with Nicole. Alex took his chance to escape.

He quickly made his way outside and began to pace. The

crisp autumn weather made him breathe easier. He pulled at his collar again and leaned against the stone lion statue guarding the front door. His mind whirled with possible disasters as a group of uniformed schoolgirls marched past him and into the museum.

There was only one thing he could do, but he was reluctant to take that course of action. Alex pulled the cell phone from his jacket and pressed the number he had hoped he would never have to use during this project.

"Yes?" The male voice was as sharp and to the point as he remembered.

"This is Alex Rafferty." He rubbed his hand against his forehead. "We have a situation with the jewels."

"Security?"

"Public relations." He paused, not sure how to word it. "It's about the princess pink diamonds."

There was a pause on the other side. Nothing ever stunned his superior into silence. Alex felt his world take a sudden tilt and he wasn't sure how he would fix it.

"There was a situation thirty years ago," the man admitted in a raspy voice. "The diamonds were never recovered."

"I saw them." He wasn't comfortable giving all the information. It felt like his loyalties were torn. "On the curator's ears."

The man bit out an expletive. "Does she know?"

"I can't tell."

"Find out what she knows. Do what you can to minimize the problem. If word got back that a commoner wore those earrings . . ."

Alex winced. "I understand."

"Keep me updated."

"Yes, sir." He disconnected the call and pocketed the device. Leaning his head against the stone lion, he looked up at the cloudy Seattle sky.

He should have known this traveling collection was going too smoothly.

What was he thinking? He should have known when he met Nicole Graham that she was going to turn his world upside down.

Chapter Four

Nicole studied the pathways she had designed for the exhibit. She had already decided that the pendants worn by the princesses at state dinners were going to be the death of her.

They were historically significant, but they were ugly. They should be given a place of honor in the exhibit, but they couldn't capture a visitor's attention like a frothy diamond-encrusted tiara created by an equally frothy but famous jeweler.

In short, the oil-paint pendants were important but boring. She could feel another argument with Alex brewing over this.

Privately, she thought the miniature portraits would ruin the look of any gown. What was the point of wearing something special if you had to include a picture of some old dead guy?

"Excuse me?" Alex's amused tone wafted over her.

Nicole froze. Had she said that aloud? Why did she find

herself in these situations? At least she knew how to get out of them. Pretend ignorance. "Hmm?"

"Sorry." He leaned back in his chair and gave her a knowing look. "I thought you had said something."

She hunched over the papers again, propping her head with her hand. It blocked her view, but it didn't do much good. She was acutely aware of him and found it difficult to concentrate on work.

As much as she had hoped Alex was an attentive man, for the past two days he had been watching her every move—and not like someone who wanted to jump her. Had that been the case, she wouldn't have been concerned.

What was he worried about? That she would steal the jewels? Mess up the exhibit? It was time to put his mind at ease, and then maybe she could get some work done without constantly being aware of him.

"I'm trying to come up with an eye-catching display for the pendants." She tossed her pen on top of the papers and stretched, shoving her hands into her hair. "Thank you for letting me use the picture of one of the princesses. It adds to the jewelry."

"You're welcome." He looked at the paper and the corners of his mouth turned down. It was as if he had regretted that decision.

Nicole bit her bottom lip as she watched him. He still had the power to veto every idea she won from their two-week negotiation. She had to keep him from doing that.

"I think the pictures help the visitor understand when and where the pendant was worn. Of course, the text helps with the why."

Okay, now she was babbling. She bit the inside of her

cheek before she said another thing. Not that the tactic ever worked, but she was willing to give it another try.

He watched her closely. "Is tradition important to you?"

"Well, no," she said with a chuckle. "But if I were a princess, I'd throw a tantrum for having to wear that pendant on my ball gown."

He folded his arms across his chest. She felt his gaze on her as if he were touching her. Nicole shifted in her seat as her breasts grew tight and heavy.

"I didn't realize you were that particular about your jewelry," Alex said.

"I'm not. I don't have that much jewelry. Except for these"—she hooked her hair behind her ears—"and I share them with my sisters."

"They are exquisite. Where did you get them?"

"My sisters and I went to a celebrity auction. Lia Dash's personal effects were being auctioned off and the money went to charity."

"Lia Dash?"

"You know, the fashion icon." His expression didn't show any recognition. "The one who showed what a woman could do if she pushed the boundaries."

"Right." He nodded. "I've heard of her."

"Well, these are hers." She felt kind of odd bragging about it, but that was the whole point of buying the earrings, right? To let everyone know that she had something of Lia's.

"No kidding." His gaze darted to her ears and she felt her lobes go hot. "Pink diamonds, huh?"

"Aren't they cool? Especially since Lia Dash used to own them."

"You're a groupie?"

Her mouth dropped open. "No, I'm not! I don't know that much about her. No one did. I have my theories that she . . . What?"

He mouthed the word: "Groupie."

"Okay, maybe I am. Just a little." She raised her hand, showing an inch between her finger and thumb. "When I was growing up, I wanted to be just like her."

"A fashion designer?"

"No, someone who had class and style. An air of mystery. Someone who made it on her own and was a lady no matter what." She glanced at Alex, who hadn't said anything. "I'm still working on it."

His expression softened. "I think you're already there," he said in a low voice.

She felt her cheeks turn pink. "I'm not quite in Lia Dash's league."

"Do you want to be?"

She felt her brow crinkle at the question. She'd never thought about something like that. "That won't happen."

"You don't think there will ever be a time when you are on the cover of your favorite tabloid?"

Nicole laughed at the improbability. "There's nothing scandalous about me."

"Don't be too sure."

She felt the pull of his gaze. Her skin tingled as her nipples furled against her bra.

He thought she could be scandalous? Boy, wouldn't he be disappointed. But then, it gave her the edge. This guy was going to think she was some sort of sex goddess.

She could live with that.

Now was the time to make her move. Show Alex that,

yes, she was exactly that. A sex goddess who knew how to give him the ultimate pleasure.

Okay, so it was a slight misrepresentation of her true nature. He didn't need to know that. Let him get wrapped up in the illusion. It's what she did best.

That meant doing it here. Not at her place—that would ruin the effect. There would be no mystery or fantasy, only piled-up dishes and dust bunnies.

She would have to do it now, before she lost her nerve. The earrings only helped her so much. But none of the suggestions Andrea had offered piqued her interest. She was going to have to improvise.

"Well, I think that's enough of the pathways for today." She stood up from her rolling chair and stretched. Her pink silk blouse came untucked from her narrow black skirt. She felt his gaze on the skin she exposed.

Alex looked away and glanced at his watch. "It's not quitting time yet."

Nicole thought his gentlemanly manners were sweet. Driving her insane, but sweet. Why wasn't he acting on the attraction? She was willing to give him a push.

"Actually, I was going to check on the movie I put together for the exhibit."

"Movie?" Alex sat straight up. "You put together a movie?"

"It's not done yet," she said as she slid her chair in. "In fact, all that is locked down is the script."

He glared at her. "When were you going to tell me about this?"

"When I needed your final approval, of course." What was the big deal? Museums often put together short movies, giving the exhibits a slant that reflected their audience. "Would you like to see it now?"

He stood up and walked toward her. "Where are you going to show it?"

"The theater." She took a step back. Alex had a very intimidating aura about him at times.

"What theater?" Aggravation clipped his words.

She gestured for him to follow. She exited the archives and headed down the spiral steps. Nervousness pumped in her blood as she took him around the temporary exhibit and ushered him through an unmarked door.

"It's really a windowless room with the audiovisual equipment." She closed the door behind her and carefully turned the lock, hoping he didn't hear the telltale snick of metal. "We can seat up to thirty people in here. Believe me, you wouldn't want any more at one time."

He looked at the carpeted steps that curved and went up three rows. "You haven't installed the chairs yet."

"You sit on the steps," she said as she turned on the equipment. "That makes it easier to maintain and clean."

"The steps?" His tone clearly indicated how undignified he thought that idea was.

She glared at the audiovisual equipment that made it difficult to start a simple movie. "We have to accommodate all of our visitors, and the steps help us do that."

"Another invention by your carpenters?"

She glanced over her shoulder. "I'm sure it will be sturdier than the empress throne."

Nicole quickly returned her attention to the wall of electronics. Why did she have to bring that up? She couldn't look at Alex. Mentioning the throne was as good as tossing a spot-light on her intentions.

She pushed the light button off and hit start. The screen flared with color and she hurriedly sat by Alex in the front row.

"Remember, this is the uncut version," she said as she shifted on the step. They were as uncomfortable as she had expected.

But she was sitting right next to Alex. Her leg pressed against his. She could reach for his hand, but would he take it?

For all of her experience, she never took the lead. Never took charge. She had been happy with that, but maybe that was the problem.

How would she approach him? Grab his chin, turn him toward her, and give him a French kiss? Stand up and strad-dle him?

Hmm . . . She might need to try something with a little more finesse. The guy was a gentleman, after all. He required something sophisticated.

Nicole glanced at him. She bit her lower lip as indecision rolled through her. Maybe it was easier to have the man make the first move.

"If you're planning to have your way with me," Alex said, his eyes never leaving the screen, "could you do it before I die of anticipation?"

Her mouth dropped in surprise before she recovered and lightly punched him in the arm. "How did you know what I was up to?"

"Gee, I don't know." His tone was very droll. "Dragging me to a dark room? Locking the door? I'm going to say it was a wild guess."

"Well, just for that, you can forget it." She crossed her arms and looked at the movie. "You spoiled the effect."

From the corner of her eye, she could see him turn away from the screen. "What would you have done?"

She leaned in closer. Nicole felt bolder now that she knew she wasn't going to go through with it. "I would have done anything you asked."

"What's stopping you?"

"Like I said"—she straightened away from him—"you ruined the effect."

"I didn't realize we were going for ambience here. Come on, Nicole." His voice dipped into a sexy growl. "Continue on with this seduction."

"No." She had lost her nerve. Not that she would tell him that!

"Do one thing I ask." His coaxing stirred her senses.

"One thing?" Hmm. It would be kind of like strip poker. She could handle that. "And then you do one thing I ask?"

"Sure." He nodded. "Are you ready?"

"Yeah." She looked at him, prepared for anything as a thrill danced along her spine.

"Take off your clothes."

Whoa. Her eyes widened. More like speed strip poker. "All of them?"

"Yes, all of them."

"Are you sure *you* don't want to?"

He looked directly at her. "I want you to strip for me."

She felt a tremor in her womb. The way he said it made her hot.

She could do this. This is what she wanted. Okay, she

thought he would do all the work, in the dark, but this was all about improvisation.

She stood, her feet wobbling, and she walked between Alex and the white screen. The projector spilled colored images against her.

"Oh, no fair!" Alex protested, but he was smiling. As if he admired the fact that she had tricked him.

"You didn't say *where* I had to take my clothes off." She kicked off her heels and paused. She had to slow down. Stripping in front of a man was not like getting undressed in the privacy of her bedroom.

She reached for her collar, secretly enjoying how the movie continued to play on her. Nicole wanted to tease Alex. She planned to draw this out as long as possible and make him pant with need by the time she was nude.

She unbuttoned her blouse, slowly revealing her lace bra. Her fingertips fumbled as she slid the buttons free. Her heart was pounding fast by the time she shucked off the pink silk.

Nicole's skin felt hot as she reached behind her waist to grasp the zipper of her straight black skirt. She didn't realize the movement would be provocative until she was arching her chest forward. The pose made her feel wanton. She rolled her shoulders back brazenly, offering Alex a better look.

Once she had dragged the stubborn zipper open, Nicole tugged the material past her hips. The skirt slid down much faster than she would have liked.

She watched Alex's face as the skirt made its journey to the floor. He seemed stunned. Stunned was good. She hoped he stayed that way.

She had difficulty seeing thanks to the projector. How

much of the movie was covering her? Probably much less than she'd like to believe.

Her hand shook as she removed her bra. By the time she was nude, she wondered where the bold girl who made this agreement had run off to.

Alex let out a tuneless whistle.

That boosted her confidence. "Okay, my turn," she said. She smiled when she saw Alex go for his tie. "I want you to kiss me all over."

His hand froze at his collar. "You don't want me to take my clothes off?"

"No, not yet." The edge of her mouth kicked up. "I want you to kiss me. *All* over."

He rose from the step and approached her. Every move whispered with lethal grace. Nicole swallowed roughly. She got the feeling that he was ready to pounce.

He stood before her, blocking the projected images from her body. She hadn't thought about that. Now she was completely naked to him. Nicole stood still, her arms at her sides.

Alex leaned down to kiss her mouth. He pulled back when she parted her lips. "Do I get to use my hands?"

Did he? She didn't know. All she knew was that his voice was like silk. "Only to keep your balance."

His slanted smile took her by surprise, but not as much as his long, wet, thorough kiss. She thought he would have rushed to complete his assignment, but no. He went over every inch of her, sometimes twice. He left her slick, puffy cleft for last.

The movie was long over, and she stood in front of the harsh, white light. She squinted, unable to see well, and she felt most vulnerable by that missing sense.

Her body trembled; her sex throbbed with anticipation as Alex knelt before her. Her legs were parted as he clamped his mouth against her clit.

She bucked against him. Alex lashed his tongue over the swollen clit before he suckled and nipped at it.

Nicole tried to keep still. She gripped his head with her fingers, but when he pumped his tongue into her channel, the sparks swept through her like a wildfire.

He held onto her waist as he stood up. "Now it's my turn," he said as moisture gleamed from his mouth.

She nodded, not trusting her voice.

"Go over to the first row of steps and kneel on it."

Kneel on it? What did he plan to do? She slowly made her way, blinking as she stepped out of the bright white light and into the darkness.

She found the step, and made her way into a kneeling position facing the wall.

"With your hands and knees," Alex corrected her.

She bent down, her fingers resting against the edge of the next step. Her muscles quivered as his hands roamed over her. His fingers teased and plucked her nipples until they stung. He tugged and played with her breasts and cupped her bottom.

Nicole closed her eyes when Alex slid his finger along her wet slit. Back and forth, back and forth. He continued to tease her until she thought she would scream. When he finally dipped his finger inside, her flesh gripped him tight.

Alex leaned over her and she realized with a start that he was still fully dressed. "Your turn, Nicole," he whispered in her ear as thrust his finger inside her.

"Alex." Her voice came out in a rasp.

"Yes, Nicole?" He pumped his finger faster and pressed against her clit with his other hand.

"Please." The word was barely whispered.

"What do you want?"

She rested her head on the second step. The rough carpet felt cool against her sweat-slicked skin. "Please, Alex. I need you in me. Now."

She whimpered when he pulled away. She heard the sound of zipper and foil before Alex clamped his hand onto her hips. With one deep thrust, he drove into her.

Nicole groaned and dipped her spine as she accommodated him. She noticed how Alex remained motionless. She felt his hands tremble on her hips.

She clenched her inner muscles around him. Alex dug his fingers in her skin and thrust hard.

Her palms and knees stung as he continued to thrust. She couldn't predict his moves. Long, short. Deep, shallow. Need coiled inside her, squeezing tighter with every thrust until she couldn't take it anymore. She cried out her release as he gave her a final thrust.

Alex withdrew from her and collapsed on the bench next to her. He gulped for air. "Okay, now it's my turn. . . ."

Nicole groaned in protest as a spark flickered deep inside her.

CHAPTER FIVE

WHEN ALEX LEANED INTO HER, NICOLE dropped the sheaf of photos onto the worktable. The back of her knees tingled as he suckled the pulse point on her neck. "Let's go back to the theater," he suggested.

Nicole closed her eyes and gathered the last of her reserves. It served her right. She had created a monster. It only took a week to make the gentleman she knew turn into an insatiable man whose stamina amazed her.

"I'm sorry, Alex," she said primly as the heat simmered in her blood. "But I never repeat."

"Is that right?" His fingers dipped underneath her collar.

"Absolutely." She leafed through the pictures. Each one was beautiful but filled with a minefield of missteps. If she put the diadem before a coronet, even though they were both essentially tiaras, was that going to get her in trouble with the royal family?

"Alex, are you going to help me with this catalog or not?"

"I'm sure you have everything under control." He spanned his hands against her waist and pulled her against him. She felt every hard inch of him.

"It's the princess's dowry that confuses me." Her voice was a little high and breathy, but that could be because his hand was dipping lower. . . . "It's too complicated."

"What's complicated about it?"

She grabbed his wrist before he cupped her sex. "Alex, behave."

He chuckled in her ear. "I can't believe those words came out of your mouth."

Neither did she, so she decided to ignore it altogether. "Everything is down to a science. Like these pearls." She held up a glossy photo that highlighted the luster of the gunmetal-gray Tahitian pearls. "A princess receives one at birth and then gets a pearl every year toward her jewelry dowry."

"Nothing complicated about that," he said, kissing the tender spot behind her ear.

"You might be right, but it's not fair. The longer you hold out to get married, the longer your necklace."

"Princesses don't want to hold out too long. There's that whole childbearing requirement." He placed a proprietary hand on her stomach.

"Which is another thing. Why would a king feel the need to make a dowry for his daughters? They are princesses. Guys should be lining up for them."

"It's tradition," he whispered in her ear.

Nicole rolled her eyes. That was the answer for anything that no longer made sense. "Whatever."

She flipped through some more photos, doing her best to ignore Alex's hands skimming the underside of her breasts. She had to get her work done or deal with the consequences.

"Okay, what about this necklace?" she asked. "It's an engagement necklace. Did her dad give her that, too, in case her pearl necklace was too short?"

"No, that is something the groom gives the princess on their engagement." He brushed his knuckles along the curve of her throat, and she found herself leaning into his hand. "When he puts it around her neck, it symbolizes that she is unavailable to other men."

"That sucks!" The necklace was nothing but a glitzy collar of ownership.

"You mean if a man put that necklace on you"—he swept his fingers along her collarbone—"you would refuse it?"

She closed her eyes as she imagined Alex doing just that. "Would I get to put one on him?"

"It doesn't work that way."

Nicole opened her eyes. "It should. The jewelry is beautiful, but it hides the real meaning of the gift, doesn't it."

"Some people want the gift because of the meaning," he explained softly as his fingers splayed across her throat.

"By 'some people' you mean men." She briskly flipped through the photos and came across the diamond earrings. "Hey, I didn't notice this before."

"What?" He nibbled her earlobe.

"These diamond earrings." She tapped her finger on the glossy photo. "They're pink like mine."

He slowly let go of her ear and looked over her shoulder. "I guess pink diamonds aren't as rare as you thought."

"Guess not." She studied how the facets captured the light.

Did her diamonds do the same? "Why do the princesses get pink diamond earrings?"

Alex picked up the photo and studied it. "I can't remember. I'll have to look it up."

"I must tell my sisters about this. They'll get a kick out of it. Oh!" She slapped her palm on her forehead. "I forgot."

He looked down at her. "What?"

"I'm having my sisters and their fiancés over this weekend. It's kind of a double-engagement dinner party. Would you like to come?"

"A family gathering?"

"Your diplomatic skills will come in handy." She turned and placed her hands on his shoulders. "Run interference. Keep me from offending my future brothers-in-law."

He tossed the photo back on the table. "I don't know. Family get-togethers aren't my thing."

"My sisters and I are cooking everything from scratch. It's tradition." He seemed big on the word. She wouldn't mention the fighting that came along with sharing chores in that small a space.

A pleasure so intense and primal flared in his eyes. "Home-cooked food? I'm in." He cupped the back of her head and kissed her hard. "Let's cut out of work early."

"Are you trying to get me fired?"

"Come on, Nicole." His voice dipped into a sexy growl as his hands trailed to her bottom. "My place or yours?"

"Yours, Alex," she said as she kissed him. "I have this thing for maid service."

Nicole raised her glass as a toast. "Welcome to the family, Dominic. We could always use another thief."

Alex took a healthy gulp of the red wine. He didn't need to bother himself by running interference. Nicole's sisters were already handling that.

"Nicole!" Lindsay gave her the glare older sisters have perfected through time. "You're wearing the diamonds, so just let it go."

"I would," she said against the edge of her wineglass, "if Dominic and Ian would stop staring at my ears."

"Nicole!" Sabrina groaned.

Alex noticed she didn't include him. But that was only because he couldn't keep his eyes off her low-cut blouse. Why didn't she wear something daring like that at work? No, scratch that. He wouldn't get anything done.

"Now Dominic," Nicole continued as she set her glass down on the table. "I have some questions for you. Just so we can clear the air. No family secrets and all that jazz."

Lindsay groaned and slammed her elbows on the table. The silverware clattered as she covered her face with her hands.

"What do you want to know?" Dominic continued eating as if he had expected an interrogation.

"A few things." She propped her chin on her hand. "Which mobster had the diamonds in the first place?"

His fork hovered in midair. "Mobster?"

"Yeah, you see, while Lindsay was seducing you in Hawaii"—Lindsay's groan grew longer and stronger—"my job was to find out the history of the diamonds."

Alex choked on a piece of carrot. He wasn't sure if it was a good thing or not to be witness to this.

Nicole cast a sideways glance at him. "Are you okay?"

"Down the wrong way," he said between gasps.

Nicole thwacked him on the back and turned her attention

to Dominic. "Some bigwig commissioned your parents to design this pair of earrings."

Alex held up his hand. "Wait. Your parents designed those earrings?"

Dominic nodded, and Alex turned his attention to his plate. This was worse than he imagined. He expected some sisterly squabbles, but Nicole forgot to mention some important details!

"And I figured there was only one way to keep your name out of this kind of scandal," Nicole said. "If you were a member of a syndicate. Organized crime, that kind of thing."

"Interesting theory," Alex said as he crumbled a roll in his hands.

"So"—Nicole wiggled her ears—"which mob did these heirloom diamonds belong to?"

"Nicole," Lindsay said through clenched teeth. "You've been reading too many tabloids."

"But it makes sense," Nicole said.

"And that car accident my dad died in later that year was really a mob hit?" Dominic guessed.

"Exactly!" She tossed her hands in the air with a flourish. "I'm right, aren't I?"

"Sorry, Nicole," Dominic said, not missing a beat as he ate, "but there was no mob."

"You're sure about that? Or are you protecting—ow!" Nicole's knee banged on the table and she glared at Lindsay. "Stop kicking me."

Alex didn't like how certain Dominic was that the mob had nothing to do with the earrings. Or how Dominic avoided looking in his direction. The guy knew exactly whose diamonds those were but he wouldn't give the answer freely.

Nicole leaned back in her chair and twirled the fork in her hand. "Okay, then who was the woman who ran away with the earrings?"

That caught Dominic by surprise. He jerked his head back before swiveling his attention on Lindsay, who sat by his side. "You mean you guys haven't figured that out?"

Alex's stomach cramped, and no antacid was going to soothe it.

"No," Lindsay answered carefully.

"If we know who it is," Sabrina said, "does that mean it's someone famous?"

"Ooh! Ooh!" Nicole held her hands out, trying to stop everyone from blurting out the answer. "Let me think."

Dominic put down his silverware. "I thought you already knew."

Aw, man. Dominic was killing him.

"What are you talking about?" Nicole asked. "We bought them at . . ." Her voice trailed off as understanding hit her square in the eyes.

Lindsay was next to figure it out. It was like a domino effect. "*No.*"

Dominic nodded. "Yes."

"*Lia Dash* is the thief?"

Alex shoveled food faster into his mouth. This was getting worse than he imagined. He was never going to another family dinner. He would rather go through territory negotiations with bloodthirsty feudal lords than sit through another Graham get-together.

It was unnaturally quiet at the table. Alex looked up from his plate and watched the stunned expressions on the sisters' faces. Dominic kept eating as if he were discussing the weather. Then again, he grew up with this information.

Ian seemed to handle the news well as he topped off everyone's wineglass. Yeah, he was going to have to keep an eye on that one. Ian West was trouble.

Nicole was the first to recover. She squared her shoulders back and jutted her chin out. "I'm sorry, but I refuse to believe that."

Dominic cocked his eyebrow up. "Because she's Lia Dash?"

"Yes!" Nicole and her sisters said in unison.

"If you knew that Lia had the earrings, why didn't you send the cops in her direction?" Sabrina asked.

"My mother and I wanted to distance ourselves from that mess," Dominic said, punctuating it with a heavy sigh. "Going after Lia Dash would open up that wound again."

"Oh," Sabrina said as her sisters nodded in agreement. Ian's look of disbelief was almost comical.

"That," Dominic said as he picked up his fork and knife, "and my mother didn't want to talk to the police since she fenced jewels for a living."

Sabrina clapped her hands on her cheeks. "Oh!"

Nicole turned and looked at Alex, shaking her head. "I can't believe this."

"Neither can I." He took a sip from his water goblet as the knot in his stomach eased. "I had no idea you cooked this well."

Her mouth twisted to the side as she glared at him. "I'm talking about these secrets that are popping up."

"I thought that was what family dinners were all about."

He gestured toward the large platter on the other side of the table. "Can you pass me the roast beef?"

When Nicole had said good-bye to the last guest, she gently closed the door and pressed her forehead against the wood. "I wish I hadn't asked." The wood muffled her voice.

Alex wanted to hold and comfort her. He hated seeing Nicole wrestle with disappointment, be disenchanted.

But would he be dishonest if he tried to comfort her? Let her believe in the fractured fairytale? He didn't know. Alex stuffed his hands in his trouser pockets. "Ask about what?"

"Lia Dash." She pushed away from the door and walked to the dinner table. "It's not true."

"Why would Dominic lie?" Wait, what was he doing? Questioning Dominic's veracity would work in his favor down the line.

"I don't think he lied." She blew out the candle. "I think he was misinformed."

Dominic didn't strike him as the misinformed type. It didn't take long for Nicole to defend that idea.

"Maybe his mother thought it was someone who looked like Lia Dash," Nicole guessed. "Or maybe Lia had an affair with Herb around the same time as the thief took the earrings."

"Why does it matter?"

She whirled around and stared at him. *Why does it matter?*

Alex shrugged. "Lia Dash has always been fodder for the tabloids. Secret babies, scandalous affairs, breakups, makeups, alien encounters. *That* doesn't bug you."

"This is different," she insisted.

He clenched his hands in his pockets. "Because . . . ?"

Nicole sighed in defeat. "Dominic isn't one who would

make an accusation unless he was one-hundred percent sure. I believe him even though I don't want to."

"You know this after one meeting?"

A long sigh escaped out of her chest. "Yeah, strangely enough." She reached up and fiddled with the right earring.

He couldn't take much more of this. Alex rubbed the back of his neck with a tense hand. "Okay, let's say Lia took the earrings. You know this for a fact and you have proof. What are you going to do about it?"

"Do?" She reached for her left earring.

"Are you going to call the tabloids? Splash it all over the Internet?"

She stared at her hand. He looked at what was so fascinating to her and discovered the pink diamonds in her palm. She had taken off the earrings. That was the one thing he hadn't expected from her.

"Well, Nicole?"

"Nothing." She clenched her hand into a fist. So tightly Alex knew the metal had to bite, but she didn't flinch. "I'm going to do absolutely nothing."

"For now?"

"Forever." She walked to the bedroom and he heard the clink of the earrings on her porcelain ring tray.

It was safer this way. He should be happy. But how could he be happy when the woman he loved had just lost the fairy tale she had always believed in?

CHAPTER SIX

NICOLE LEFT EARLY TO WORK ON the catalog. She had to get it to the printers in time. She didn't know what her problem was, other than Alex's frequent erotic interruptions. She was working around the clock, but she found no excitement or joy in the project.

It was all Lia Dash's fault, Nicole decided with a scowl. She'd pretended to be someone she wasn't.

No, Nicole decided, letting her shoulders sag. It was *her* fault. She shouldn't have made the woman into something she wanted. A hero. An icon. A template. She shouldn't have believed in the illusion and avoided the real woman.

She was approaching Alex in the same way. She wanted him to fall for her—but the illusion of a sex goddess in human form wasn't the real woman.

The real Nicole couldn't keep his interest, and she had to

accept that, but the bold and sophisticated version had a chance.

Okay, neither had a chance.

Come on, concentrate. She put aside the tiaras and decided to work on the earrings next. Nicole took a deep breath. She must be a glutton for punishment.

She didn't want to do earrings. Think about them, work on them, or even look at them. Her ears felt naked as it was, but glancing over these pictures made the sensation stronger.

She systematically went through the earrings. They were just bits of metal and stone, that's all. She double-checked the facts, checked off the photos, and finally came across the pink diamonds.

This was her job, she reminded herself fiercely. She could work on these and not think about Lia's earrings. She was a professional. Anyway, these earrings weren't the same grade of clarity as hers.

Okay, maybe they were. But they weren't the same size. She glanced at the carat. Her eyebrows dipped in a frown. Huh, that was strange. The diamonds in the pictures were the same cut and carat as—

Her shocked gasp rang through the workroom. Nicole slapped her hand on the picture and looked around the room. No one was here. *Duh.*

Nicole raised her hand just a little and took a peek. She slowly uncovered the picture and studied the pink diamond earrings. It was a different setting, but those looked a lot like the ones she had been wearing.

There was one way to find out. Nicole rose from her chair and nonchalantly walked out of the workroom and strolled down the hall. When she remembered that no one was there to see her, she bolted for her office.

She slowly closed the door, just in case someone decided to come in early. The closed door would probably be cause for alarm, but she wasn't taking any chances. No one could over-hear her conversation.

She went to the phone and dialed Lindsay's number. So what if was early? Lindsay was already at work anyway. The woman was a workaholic.

But Nicole would leave a message and hope Lindsay re-turned the call.

She was waiting for the answering machine to pick up when someone answered. "Dominic Stark."

"Dominic?" Yes! She wasn't going to have to wait all day for the answer.

"Yeah?"

Ooh. He sounded about as friendly as a bear woken during hibernation season. "This is Nicole."

"Hello, Nicole. What is it you want to know about the diamond earrings this time?"

"How did you—never mind." She was not that predict-able. She knew she wasn't. "I need to know who commis-sioned the earrings."

"Why do you need to know?"

Hmm . . . he was deflecting. He knew the answer and it had to be a good one. Probably something juicy and scandal-ous. She couldn't wait to find out. "I'm working on the jew-elry collection at the museum," she began.

"I remember."

Alrighty. He was a cut-to-the-chase kind of a guy. She

could respect that. "And I see these pink diamond earrings and they look a lot like the ones we wear."

"What's your question?"

Nicole made a face at the phone. "Did the royal family commission the design of the earrings from your parents?"

"Yes."

She froze and thought that she might launch into her happy dance. "Yes? That's it?"

"Yes, now stop bothering me about it."

Wise guy. "Okay, I'm going to have to get back at you for that. You are being forewarned. I am going to shower every child of yours with the noisiest and most annoying toys ever made."

"I expect nothing less."

"And for that comment, I'm throwing in a jumbo pack of batteries with every present. Oh, and Dominic?"

"Yeah?"

"Thanks."

"Okay."

"And Dominic?" she said sweetly.

"What now?" His voice turned gruff.

"Fine, I won't point out your tactical error." She glanced at her nails and buffed them on her blouse as she waited for Dominic to take the bait.

"What error?" He bit out each word.

"That because of you, I know something Lindsay doesn't know yet." She hung up before she could hear his reply. She shouldn't have given him that freebie. Then again, the guy was new to the family. How else would he learn?

Wow. She had a pair of earrings that not only belonged to

Lia Dash but to a royal family. She staggered to her desk and sat down. Huh. How about that?

Wait . . . She sat up straight as a horrible thought occurred to her. She was wearing stolen royal jewelry and now knew about it.

Nicole grimaced at the implications. What was the statute of limitations on grand theft? And did she have to return them if she wasn't the one who did the stealing?

Nicole rolled her eyes. Of course she did. Bummer. Her sisters were going to kill her.

Oooh . . . She hissed as she imagined the fight that would ensue. Now she really, *really* wished she hadn't asked.

Alex stood in the workroom and looked around. Where could Nicole be? Her note on the bathroom mirror said she had come in early to work on the catalog.

"Hey, Alex?"

He pivoted on his foot and saw her standing at the doorway. His heart clenched when she approached him hesitantly. "Can I talk to you for a minute?"

There was something wrong in that simple request. He could feel it. "Sure."

"Outside." She whispered and jerked her head in the direction of the window.

"Outside?" He frowned. Was she okay? Did the news last night take her over the edge? "Uh, Nicole, it's raining outside."

"It is?" She glanced at the window and was genuinely surprised by the black clouds coughing up sheets of rain. "Oh, well, then, let's go to my office."

He wasn't going anywhere. Not yet, anyway. "What's going on?"

Nicole visibly took a deep breath and leaned against the door after closing it. "I noticed that my pink earrings had a lot of similarities to those in the royal family's collection."

Uh-oh.

"So I talked to Dominic about it." She nervously chewed her bottom lip. "I found out that they once belonged to this royal family."

He folded his arms across his chest and struck a thoughtful pose. "I see."

She hunched her shoulders. "That's all you have to say? You see?" Realization hit and she pointed an accusing finger at him. "You knew?"

He winced. "Yes, I knew the moment I saw you wearing the earrings."

She strode over to him. "And you didn't tell me? Didn't you think I would want to know?"

Oh, yeah. That was the problem. "What purpose would it serve?"

"Oh, I don't know." She gave an exaggerated shrug. "Maybe so I wouldn't think I was going crazy thinking something was strange about my earrings matching a princess's?"

"The problem is," he said in a low voice in hopes that she would follow suit, "only princesses are allowed to wear those particular earrings."

She dipped her chin and stared at him. "You're kidding, right?"

"No. If it became known that someone who wasn't from the royal family wore those earrings, it would be a scandal."

Nicole nodded and rotated her hands. "And for a family that values privacy over everything else . . ."

"It was best to keep quiet altogether." He leaned against

the edge of the worktable. "That may have been the wrong decision, but it's the one I went with."

She tugged at one of her ears. "Who else knows that I'm wearing these?"

"As far as I know, it's you, me, my superior, and Dominic."

A guilty blush stained her cheeks. "You might as well add Lindsay, Sabrina, and most likely Ian while you're at it."

"You told them." It wasn't an accusation. More like a statement of fact.

"Sort of." She bobbed her head before she let it all out. "Well, okay, yes, I did. I had to."

"Why?" He wasn't totally against the idea, but the fewer people who knew about it, the better.

"I needed to explain why I was giving them back to the royal family."

"You are?" Alex's hands gripped the edge of the table. He hadn't expected her to make that kind of sacrifice. The most he had hoped for was that she'd sell it to the family for an exorbitant price. Which he knew Nicole could never do. She could never part with the earrings.

She nodded slowly, as if she were gearing herself up for something extremely difficult. "Well, yeah. This is stolen property, right?" She reached for her ear to take off the diamond.

Alex stopped her. He placed his fingers over hers and guided her hand down. "You're going to give away these expensive earrings?"

"I'm giving them *back*," she corrected. "It's the right thing to do."

"Nicole, sit down." He assisted her to a chair. "There's something I have to tell you."

She sat down, eyeing him suspiciously. "What? I don't think I can handle any more secrets and surprises."

He held her hand, for his courage or hers, he wasn't sure. But once he had divulged this information, there was no going back. "Nicole, despite what you read in the reports, the earrings weren't exactly stolen."

She looked at him strangely, then made a face and clucked her tongue. "What are you talking about, Alex? Of course they were. Dominic's family was destroyed because Lia Dash stole the earrings."

"Well, yes, the earrings were stolen, but they weren't." Alex realized that sounded convoluted. He rubbed his forehead and tried again. "It's kind of a gray area."

Her eyes narrowed with confusion. "Am I supposed to understand that?"

Alex knew he was making a mess of it. Surprising, considering his job. "Lia Dash did take the earrings. I know you don't want to hear that, but she did."

She blinked slowly as her face took on a pinched look. "Okay," she said, her lips barely moving.

"She did have an affair with Dominic's father," Alex admitted, knowing that he was hitting hard with the stone-cold truths. "He refused to name his girlfriend for various reasons."

"Why, if she stole the earrings?"

He felt the corner of his mouth rise. This was going to be difficult. "I said she took them. Dominic's father gave them to her."

"He gave them to her? Even though it would ruin him? Why would he do something like that?"

"Well, a couple of reasons."

"Was he that far gone in love with her?" she asked, her voice raising. "Which, by the way, is disgusting. She was barely out of her teens when he met her." She shuddered with repulsion.

"Because . . ." He paused. He'd gone this far; he might as well say it. Nicole needed to hear these words. "The earrings belonged to her."

Nicole frowned. "Okay, now you're confusing me. How is that possible? If they belonged to Lia, then that meant—" Her mouth slowly fell open.

"The diamond earrings belonged to her jewelry dowry," he continued. "She met Dominic's father while she was deciding on the design."

She jumped from her seat and her chair knocked over onto the floor with a crash. "She was a *princess*?"

"Yes." He motioned with his hands to quiet her down. "Lia's real name is Liyakat."

Nicole scrunched her nose. "I can see why she changed it," she said in a murmur.

"She took the diamonds, ran away, and created a new identity." There. He'd done it. He'd broken the rules and told Nicole. And he didn't regret it.

"Why did she run away?"

"I don't know all the details, but the deciding factor was when the family discovered her affair."

"Why didn't they go after her?"

"She was considered ruined and was then seen as a liability," Alex explained. "There was no way they could marry her off."

Her eyebrow arched high. "*Ruined?* Marry her *off*? Did you just say *liability*?"

Alex was not going to listen to another tirade this early in the morning. "So she gave up her family name, all the rights and privileges she had as a princess—"

"I'm guessing there weren't that many."

He ignored that. "But she wouldn't give up the earrings."

"Because they were connected with her lover, right?" She frowned as she considered that reason. "No, I bet there was something more. Why did the royal family want the diamonds so much?"

Alex's mouth twitched. Nicole wasn't going to be pleased when she heard this. "The earrings have deep spiritual symbolism. As you know, earrings were first created as amulets to ward off evil spirits. . . ."

She shifted her jaw to one side. "Spill it, Alex."

"The pink diamonds represents a princess's modesty, chastity, and subservience."

Her eyes widened with outrage. "Say what?!"

"These are very important attributes to be a good princess."

"I don't believe this." She shoved her hands in her hair.

"I guess the earrings were Lia's way of thumbing her nose at the yardstick she was measured against."

"This is . . . this is . . ." She paused and looked at him in horror. "Why are you telling me this?"

He thought it was obvious. "Because you needed to know?"

"No, no." She stomped her foot. "You shouldn't have told me this. I'm a blabbermouth. I gossip." She clapped her hands over her mouth. "I—I can't keep a secret to save my life."

"Yes, you can. I believe in you."

"Oh, Alex." She grabbed his hands and looked earnestly into his face. "You shouldn't."

"I can't sit by and see the woman I love lose her faith in fairy tales."

She pressed her lips together as tears shone in her eyes. "Thank you," she whispered.

"For telling you the truth?"

"For loving me back." She gently pressed her mouth against his.

She loved him. He felt the bands of tension breaking free from his chest. Alex wanted to swing her into his arms and claim her mouth with his. He had to restrain himself for just another moment.

Alex pulled away from her, his lips clinging against hers. "How do you feel?"

"Good," she said with her eyes closed. "But it might wear off, so kiss me again. Quick."

A laugh tickled in his throat. "I meant about knowing the truth."

"Oh, that." She opened her eyes. "I don't know. I have to think about it. I thought Lia Dash was one thing, but it turned out she was much, much more."

She paused and looked out the window before she returned her attention to him. "She created her own fairy tale, didn't she?"

"Yeah, I guess she did." Trust Nicole to look for the fairy dust. Alex wasn't sure, but that could be the strongest act of courage he'd seen.

Her eyes lit up with anticipation. "You do realize I have to tell my sisters about this?"

Alex winced. "Do you have to? Can't you keep it to yourself?"

"Of course not! Alex, there is one thing you should know by now. The only thing a sister is required to share is the secrets."

IN THE PINK

CHAPTER ONE

Mercer Whitley-Cooke lunged forward as the stack of silver trays cascaded from her hands. She managed to catch one as the rest crashed onto the hardwood floor.

The silence that followed was almost as deafening.

"Mercer!"

She jumped, and the remaining tray slipped from her fingers. It crashed on the floor like a cymbal, punctuating her boss's yell. Mercer winced, waiting to see Ellis storm from the kitchen. How did the catering manager know it was her? Did the guy have X-ray vision or something?

"Sorry!" she called out as she hastily picked up the trays before Ellis could walk in to see the mess. Why did these things happen when she was in his hearing range? She had to be careful and not make another mistake.

Mercer rolled her eyes at that idea. Okay, *that* wasn't going

to happen. How about no mistakes in the next twenty
minutes?

She cast another look in the direction of the kitchen,
grateful that her boss had decided to stay put. The last thing
she needed was to get fired. Not now. Not tonight.

The sad thing was, she wasn't hanging on to this job for
the money, even though she needed it. Minimum wage was a
pittance compared to what she once enjoyed. And being em-
ployed was always a good thing. The way her probation officer
acted, it was a necessity.

Mercer wasn't thinking about that. She needed this job for
tonight. The elegant housewarming party was for Dominic and
Lindsay Stark. Lindsay, Sabrina and Nicole Graham were
rarely at these parties. They weren't socialites by any stretch of
the imagination, which made Mercer's plan more difficult.
Still, she kept at it, believing that one night she would work at
a party where one of the sisters would wear the earrings for a
special occasion. That night was tonight. Lindsay would wear
earrings once owned by Lia Dash.

Mercer wasn't a fan of the famous woman, but the pink
diamonds sparked her interest. She closed her eyes and envi-
sioned the jewels, remembering everything from the brilliant
cut to the pink champagne color. That memory kept her going
during her dark days of forced retirement from pickpocketing.

"Stop daydreaming," one of her coworkers warned in a
harsh whisper as she walked past.

Mercer opened her eyes and quickly followed the others to
finish unpacking for the party. She positioned herself in the
circle of employees, doing her best to blend in. She industri-
ously polished the trays, which seemed to attract fingerprints,
as the other workers chatted around her. She occasionally

joined in the conversation, being careful not to talk too much about herself. The fewer questions asked, the better.

It wasn't because she was an ex-con. This group didn't care about that. In fact, she might even gain some respect because she put one over on the upper class. But she didn't want them to know that she once belonged on the other side of the serving tray.

Mercer looked up at the painted vaulted ceiling, and memories flickered before her eyes. Hard to believe that she was once invited to these high-society parties. Her coworkers definitely wouldn't appreciate that she used to belong to the other team.

Little did they know that she worked hard at these parties. She became quite adept at lifting wallets and money clips, usually from lecherous men who were distracted by her plunging necklines. Air-kissing the society matrons while grabbing their bracelets required more bravado and quick thinking.

It came as a surprise that she didn't miss the parties at all. Or the endless salon and spa visits to have every inch of her pulled, dyed, injected, buffed, varnished, waxed, tweezed, or punctured.

Pure torture. Mercer gave a shiver. It was amazing women found those visits a form of relaxation. Pampering. Whatever. That she could do without.

The waitress next to her looked in her direction. "Cold?"

"Just a little chilly." Mercer rubbed her arms briskly. "These uniforms are thin."

"And ugly."

She looked down at the scratchy white shirt, polyester black pants, and red brocade vest. "That, too." The shoes with the squeaky thick rubber soles sent the outfit straight into the fashion failure category.

Mercer finished polishing the trays and decided it was time to learn the layout of the mansion. The more comfortable she was with her surroundings, the better chance she had of getting her hands on the diamonds.

Acting as if she was heading back to the catering truck, Mercer went to the grand entry hall and looked around. One thing was for sure—this house on the lake was amazing.

She'd seen plenty of mansions on the east side of Seattle—even lived in one—but this was something else. Mercer decided to venture deeper into the house, noting that the walls were painted warm, vibrant colors. The clusters of sofas, chairs, and ottomans in the formal living room were top quality.

Stop gawking. She needed to memorize the walk paths and exits. Big parties were difficult to predict. They could hide you or block you. Every thief knew that grabbing the most coveted item in the most amazing manner meant nothing if you couldn't get away.

Her gaze swept down the hallway and jerked back when she saw a familiar figure. Her stomach made a sharp twist when she recognized the lanky male in the dark suit. Her eyes widened.

What was *he* doing here?

As if he felt her gaze, Detective Tony Jackson turned and looked directly at her.

Wow. Tony's brown eyes could always pack a punch. Her breath caught in her chest as she felt the warmth spread through her body. The heat radiated to the tips of her fingers and toes, zipping through her blood and dancing just underneath her skin. It tingled in her breasts and flooded her sex.

He looked good. A little too good, which irritated her.

Tony Jackson seemed to have flourished during her yearlong absence.

She noticed everything, from the expert cut of his light brown hair to the fine quality of his shoes and the designer of his black suit. The white shirt was expensive, but trust Tony to dismiss the black tie and leave the top button open. His shoulders were perfect to cling to often, and his lean hips were just right to wrap her legs around and hold tight.

Mercer should have known that Tony would have changed. She'd like to think time would have frozen when she was gone, waiting to start up again when she got back.

But all that time she had missed Tony. It had been a physical ache that seeped into her bones. It weighed her down until this moment. Suddenly she felt stronger now that she'd seen him, and the pain surrounding her fell away.

As much as she longed to run to Tony and jump into his arms like she always wanted to, she also fought the urge to hide. She wasn't ready to see him. Not now. Not *tonight*! She had wanted to be the new and improved Mercer Whitley-Cooke before he saw her again. This could ruin everything.

Her back foot was positioned to make a quick pivot and turn away, but she knew it was too late. A quick recovery was in order. Mercer smiled and strode forward as if she still looked like a million bucks. "Hey, gorgeous."

"Mercer." His brief scan made the back of her knees tingle. "Long time."

"It didn't have to be that way." She moved to flip her hair, then remembered she wore it short these days. It was also light red since she couldn't maintain the costly highlighting regimen. Not that it mattered. She wasn't trying to disappear in a room filled with blondes anymore. She hoped Tony liked redheads. "You could have visited me."

Tony rolled his eyes. "That would have been fun."

"You always wanted to see me behind bars." Mercer gave a playful pout, but Tony didn't seem to notice. Guess she needed to be pumped up with collagen for that move to be more effective.

"You weren't in for long," Tony pointed out, "thanks to your hotshot lawyer."

"He was worth every penny." Even though it meant she had no money left, but Tony didn't need to know that.

"The sentence was ridiculously light," Tony said as he braced his legs apart and slid his hands into his pants pockets.

"The justice system hard at work."

"And you went to a prison that makes a five-star hotel look shabby."

"No, not quite." She leaned closer to confide with Tony, fighting the urge to touch him. "There was no valet service. If you leave your shoes outside your door, you won't get them back."

"And then you had your sentence shortened for"—he shook his head in disbelief—"good behavior."

"I can be good. It's been known to happen." She put her hands on her hips. "In fact, I have been a responsible citizen since I was a guest of your lovely Department of Corrections."

"Then what are you doing here?"

"Working." She drew the word out, wondering if it was a trick question.

His gaze leisurely traveled down the length of her body. "Do I need to frisk you?"

Yes, please. She imagined his hands on her, and her sex clenched. "I usually insist on dinner and a movie first, but I'll make an exception for you, Gorgeous." She lifted her arms in the classic ta-da pose and twirled around. "Sure you don't want a female officer to do it?"

"I'm not with the force anymore."

She dropped her arms. "You finally came to your senses. It's about time." The relief pouring through her body immediately congealed into a lump in her stomach. The guy was a little too smart for his own good, but the red tape usually tangled him up.

No big deal. Tony was a civilian now. Even if he planned to do a citizen's arrest, it wouldn't happen. He had never caught her, and that was back when she wore high heels and couture gowns. She would be faster than ever this time around.

"Doesn't look like you came to your senses," Tony said as he studied her uniform.

She gave a coquettish tilt of her head. "Why would you think that?"

"You're working at a party where there will be someone wearing the pink diamonds you once tried to steal."

Mercer shrugged and looked away. "Not my fault. I don't make those decisions. I was told to show up here, and here I am."

"And you're going to be in the same room as the earrings."

She waved the concern away with a flick of her wrist. "I'm around a lot of jewelry these days, but I can't do anything about it. My hands are usually full of canapés."

"This is no coincidence. You want those diamonds. They are the only jewels you failed to grab."

She felt the sting of that word. *Failed.* Gee, did he have to bring that up?

"I know you're after them again," Tony said, watching her face intently.

"Think what you want"—she made a show of looking at her manicure, or rather lack of one—"but it doesn't concern you."

"Yes it does."

"You're not a policeman anymore," she reminded him with a smile.

"True, but I'm still in the business." He pulled out a slim leather wallet from his jacket and flipped it open to reveal his identification. "I'm a private investigator."

Mercer reluctantly took the wallet, her head spinning as she studied Tony's license. "Six-feet-two? You wish."

Tony ignored that remark. "And the security team on this party works for me."

Alarm skipped down her spine. "If the Starks are afraid the guests will take the silver, then they need a better set of friends."

"They are more concerned about thieves targeting their friends. So I'm keeping my eye on you," he announced as he slipped the wallet back into his jacket. "It'll be like old times."

"Oooh." Mercer smiled weakly. "Fun."

Tony watched Mercer with satisfaction. He'd managed to rattle her. Good. Now maybe she would think twice before swiping the earrings.

Then again, this was Mercer. Nothing was going to stop

this woman from going after the pink diamonds. He could almost admire that level of determination, but she used it for the wrong side of the law.

"I'll see you around, Mercer." Tony moved to leave. "I have to check the security measures before the party."

"Security measures?" she mimicked loftily. "You make it sound like you've set up a web of lasers."

"Nice try, but I'm not falling for it." He knew what she was trying to do, but he wasn't going to boast about their line of defense.

"Well, excuuuse me. I know how you men love to talk electronics." She patted his chest with her hand. "Gets the testosterone running."

The flirty touch was like an electric jolt to his system. He wanted to cover her hand with his and press her palm against his chest. Then she could feel how she made his heart thud against his ribs.

As he fought to keep his reactions in check, he almost missed the light, stealthy move. "Give it back, Mercer," he warned her softly.

She stiffened in surprise. He saw the uncertainty flash across her features before she made an exaggerated face. "I was going to," she said as she brandished his wallet with a theatrical flair. "There's not a good market for a P.I. license."

"I'm waiting."

Mercer's eyes narrowed. She wordlessly slapped the wallet into his waiting palm.

"Thank you."

"You're welcome," she answered in an ungracious growl.

The French doors opened behind them and the short

catering manager bustled in. "Mercer, there you are." Ellis tossed his silk red scarf over his shoulder. "Stop flirting and get back to work."

She scowled at her boss's retreating figure. "I'm not flirting."

"You call everyone Gorgeous?" Tony asked, and he slid his wallet back in his pocket.

She looked at him from the corner of her eye. "It saves me from remembering names. I gotta go. I'll see you later."

"Bet on it." He allowed her to take a few steps. "And Mercer?"

She paused in mid-step, but didn't turn around. "Yeah?"

"My watch."

"Oh, come on." Mercer stomped her foot and whirled around. "You couldn't have seen that. You had a hunch, right?"

"And I also guessed that you put it in your left front pocket?"

Her hands bunched into fists before she stretched her fingers out. She walked to him and pulled the watch from her pocket. "I was testing you, you know."

"I know." He took the timepiece she dangled from her fingers and put it back on. "It has a loose clasp, which made it easier."

"I don't need any help," she muttered as she watched him struggle with the strap. She stepped closer, and her soft breast skimmed her hand. "But you do. Here, let me."

Her fingers were light and quick as she cinched the wristband. Her feminine grace fired his imagination. Having those fingers roam his body would be a mind-blowing experience.

"Mercer!" Ellis made her name sound like a sharp bark.

"All right, all right!" she called over her shoulder. "I have to go." She turned and rushed down the hall and around the corner.

Tony watched her retreat. He couldn't keep his eyes off the sway of her hips. When she disappeared, he slowly exhaled and dragged his fingers through his hair. He knew Mercer would be here and that she wouldn't be able to stay away. The prior knowledge didn't help. He didn't know how much longer he could act indifferent.

He could predict almost everything Mercer would do. If there ever was a job for a Mercer Whitley-Cooke expert, he would be overqualified. Then again, he wouldn't get the job because of how he felt. The more he learned about Mercer, the more fascinating she turned out to be.

He was crazy about her, but there were two things that had stopped him in the past from doing something about it: Mercer had been married, and she had been a thief.

She might be single these days, but the woman continued to be up to no good.

It didn't matter. He still wanted her. Tony shook his head. They might as well shoot him now, because if Mercer knew how he felt, she would use it to her advantage.

She had no idea that her flirting got to him, that it was like needles grazing sensitive skin. He used to think that she was playing him, but he had been wrong. She wanted him as much as he wanted her.

Just a few moments ago, he wanted to sweep her into his arms, hold her tight, and never let go. She had teased him about not visiting her while she had been incarcerated, but it was something he couldn't do. Seeing her behind bars, no matter how much she deserved it, would have killed him.

It was no wonder he never caught her. His heart wasn't

fully into it, and once he realized it, he quit the force. He wasn't doing any good there.

He had better keep his distance from that woman. She was dangerous. It didn't matter that he saw the creative spirit inside her, or the way she strove for excellence, or even her generous nature. She was trouble, and he needed to keep away.

Shrugging off the dark thoughts, Tony raked his fingers through his hair again. Time to get back to work. He checked his watch.

His cuff link was missing.

He pressed his lips together as a smile tugged at the corner of his mouth. Tony walked down the hallway and searched for Mercer. He found her in the butler's pantry, unpacking glasses from crates.

"Mercer?"

She glanced up. Her look was perfectly innocent.

That was the tip-off. There was nothing innocent about the woman. Tony lifted his hand and pointed at his sleeve. "My cuff link."

Mercer smiled. "It took you long enough."

Chapter Two

MERCER LEANED AGAINST THE WALL OUTSIDE the kitchen, enjoying the cool summer breeze while mentally going over her plan once again. As the other workers puffed on their last cigarettes and gossiped before the party started, she stood off to the side, working a quarter over the back of her hand.

She could still do *this*, she noted wryly as the coin flipped over one knuckle after the other. She'd done this every day for ten years. A musician had scales, athletes had stretches, and she had these warm-ups.

But the faithful practice didn't keep her at the top of her game. She couldn't understand how Tony knew she took the wallet. Or the watch. How did she expect to get the earrings without anyone noticing? She was going to get caught and go back to the slammer.

Mercer took a steady breath and pushed back the panic threatening to pull her under. There was no need to worry.

The unexpected presence of Tony surprised her. That's all. She had to adapt the plan, not abandon it.

She had been studying the Graham sisters like a hawk for months, learning their habits and tastes. Her plan was unbelievably simple. She knew that Lindsay would be wearing the earrings tonight, because hosting the party was a special occasion for the woman. But since it was the last day of the month, Nicole got them the next day. Nicole was very particular about getting her whole month's worth of earrings, so Lindsay would hand them over immediately after the party.

It was amazing what people discussed in public on their cell phones, Mercer mused as she flipped the quarter expertly to the next hand. In fact, the Graham sisters had become lax about protecting the diamonds. Walking around with ten carats of diamonds in an evening purse? Did they think nothing would happen, when the earrings were so easy to snatch?

"Wow," one of the bartenders said as he walked by her.

Mercer's hand tensed and the quarter fell to the ground. It bounced onto the patio and rolled, veering off into the bushes.

"That was some trick," he said. "Where'd you learn that?"

"My physical therapist. It's for my arthritis," Mercer lied as she rubbed the joints in her hands. She didn't want anyone to know what she was capable of doing, or that she was preparing for the theft.

Mercer pushed off the wall and walked down the stone path to where the coin had fallen. She passed by one of the large windows overlooking the view and saw Lindsay inside, straightening one of the floral arrangements on the fireplace.

Yep, she was wearing the pink diamonds. Five carats on each ear. Mercer tried not to stare. She didn't want anyone to notice her preoccupation with the jewels. But it was hard not to do a double-take at the most beautiful diamonds she'd ever come across.

She wasn't sure what she would feel when she saw the earrings again. Something more than her blood heating up. Those diamonds had been her downfall. A year ago she could have gone for more expensive jewelry or for the easier pick, but the moment she saw those diamonds, everything had paled in comparison.

The pink ice had once represented the most difficult challenge. A year ago she mapped out puzzles and possibilities. If she had gotten those diamonds, she would have been the undisputed best pickpocket. She would have become a legend. The technique would have been named after her: The Mercer.

She sighed and clucked her tongue. She would have loved that.

Mercer studied what Lindsay was wearing. The eldest Graham's upswept hair was a bit prim, but it showed off the earrings. The black cocktail dress was going to be a problem. Mercer might lose track of Lindsay among the other little black dresses.

Sparing another quick look at the earrings, Mercer discovered that she didn't feel the same fire or drive from a year ago. Did the passing of time dull her need? Or did her sabbatical from a criminal life cure her of the obsession?

Mercer gave it a moment's thought and wriggled her nose. *Naaah.* She was still here, planning to get her hands on those diamonds.

And that's all she wanted to do. She didn't want to steal them away or fence them. She definitely didn't want to own the earrings.

She wanted to get the diamonds in her hands, raise her

arms above her head, and do a touchdown dance. She wanted another try, to succeed and erase her failure.

But was she willing to risk her freedom for it? Mercer grimaced. That she wasn't sure about.

She was allowing herself just one more look at the pink earrings when a man walked behind Lindsay. It looked like Dominic, Lindsay's husband. He appeared just as forbidding as he did in the newspaper photos. From what she'd gathered during her research, he was some sort of venture capitalist who made risky gambles and came out richer than a king.

She watched as Dominic wrapped his arm possessively around his wife's waist. Mercer's stomach felt hollow at the tender gesture. Dominic leaned down to kiss the pulse point of Lindsay's throat.

Mercer blinked and looked away. She could do without the mushy, gushy stuff. She hunched her shoulders, wanting to curl up in a ball as envy snaked through her.

That's what she wanted more than anything. More than the diamonds. But it would have to wait.

She wanted someone to love and cherish her. She wanted to love and look after someone, too. Someone who was strong inside and out. Someone who made her weak in the knees, but someone she could lean on. And if she was going to be completely honest with herself, that someone was Tony Jackson.

But he wouldn't be interested in a thief. She wasn't so thrilled with the line of work anymore either. It wasn't at all that she had hoped it would be. So she would grab the earrings tonight and retire on a high note. Then she'd go after Tony Jackson as if he was the Orloff diamond.

That is, if she didn't get caught and sent back to prison.

"Places, people. Places." Ellis clapped his hands loudly at the doorway. "The guests are arriving."

Everyone scurried back inside except for Mercer, as she crouched down to retrieve her quarter. Considering what she made an hour, every cent counted.

She picked up the coin, turned toward the kitchen, and halted when she saw a flash of green next to the refrigerator.

Oh, hell. It was Sabrina West. The middle Graham sister was wearing an olive-green cocktail dress. From the Chloé collection, if Mercer remembered correctly, but she wasn't up on her designers like she used to be.

When Sabrina turned, Mercer suddenly understood the choice of designer. Chloé was known for flowing lines, and the jeweled empire waistline allowed ample room for Sabrina's very pregnant belly.

That woman was going to pop any day. And she was probably hormonal. Mercer rotated her shoulder as she felt the old twinge, remembering her last encounter with the other woman. Sabrina looked delicate, but she was a scrappy fighter. She was also trouble. Sabrina Graham was the only person who had caught Mercer in the middle of a theft—and Sabrina had been an amateur! Oh, the humiliation of it all.

Mercer took a step back and scanned the area for an alternate route. She didn't want a face-to-face encounter with Sabrina. While she didn't think the woman would make a scene—or put her in a headlock again—she didn't want to alert the Graham sisters that she was here.

She needed to enter from the side of the house, keep her head down, and have an eye out for Ian West, who was undoubtedly somewhere around here. He was the type to keep a watchful eye on his pregnant wife.

She hoped neither of them recognized her. Mercer grimaced as she imagined the possible outcomes, each scenario worse than the last. They probably wouldn't place her at first. She had different hair, less dependency on Botox, and no designer clothes.

Then again, she couldn't leave anything to chance. Mercer ducked her head and crossed the stone patio that overlooked the lake dotted with expensive houses and boats. Guests were already strolling around the mansions, and one couple had already made their way outside.

She passed the couple and gave a vague nod in their direction. Her boss was going to have a conniption, Mercer decided. Ellis treated the catering business like the theater, and he had the high-strung personality of a diva choreographer. She had a strong feeling that no matter what happened tonight, this was going to be her last day on the job.

"Mercer?"

She froze. *That voice.* Mercer squeezed her eyes shut. *Please don't let it be . . . Please don't let it be.*

"Mercer, darling. You can't even recognize your ex-husband? Has it been that long?"

"Ex-husband?" She turned to face the man in the exquisitely tailored tuxedo. "Show me the divorce papers. Or, for that matter, the marriage license."

Reginald Whitley-Cooke looked mildly amused. That irked her even more. The guy patterned his style and cool charm on Cary Grant, and Reggie was no Cary Grant.

"Now that I think about it, I haven't received an alimony check." Mercer reached out her hand. "Cough it up."

"Uh, uh, uh." Reggie shook his finger like a wise old sage

chastising a novice. "You're already slipping. What's rule number one?"

The rule flashed through her head before she could stop it. *Never blow your cover.* And she didn't. Not even when she was tried and convicted. The ploy was supposedly meant to protect her, but what good did it do? Nothing. All it did was protect her accomplice. Her partner-in-crime. Her mentor.

Mercer studied Reggie, noting a few more strands of gray in the older man's dark hair, but the change only made him look more debonair. She had to admit, the man was a master at cultivating an image. Reggie had plucked her from the streets and acted as Professor Higgins to her Eliza Doolittle. Before she knew it, she was able to pass as a trophy wife and pick pockets of the rich and famous.

Their deal had been simple: Reggie took the jewels, gave her twenty percent of their worth, and made a lot of money off her. Now that she was away from him, she realized that his rules and plans would have always made her the fall guy if things went wrong. They were also designed to let him walk away unscathed with the prize in his pocket.

Mercer shifted on one foot and crossed her arms. "I heard you were so devastated by my conviction that you had to go away. Trip to some island while things were hot here?"

"Yes, my memories here were too painful." Reggie sighed and shook his head with sorrow. "But I found someone to help me forget the troubled past."

She took a good, hard look at her successor, who wore a gold and pink strapless gown. She was stunning. It was more than the luxuriously long black hair, curves that would knock an eye out, and the exuding elegance. The woman was just too . . . gorgeous. And yes, Mercer thought with a hint of defiance, that was a flaw.

"What's her talent?" Mercer asked Reggie. "Shoplifting? Pickpocket?"

"Please, darling." Reggie stroked the other woman's bare arm. "It would be ungentlemanly for me to answer."

Mercer had to laugh at the innuendo. She couldn't help it. Reggie was probably more disinterested in sex than any man she had ever met.

His nonanswer made her curious. Mercer decided to introduce herself to the other woman. She offered her hand and the glamorous creature took it. Mercer noticed the woman's rough fingertips and unusually short fingernails.

Safecracker, Mercer decided smugly. "Hi, I'm Mercer."

"London," the brunette introduced herself.

London, England . . . Mercer Island . . . Mercer glanced at Reggie. "What's with the location names? Are these places that have outstanding warrants on you? Do you name your 'wives' so you don't forget?"

Reggie's eyes narrowed. "I see that your incarceration didn't rehabilitate your unfortunate personality."

Ah. Mercer raised an eyebrow. She must be on to something. Multisyllabic words meant his temper was flaring. When the Appalachian mountain twang filtered through his Continental accent, she would know it was time to duck.

"London"—Mercer clasped her fingers on top of their joined hands—"a piece of advice from a former Mrs. Whitley-Cooke to a future one. Don't trust this guy for a moment."

"Pay no attention to her, London dear." He plucked the woman's hand from Mercer's grasp. "She's bitter."

"For being the fall guy for our work?" Mercer asked Reggie. "I say I had good reason."

"It's not my fault that you didn't do your job properly. You were never one of my best."

Strange how the snide comment didn't bother her. It would have a year ago. "Really? How many wives have you gone through?"

Reggie stopped smiling. "Come along, London. We should not be seen fraternizing with the hired help."

Oh, he was not going to walk away after that remark. "Why are you here, Reggie? And how did you get invited? After your 'wife'"—Mercer used air quotes—"stole from them?"

"Many of our friends took pity on me. How could I have known that not only were you after my money, but you were also after my friends' jewels as well?"

"This kind of party isn't grand enough for your standards."

"It's a housewarming party," he reminded her. "I'm welcoming my new neighbors."

"You're after something. Something in their safe?" She saw London's twitch. It was slight, but a newbie mistake that Reggie hadn't ironed out yet. "No, London is still too raw for that kind of coming out."

"And you think you've been promoted to expert?"

"Oh, I'm sorry, Reggie." She flattened her hand against her chest. "Am I getting too close to your secret? Am I that much of a threat?"

Reggie struggled not to smile. "I have no problems telling you. I'm surprised you haven't guessed it. You're getting slow."

"You can keep saying that, you can even say it ten times fast, but it won't make it true."

He leaned closer to her. "I'm here for the same reason you are."

"The free food?"

"The earrings."

Every muscle tightened in her body. It hurt to breathe. "What earrings?"

"You never could play dumb, could you?" Reggie straightened to his full height. "The earrings are why you're here. That's why you took the job with the catering service. Because you knew sooner or later you would work a party where the earrings would be."

"You are delusional." Her mentor was going after the earrings the same night she was? Would she get to them first? Or would she be left taking the fall again?

Her mind stopped whirling when it suddenly occurred to her. She glared at Reggie. "Not so much of a coincidence, is it? You're planning for me to take the fall, aren't you?"

Reggie's sly smile said it all. "Mercer, darling, you give me way too much credit. Come along, London. We need to mingle with the important people."

Mercer sensed them walking away as her skin went from hot to clammy cold. The detective who could predict her every move was watching her. The person who caused her to fail the last time was here. And now the guy who taught her everything she knew was going to steal the earrings and make her take the fall.

This theft just got way more complicated.

CHAPTER THREE

MERCER CRANED HER NECK OVER THE well-dressed crowd as she carried a tray of smoked salmon and caviar éclair hors d'oeuvres. Where was Nicole? What was keeping the youngest Graham sister from the party?

She pressed forward and then dodged a couple who almost backed into her. Mercer bumped into a table edge, stifled her yelp of pain, and held onto the tray for dear life.

Nothing spilled. She was somewhat shocked. Mercer paused for a moment longer, waiting for something to knock her to the floor or tip the tray, but luck was on her side this time. She gave a sigh of relief and slowly made her way through the large media room and back to the kitchen.

As usual, she recognized many of the guests. None of them noticed her, much less remembered her from previous guest lists. She must have done her interchangeable trophy wife bit well, but it was a tad disheartening. Mercer would have liked to have been memorable.

Worse, she realized now that she would have had a more successful pickpocket career as a catering employee than as Reggie's arm candy. She wished she had known that earlier. It would have saved her a lot of headaches. Pain and agony. At least some of her dignity.

But now that she was working for a caterer—at least for the moment—the knowledge wasn't much use to her. She could really use the money, but she wasn't interested in career advancement as a criminal.

Her timing really sucked these days.

"Oops!" She collided with one of the tuxedoed guests, and the last hors d'oeuvre plopped onto the carpeting. "Sorry."

"Watch where you're going." The distinguished gentleman glared at her and turned his back to resume his conversation.

"Yes, sir," she muttered, hesitating when she saw the salmon caviar éclair next to the man's foot. Mmm . . . nope. She wasn't going to try.

She hurried away before the guy took a step back. All the way to the kitchen she thought of quite a few put-downs she could have used. The guy was lucky she had been rehabilitated, or she would have picked him clean.

She knew she could, and wasn't even going to pretend to be modest about that talent. Pickpocketing was what she did best. She excelled in it. She missed that feeling.

These days she seemed to mess up at every job she worked: cleaning service, indoor painting, and gardening. She hadn't found anything that made her feel good about a job well done. More like "why can't you do anything right?"

Mercer headed for the swinging kitchen door as if it were a lifeline. She slapped the door with her palm and watched it fling open before it stopped abruptly just as Ellis cried out.

She grabbed the door as it swung back at her. "Ellis?" Mercer cautiously peeked around and saw the catering manager pressing his hands against his forehead. "I am so incredibly sorry."

Her boss didn't say anything. Didn't move. Didn't open his eyes. Either he was suffering from a concussion, or he was counting to ten before he let loose.

Maybe she wasn't fully rehabilitated, Mercer thought, because she was really hoping for the concussion. That would make her boss too busy at the hospital to fire her.

"Mercer."

She hunched her shoulders. "Yes?"

He dropped his hands and looked directly at her. She noticed the red mark on his forehead was about three times darker than the flush of anger rising in his face. "I've had it."

Please don't fire me. . . . Mercer made a fierce wish. *Please don't fire me . . . Please don't fire me. . . .*

"Do everyone a favor," Ellis said through clenched teeth as he grabbed her silver tray, "and work the gardens."

"You want me to go outside?" She glanced at the patio. It would soon be dusk. "Are you sure? There are steps. Wet surfaces. Bees." That went way beyond her serving capabilities.

"I don't care," Ellis said as he pressed the edge of his scarf onto his wound. "All I want is for you to be out of my sight."

Unfortunately, she would be out of the house and away from where the Graham sisters were. Mercer opened her mouth to argue, but the words died in her throat when she saw her boss's expression. Mercer shut her mouth with a click, wordlessly took a fruit and cheese tray, and headed outside. She closed the door behind her, paused at the doorway, and saw only a few guests meandering through the grounds.

She soaked in the quiet as the breeze tugged at her hair. It was definitely cooler outside, with less people to serve, but there was no Nicole.

Mercer shook her head in self-disgust. She should have stayed focused. Now she was banished from the house.

Not only did she need to find an opportunity to get her hands on the diamonds, but she also needed to protect herself. Reggie was going to grab the diamonds and make it look like she took them.

Mercer jumped at the tap on the window and saw her angry boss motioning for her to move. She rolled back her shoulders, put on a smile, and approached the guests.

She slowly made her way around the gardens as the sun dipped toward the horizon. The scent of the flowers mingling with the fruit and cheese was getting to her. Her mouth watered at the aroma.

She always got hungry during a theft. No idea why. Probably had something to do with nerves. But with her stomach grumbling, she was finding it more and more difficult to focus.

Her stomach clenched. Wow, she was *really* hungry. Mercer rubbed her stomach through her brocade vest. Did that mean she was really nervous? Maybe not. She didn't remember being this hungry on her most daring maneuvers. But back then she could eat whenever she wanted. It was one of the advantages of masquerading as a guest.

Mercer glanced at the food on her tray. There were only a few pieces of fruit left. Maybe just a nibble . . .

No. She snatched her hand back and balled her fingers into

a fist. Ellis would toss her on her butt for sure. It was his most sacred rule.

But her boss couldn't see her right now.

No. Mercer marched down the steps to the waterfront. She wasn't going to push her luck. Someone would see and complain. It was how her day was turning out to be.

Was that an omen? Mercer hesitated as she took the steps to the dock. Was all this bad luck a warning, telling her not to try for the pink ice?

Naah. She wasn't superstitious, and she wasn't going to start to be now. Mercer stepped onto the dock and saw Tony standing on the far edge by himself. The heat flickered deep in her belly.

"Planning to jump, gorgeous?" she called out. Tony turned around, and she felt the glow rushing inside her.

"What?" he asked. "No sneaking behind me and giving a good push? You're losing your touch."

Ha. He didn't know the half of it.

"What brings you out here?" Tony walked the length of the dock and stopped in front of her. "Are you checking alternate escape routes? I should warn you that one of the security men will be back to guard this area."

"Oh, please. Getaway by water is so déclassé if you can't do it by yacht." She held the silver tray between them. "Care for a strawberry?"

"Why?" He studied the fruit slices with suspicion. "What did you do to it?"

"Nothing!" Her mouth dropped open in outrage. "I'm not allowed to touch the food. Or sample. Even when it all smells so wonderful."

His gaze flicked over her face before he chose a strawberry

slice. Mercer felt the pull deep inside her as she watched him bite into the fruit. She couldn't tear her gaze away from his straight white teeth sinking into the pink, juicy strawberry. The tip of his tongue darted past his firm lips, lapping at the drop of juice.

"Mm. Pretty good."

Uh-huh. She swallowed hard. She bet he was better than good. She'd like him to use that move on her. Mercer clenched her thighs together at the forbidden thought.

"Here." He held the half-eaten strawberry out to her. "Try."

Mercer opened her mouth in surprise, inhaling the strawberry scent as Tony rubbed it against her bottom lip. He slid the fruit past her lips before she closed her mouth. Mercer instinctively lowered her eyelids as the flavors danced along her tongue, deciding it was the most delicious thing she had ever tasted.

Tony watched her savor the fruit as he gently trailed his thumb down her lip. Her mouth felt soft and inviting. The joy shimmering from her face nearly undid him.

He desperately wanted to claim her mouth, kiss her with slow pleasure until she clung onto him.

Nothing was stopping him.

Except for the possibility that Mercer was using him. Trying to distract him. That should have diminished the raw need slamming through his body, but it didn't have any effect. He wanted her even if she *was* up to her old tricks.

"Oh, yeah." She smacked her lips. "That's good."

Tony struggled to hide his feelings behind a blank expression as she opened her eyes. He really wanted to kiss her. He regretted not taking a chance in the past. But back then, Mercer was another man's wife.

"Have the last one," he said, nodding at the tray.

She stared at the food with regret and shook her head. "I shouldn't."

"Since when have you been so principled?"

She stuck her tongue out at him.

Tony's chest tightened as he considered what he would do with that tongue. "Sometimes rules are made to be broken," he said, wishing his voice didn't sound so gruff.

"This isn't one of those times." She grabbed the last strawberry off the tray and offered it to him. "These are for the guests."

"I'm working the party, too." He leaned forward to take a bite, but she pulled it out of reach.

"That's true. You shouldn't have it either." She waved it under his nose. "Too bad."

Tony stood still. His body was tensed and ready as he watched Mercer's blue eyes sparkle. She had looked just like that when he first fell in love with her. And she had been teasing him that time, too.

"Don't you want it?" she asked in a singsong tone.

Yeah, he wanted. Her. More than anything.

Tony moved quickly and captured the strawberry between his teeth. Mercer jerked her hand back when he grazed her fingers. "Hey!"

He knew his grin indicated it wasn't accidental.

She shook out her fingers. "That hurt."

Tony raised an eyebrow in disbelief. "Who knew that you were so fragile?" He reached out and cradled her fingers with his hand. He gave a courtly, mocking bow before brushing his mouth over her fingers.

The gentle touch shouldn't make his heart race. He wanted

to show her his tender side, but all he could think about was brushing his lips lightly over every inch of her soft skin. He looked up into her eyes, enjoying the faint blush streaking up her cheeks.

"A kiss to make it better," he assured her.

"You do that well. Reggie would—" She stopped abruptly and pressed her lips.

Tony straightened as jealousy pressed against his chest, making it hurt to breathe. It wasn't logical. The man was no longer married to Mercer, but he had been the one thing that had prevented Tony from getting what he really wanted.

"I saw that Reggie was here. With his fiancée." Okay, that was cold, bashing her over the head with the fact that Reggie had moved on with ease.

Mercer nodded and looked away. "I bumped into them."

"Literally?"

"Ha, ha." Mercer held the tray against her.

"Is this the first time you've seen Reggie after the divorce?"

"Hmm?" Her eyes clouded with incomprehension. "Oh, yeah. It is." She lifted her hands and shrugged. "No big deal."

Tony frowned as he watched her take a step away and then another. Something had spooked her. It had started when he mentioned her ex-husband. But there was more to it. In fact, it had taken Mercer a moment when he mentioned the divorce.

"If you have a craving for more fruit, I'll send some over." She turned and headed for the house.

The possibility shot through him like fire, rippling through his gut. "Mercer."

His voice was low, but there must have been something in his tone because the word broke her stride. He pressed on.

"Are you still"—he hated to say it out loud—"married to Reggie?"

She froze and didn't look back.

He wanted to follow her. Tony needed to get the answer and shake off this bad feeling. But something about Mercer's body language indicated that he wasn't going to like what she had to say.

"Are you hoping for a reconciliation?" He didn't know why she would want that. Unless he'd been wrong about her all this time. That she wanted the high-society life and would sacrifice everything to get it.

She turned her head and hesitated. It was as if she wasn't sure what to do. Tony had never seen her like this. Her uncertainty was clear to him.

"Mercer?" He didn't know if he should reach out and hold her. Or if someone should be propping *him* up.

"I . . ." She moved her head so he couldn't see her. "I was never married to Reggie."

CHAPTER FOUR

His fingers wrapped around her arm before she took a step. "What do you mean you weren't married?"

He sounded bewildered. Mad. She wasn't sure how she wanted him to respond, but anger wasn't it. Mercer wished she had kept her mouth shut. Why did she think she could have walked away from Tony after revealing that?

And why did she feel even more vulnerable than before? It was because she was breaking the rules she had blindly followed for years. Nothing was going to protect her now. Should she backtrack? Tell him she was joking?

"Mercer?" His hold tightened.

It was time to retreat. "I have to get back to work." She couldn't look at him. Tony always made her feel as if he could see what was going on inside her head.

"You were never married?"

"Let's keep this between us, please?" She shouldn't have

said anything. She didn't know what this would do, if it would get back to Reggie. The guy probably had been holding a lot of dirt on her. He was the type to have that kind of insurance.

"Why is it a secret?" He moved to stand in front of her, and Mercer looked to the side. "Why pretend in the first place?"

"It's complicated." She wasn't sure if she could trust him. Why hadn't she thought of that a minute before? What had she hoped to achieve by telling him this?

"What's going on, Mercer?"

"I don't know. Please let go of me."

He showed no sign of releasing her. He blocked her escape. She felt surrounded. So it made no sense that she had the urge to press her head against his shoulder and have Tony wrap his arms around her.

"Is Reggie making you say you were never married?"

Mercer went rigid. "Don't say anything to him, okay?" She had just broken the number-one rule. And to an ex-cop!

"Why are you going along with it?" Tony hooked his finger under her chin firmly to direct her face to him. "Does he have something on you?"

Probably, but she wasn't going to speculate out loud on what that could be! Mercer did her best at keeping her expression blank. "Tony, you're out of the police force. You don't have to interrogate me."

"If he's blackmailing you, that's a crime."

Not like she was going to call Reggie on it if her crime was more severe. "I'll keep that in mind."

"You know that if you need anything, you can ask me."

His gentle tone slayed her. "I . . . can?"

"Sure you can."

Tears unexpectedly began to burn in the back of her eyes.

Huh. She thought she lost the ability to cry. She tried to bra-zen her way out. "What's the catch?"

"No catch."

"Gorgeous, there is always a catch." She jerked her chin away from his hand. She blinked rapidly, trying to hold back the tears when she saw Ellis by the kitchen door. "My boss is on the prowl. I have to go."

She didn't know if she should feel relief or disappointment when Tony reluctantly released his hold. Mercer felt his gaze on her as she walked toward the house. The guy had no idea what he was offering. One didn't volunteer to help a girl like her. It got you nothing but a headache and a rap sheet.

"Where have you been?" Ellis whispered fiercely as she walked across the patio.

"I was chased by a swarm of killer bees," Mercer lied, her voice dull, as she walked past him.

"So?"

Nice to see that he cared. "So I ran to the dock to jump in the lake."

Ellis caught up with her and walked by her side. "You're still dry."

Very observant. "Because the bees made a turn when they got one whiff of that Merriweather woman's perfume. That's what she gets for putting on too much."

"Ssh!" He frantically looked around. "Someone might hear you."

"It's not a secret. Everyone knows she pours it on."

"Mercer, do me a favor and keep your opinions to your-self."

"I'll try."

"Most of the guests are back in the house." Ellis motioned

at the kitchen door. "Get another tray and work the main floor."

"Yes!" She hissed the word out. That was the best news she had heard all night. She froze when she saw the strange look Ellis gave her. "What?"

"One more mess-up and you're out. Remember that I'm watching you."

Get in line, honey. His warning didn't bother her, because her luck was changing tonight.

She hadn't been married.

Tony stared at Mercer as she hurried away. He stood still, the warring emotions swirling inside him.

She. Hadn't. Been. Married.

Was she telling him the truth? He didn't like how long it took to consider that possibility. His gut instinct said she wasn't lying. If she was, why would she do it now, and not a year ago?

"Okay, Tony," the security guard said as he came back. "It was a few teenagers causing some noise."

Tony nodded his head, but he wasn't listening. Why did Mercer lie about the marriage back then? It's no scandal for couples to live together. No need to hide it. The secret didn't make sense.

"You okay?"

"Yeah." He headed for the house, mulling over the puzzle. Why would a multimillionaire who was born with a silver spoon in his mouth pretend to be married? Inheritance? Tax purposes? Or was it a mixup with the paperwork that Reggie had chosen not to correct?

Tony knew he could figure out the answer if Mercer

wasn't a part of the equation. She was his blind spot. His Achilles' heel.

And the woman hadn't been married.

Tony stopped and glared at the darkening sky. All this time he had lusted after Mercer but didn't act on it. He loved her from afar, but never touched her because he thought she was taken. He had wrestled with his conscience about coveting another man's wife when she hadn't been.

He stood to the side of the large windows and looked into the party, searching for Mercer. He easily found her as she walked slowly through the crowd. Her graceful moves were noticeably absent as she carried a tray of appetizers, but it didn't diminish her beauty. It was more than her looks that twisted him into knots. She had a presence that stopped him in his tracks.

Mercer paused and looked to the side of the room. There was something about the move that alerted Tony. He followed her line of vision and saw Nicole Rafferty, the youngest Graham sister.

Nicole wasn't doing anything to cause attention. The bold pink cocktail dress she wore had no back, but that wasn't enough to gain Mercer's interest. The only thing Nicole was doing was talking to her husband.

From the way Nicole and Alex Rafferty stood next to each other, their heads nearly touching, anyone could tell that they were newlyweds. They created a small, intimate circle for two in the midst of a crowd.

But what made Mercer interested? He looked back at Mercer and realized she wasn't looking at the youngest Graham sister anymore. She was mesmerized by the one wearing the pink diamond earrings.

She was going to make her move. Anticipation buzzed through his veins. He knew Mercer's methods. The more crowded, the better. All he had to do was stand there in the shadows and observe.

He watched her slowly make her way toward Lindsay. The tension climbed up his chest. A part of him wanted to get this over and done with, while another part wished Mercer would stop and head for a different direction.

Patience . . . Tony stayed perfectly still. Most of his job was about waiting. He was good at being patient.

Mercer was only five people away from Lindsay.

The tension clawed up his throat. His muscles shook with the need to move, do something.

Four people . . . three people . . .

His head throbbed with tension.

Two people . . .

Enough! He couldn't take it anymore. He had to stop Mercer before she made the same mistake that had cost her her freedom. But he'd waited too long. He didn't know if he could get to her in time.

Forget the party's security. To hell with the earrings. Tony was determined to protect Mercer from herself.

He opened one of the patio doors and entered the house. A group of men in tuxedos were in his way. Tony jostled around them but lost sight of Mercer.

Shouldering his way toward Lindsay, Tony gave terse apologies left and right as he forged a path. He spotted Mercer. She had passed Lindsay.

Failure crashed through Tony.

He reluctantly glanced at Lindsay, torn at the prospect of seeing Mercer's grandest achievement.

The pink ice twinkled at him.

Lindsay still wore the diamonds. Both of them. The hostess of the party continued to chat to a guest as if nothing had happened.

Tony breathed out a shaky sigh of relief. He had been wrong. Mercer didn't take the earrings.

Yet.

But she'll try before the night is over. He'd stake his agency on it.

And it was up to him to stop her before she made the attempt. How would he keep her away? He looked around the party, wishing inspiration would strike.

His gaze rested on the entryway, and a smile crept along his mouth as the idea formed. . . .

Those were the real diamonds. The knowledge tickled Mercer as she walked by Lindsay. She didn't need to take a jeweler's glass and study it. Ten carats total were big enough to tell the earrings were the real deal.

Nicole was finally here, too. Mercer was ready to sag with relief. The transfer of the diamonds would happen tonight, and she would be ready to intercept.

It might not be quite "The Mercer" move she wanted. In fact, the lift would be relatively tame—almost too easy. She could get too confident and flub it up. Or someone would flub it for her.

The fine hair on the back of her neck stirred. Was he watching her? Mercer glanced around the room but couldn't find Reggie. Was he already making his move? The competitive spirit kicked her hard.

She scanned the room again, slowly this time, as her

heartbeat pounded in her ears. Reginald Whitley-Cooke wasn't the life of the party, but neither did he blend into the woodwork. Everyone would remember he was at the party, although they wouldn't quite recall what he said or did. Parties were always the perfect alibi for Reggie.

She stopped when she finally spotted him. He was across the room, with London artfully draped at his side. A drink was in his hand, and a few guests were chuckling over something that the beautiful woman said.

But Reggie was looking straight at her. No smile. No aura of elegance. As if he forgot to put on his Cary Grant persona. And then it suddenly appeared. The wry gleam in his eye. The suave sophistication cloaking him.

He nodded and raised his glass before taking a sip. The mock salute grated on her nerves. It was like he had a secret that he was keeping from her.

No. It was all part of the game to him. Messing with her mind. *Don't let it fluster you.*

Mercer would have loved to fling her silver serving tray like a Frisbee and watch it clip his head. Knowing her luck, Reggie would catch it and lob it back at her, only showing more panache while doing it.

She rolled her eyes at the thought and turned away, offering appetizers to more guests. It was a good thing Tony didn't know *exactly* what went through her mind. He wouldn't get near her if he did.

He probably thought she was a sweet girl underneath it all. There was nothing sweet about her, but Tony was too much of a knight in shining armor to get that. He also didn't seem to realize knights were obsolete these days.

That's probably why she had no idea how to deal with

Tony. Guys like that were exotic creatures to her. Fascinating, hot, and sexy, but hard to figure out.

Mercer slowly worked the room until the last appetizer disappeared from her tray. She stepped into the grand entrance, which was barely occupied. A group of women were making their way up the staircase, and Tony was standing by underneath the steps. He opened the closet door that was seamlessly hidden in the woodwork and peered inside.

Okay, she couldn't avoid him. That was too obvious. He'd know she was uncomfortable about what they had discussed and it would give the topic far more importance.

So she'd breeze right by him, say something meaningless, and keep going. She could do that, Mercer decided, and started a brisk pace.

"You're checking the coat closet?" Mercer asked him as she walked by. "Do you really think a thief would hide in there?"

"Why not?" He reached out and wrapped his arm around her waist before pulling her against him.

Mercer's voice squeaked from her throat as her muscles went rigid. Wow, the guy was all muscle. Warm, sculpted muscle. "What are you doing?"

"What does it look like?" he asked, pulling her into the closet with him and shutting the door.

CHAPTER FIVE

"COME ON, TONY," SHE WHISPERED FIERCELY. "Stop playing around."

"I'm not." The closet was dark except for a strip of light at the bottom of the door. He couldn't see a thing.

It was cramped, too. His back pressed against the door and he stood toe to toe with Mercer. As far as he could tell, she was being swallowed up by the coats.

"If this is about Reggie"—her voice sounded muffled— "then you are wasting your time. That is not up for discussion. Not now. Not ever."

"It's not about him. I'm making sure you don't steal the diamond earrings. Ow! What was that?" he asked as he rubbed his shoulder. It must be the serving tray she had been carrying.

"So you're locking me in a closet? How lame. All I need to do is scream my head off."

"Do you really want to draw attention to the fact that you are in a closet with a guy?" He reached out but got a handful of a coat. Tony pushed it down the clothes rod, the screech of metal against metal extra-loud in his ears. "How is that boss of yours going to feel about that?"

Her gasp echoed around him. "You aren't saying anything to Ellis!"

"Then be good and keep your mouth shut." His fingertips brushed against flat metal. That had to be the serving tray. He snatched it out of her grasp.

"Move." She flattened her hands against his chest and pushed. "Get out of my way."

"Nope." He ditched the tray on the floor.

"I get claustrophobic," she announced.

"No, you don't." But he was feeling the effects of her standing close. Her scent curled around him like smoke.

"Yes, I do."

He reached up and grabbed the clothes rod. Anything to keep his hands off Mercer. "I remember the night of the Tolliver heist when you sat in—"

"All right, all right," she interrupted. "I lied. I don't get claustrophobic."

"Knew it."

"I'm afraid of the dark."

Tony scoffed at the statement. "That didn't stop you in the Shaw case."

"Did I say dark? I meant that I'm highly allergic to wool." She batted at the coat at her left, then at her right. "And fur. And—ooh . . . is that mink?"

Tony rolled his eyes. "Mercer."

"All right! I'm not allergic. What are you? A walking encyclopedia on me? Uh, not that I am admitting to any participation in those cases you mentioned."

"Of course not."

She exhaled sharply. The puff of breath played against his collar. That meant her lips were right—no, he wasn't going to think about it. Tony held tighter onto the metal rod. He tried to ignore how close she stood, and how her breast grazed his chest, and her leg bumping against his. . . .

"So now what?" she asked. "I just stand here?"

"Yeah, pretty much." He froze when her hair brushed under his chin. The softness teased his senses. It was going to be a long night.

"I don't think that's necessary."

"Think again." He'd do whatever it took to keep her out of trouble.

"No, really, Tony. This time-out has allowed me to see the error of my ways."

He wondered if she was saying that with a straight face. "Sure it has."

"I'll be on my best behavior."

Tony imagined her crossing her heart with one hand and crossing her fingers behind her back with the other. "Is that supposed to reassure me?"

"You can let go of me now," she said sweetly against his ear.

His fingers squeezed the metal rod. He liked how she said that. A breathy mixture of innocence and naughtiness. But it wasn't going to change his mind. "No way."

Tony felt her stiffen before she leaned back against the wall. Her frustration was almost tangible. "Then how about if you leave?" she asked.

"That's not part of the plan."

Tension vibrated from her. "You're staying here with me all night?"

"Looks that way." And he'd keep his hands on the closet rod all night if it was the only way to keep them from roaming all over her body.

"I have a job to do," Mercer reminded him.

"I know."

"My catering job," she clarified. "If I'm stuck in a closet, Ellis will find out and he'll fire me."

"I'll help you find another job," he promised.

"There you go again. Offering help without knowing what you're getting yourself into. You have no idea how hard it was to find this one."

The weary thread in her voice got to him. He never wanted to see her defeated. "Then you can work for me."

"Ha!" Her laugh bounced against the walls. "Oh, you were serious?"

"Yeah." Strangely enough, he was. He hadn't thought about it before, but Tony was sure he could use someone with Mercer's talents.

"I can't work with you!"

Okay, maybe that was a bad idea, but he still kind of liked the possibilities. "I'll think of something."

"Think about it somewhere else. I'm still working for El-lis." She gave his chest another push.

"You're not leaving."

Her silence surprised him. She didn't utter a word for several beats before she finally said, "Fine."

"Fine?" His instincts went on full alert. He didn't like that answer. Or the tone. She wasn't backing down; she was changing tactics.

"Yeah, fine." Her vest rubbed against the wall as she found a comfortable spot. "We'll stay here. I could use a break."

As the silence stretched, he listened intently for any telltale moves. Was she going to ambush him? His suspicions came in waves, one rolling over the other, growing bigger, stronger, before crashing against his head. What was she going to try next?

"It's getting hot in here. Don't you think so?"

His skin felt flushed, and he was very aware of the drop of sweat rolling down the length of his spine, but it had nothing to do with the temperature. "No."

"Really? I think it is."

He heard something ripping. Or was it a rip? Tony squinted in the dark, unable to place the sound. "What are you do-ing?"

"I'm getting naked."

He reared his head back at those three little words. "No, you're not." His voice was hoarse.

Something soft and heavy hit the ground. "Yes, I am."

"I don't believe you." But his body did. His cock stirred. His skin tightened.

"Open the door and see for yourself."

Tempting. Very, very tempting. "I'm not falling for that."

"Suit yourself," Mercer said.

Something snapped. Or unsnapped? His fingers dug into the metal bar as he heard it again . . . and again.

Her shirt? Did her shirt have buttons or snaps?

Another snap.

She wasn't removing her shirt. In front of him. During a party. Was she? He wanted to fling open the door. The need ached inside him. He was desperate to see the curves that he dreamt about.

Snap.

He heard the shirt gliding off her shoulders, down her arms, before falling onto the floor.

Tony clenched his jaw when he heard the metallic sound of a zipper. The muscle in his cheek bunched as Mercer pulled the zipper down with agonizing slowness.

It had to be her pants. He heard the fabric brushing against her skin. In his mind he could see her peeling off the black pants, revealing long, bare legs.

"Stop it, Mercer," he said through gritted teeth.

"Stop what?"

He heard her moving. He wanted to follow. Guide her hands. Help her with the rest. "Stop teasing me," he nearly begged.

"Aw, you don't really mean that."

He flinched when something silky landed against his cheek before slipping onto his shoulder. Tony clung onto the metal bar, but it wouldn't take much more to let go.

The silk slithered off him. He didn't remember her wearing anything silky. Unless . . . Her panties. Tony swallowed back a groan as his restraint slipped precariously. "Mercer, you don't want to tease me."

"It's my favorite hobby."

Did she think he had superhuman patience? That he wouldn't take her against the wall? Tony winced, his cock hardening, as he imagined doing just that. "I might take you up on your offer."

"I live in hope."

He didn't need to see her saucy smile. He could hear it in her voice. The woman loved to live dangerously.

Something fell onto the floor. He wouldn't let himself imagine what it could be. He needed this torment to end.

"Oops." She collided against his chest. He flinched back as

if he were burned on contact. "Sorry," she whispered. "My arms got tangled in my bra."

He let go and grabbed Mercer's wrists. He held them high against the wall behind her. Tony ducked under the clothing rod and then rose to his full height. He accepted the bite of metal against his shoulders if it meant he could press his body against Mercer's.

His hands shook. The darkness swirled in front of his eyes. And then it hit him. "You're still dressed."

"Don't let that stop you." Mercer tilted her head and brushed her mouth against his.

His mouth covered hers. It wasn't the hard, quick claiming she expected. Instead his mouth pressed against her lips. She felt the shudder sweep his body. Mercer wasn't sure if it was a reaction based on surrender or victory.

Tony rubbed his lips against hers. She parted her mouth as he captured her bottom lip between his teeth. She gasped as the sting set off a chain reaction from her nipples to the tightening coil low in her belly.

Mercer arched against him as their kisses grew fierce. Untamed. She wanted Tony to cup her breasts. Her sex. Kiss her until she came, and came hard.

She tried to pull out of his grasp, but he wouldn't release her wrists. Instead he nudged her legs apart with his knee. Tony settled against the cradle of her hip, and she rocked her pelvis against him.

Her knees almost crumpled when she felt his hard arousal. She wanted to touch him, taste him.

Mercer pulled at his hands again. This time he let go. Before she could put her arms down, Tony cupped the back of her knees. She reached out for him, grabbing blindly until she clawed his jacket, as he hooked her legs over his hip. She leaned back, snugly fitting her legs around him until his cock pressed against her hot core.

Their clothes were a frustrating barrier. She thought Tony would rip them away, shred them. Instead he reached for her face, his fingers bumping against her cheeks.

The only thing she could hear was their uneven, harsh breaths and her pounding heart as he tipped her chin up. He kissed her hard, driving his tongue deep into her mouth. She groaned with pleasure, gripping the back of his head, tangling her fingers in his hair, and bringing him closer.

A flash of light swept across Mercer's closed eyes. Cool air rushed over her as the party chatter swelled to an unexpected crescendo.

"Oh! Sorry!"

The interruption was like a slap in the face. Mercer dragged her swollen mouth away from his. Her legs slipped off of Tony as they were plunged back into the darkness.

"Someone found our hiding place," Tony said against her ear.

"I—I have . . ." Mercer shied her face away from the door, praying that no one else would check what was going on in the closet. She had to leave before someone else found her, but she didn't know who would be standing outside the door.

"I'll go first," Tony offered as he straightened out her vest.

"No, that's okay." She moved to the side, her feet tangled up in the coats and scarves she had used to fool Tony.

"Mercer." Tony blocked her way. She froze until he placed a gentle kiss on her brow. "We'll continue this later. Understood?"

"Yes." Her breasts felt tight and heavy. Her legs shook and she felt light-headed. He didn't seem to realize that she would hunt him down to finish this tonight.

Tony seemed satisfied with that answer as he stepped out of her way. Mercer ran her hands through her hair before reaching for the doorknob. She took a deep breath and opened the door.

She sidled out of the doorway, praying she would be undetected. A few people noticed her furtive moves and cast questioning glances, but no one called her to everyone's attention.

Mercer looked around. No Ellis in the room, thank goodness. Now she needed to pinpoint Lindsay's and Nicole's locations.

She edged toward the formal living room where she'd last seen them. Mercer didn't see either of the women. She checked the other rooms on the floor to no avail. Mercer stepped outside and hastily hid behind a tree when she saw Tony stride down to the dock, but she didn't see any of the Graham sisters.

Mercer snuck back in the house and felt a flash of relief when she saw Nicole's pink dress in the entryway. Mercer made her way through the crowd.

Nicole started climbing the stairs to the next floor. Lindsay was right behind her.

They're going to make the exchange now? Why? She wasn't ready!

"Miss! Oh, miss!"

Was someone trying to get her attention? If so, they were in for a long wait. Mercer ignored the insistent call until someone tugged her shirt. She reluctantly turned around and saw London standing in front of her.

"I'd like a Lemon Drop, please."

"I'm sure you would." *Get your own drink, hon. I'm busy!* Mercer took another step to the entrance, but London tugged on her shirt again.

"Now." Urgency crept into London's voice.

Mercer understood exactly what was going on. London had been given a job to stall the competition. "I'm on a break," she lied, "and I don't have my tray. But one of my coworkers would be happy to assist you."

"You don't want to do that. Not while Reggie and your boss are looking at us, discussing the possibility of catering my wedding." London glanced to her right.

Mercer followed the woman's gaze and saw Reggie was indeed talking to her boss. Or rather, Ellis was doing his sales spiel while Reggie watched Mercer.

Clever. She had to give Reggie full marks on that maneuver. Although she wasn't sure how that got him closer to the earrings.

Mercer smiled tightly. "One Lemon Drop coming right up." She turned on her heel and walked to the bar that was located a few feet away.

She placed the order, drumming her fingers against the counter. Okay, this was not a setback. It wasn't even a problem. If Lindsay came down without the earrings, she would follow Nicole. No big deal.

Once the bartender finished making the drink, Mercer grabbed the glass and marched back to London, only to find that she had disappeared.

Of course. Mercer set her jaw. Now she had to hunt London down. She would probably be in a spot that was the farthest away from the staircase and the earrings. Hmm . . . that would be outside.

Mercer headed for the patio and spotted the gold and pink dress in a group of three or four people. Mercer hurried toward the huddle of guests, doing her best not to slosh the drink before she delivered it. If London was surprised she was found so quickly, she didn't show it.

"Thank you, Mercer," London said before taking a healthy sip of the mixed drink.

"You're welcome." Mercer gave a short nod and noticed Reggie was at London's side again. That might explain London's dire need for sustenance.

"Mercer?"

Uh-oh. She didn't recognize the voice, but the tone warned her it wasn't going to be pleasant.

"Not *the* Mercer."

That was never a good sign.

"You've met before, haven't you?" Reggie said at his most affable. "Mercer, darling, don't you remember Ian and Sabrina West?"

Mercer swallowed hard and knew she had paled. It took every ounce of courage to turn and face the Wests. She was so angry at herself. She should have noticed the olive-green Chloé dress, even in the shadows.

"Of course I do, Reggie," Mercer said with a polite smile. "The last time I saw them, they had me arrested and I was put away for a year."

Sabrina continued to stare at her in disbelief. Mercer shifted from one foot to the other as Ian's cold stare penetrated her nerves. Reggie seemed to be waiting for the fireworks to go off.

"Well . . ." Mercer said as the awkward pause got to her. "Enough about me. What have you guys been up to?"

CHAPTER SIX

I⊤ WAS ALMOST MIDNIGHT WHEN SHE bumped into Tony again in the entrance hall. Mercer was bone-tired, her feet ached, and her nerves were frayed, but one look at Tony Jackson made her forget about that. Suddenly she had a bounce in her step and it felt like the angels were smiling upon her.

She wondered if she had that effect on him. Ha. Unlikely.

"The party is winding down," Tony said as he scanned the room. "Just a few stragglers left."

"About time," Mercer said in a grumble as she picked up discarded napkins and piled them on her tray. "This night was the absolute worst."

"It wasn't *all* bad."

She felt Tony's gaze on her mouth. Her face grew warm as her lips tingled. "You think? I'd say it took a disastrous turn right about the time I was reintroduced to Ian and Sabrina."

He stood to attention. "What did they do?"

His gruff voice startled her. She paused, uncertain of what she did wrong. Oh, wait. He was feeling protective toward *her*. She kind of liked that. A lot. The knowledge sent something warm and light fizzing inside her.

"Besides watching me like a hawk?" she asked. "Nothing. They didn't have to."

"Then what's the problem?"

"Every other guest found out who I was and kept their distance." She wasn't sure who started blabbing, but she placed her bets on Reggie.

And boy did the tension escalate anytime she was in the room with Lindsay, who still wore the earrings. It had turned out that the Graham sisters hadn't transferred the pink ice while she was getting the Lemon Drop.

Not much good that did her. Every time she entered the room, Lindsay seemed to immediately exit, along with anyone else wearing serious jewelry. Mercer wanted to believe she was being paranoid, but even her coworkers noticed the long looks and heard the whispers.

"Do you know how hard it is to serve people who try to keep at least three feet away from you?" she asked Tony.

"I can imagine," he said, leaning against the wall and crossing one ankle over the other. "But you didn't let it get to you."

"Oh?" She rested her hip against the side table. "Were you watching me, too?"

His smile was slow and seductive. "I can't help it."

"Yeah, yeah, yeah." She busied herself by collecting a few empty wineglasses. "Part of your job."

"No, that's not it."

She gave a quick glance at him, but couldn't look away. Urgent need was flaring in his eyes, but it was the promise of something more that pulled at her.

"Do you need a ride home?" he asked.

Her knees wobbled. She wanted to take Tony home. Take him to her bed. But she had to finish something first. Only then could she have a future with him.

"Uh," she stammered. What's the question? "There's a seat for me on one of the catering vans."

He shrugged. "So?"

"You don't need to hang around for me." It would actually be better if he left the premises. If anything went wrong, she didn't want him to witness it.

"I'm here until the last guest and worker"—he emphasized—"leave."

Yeah. She had been afraid of that. Tony might want her, but he wasn't blinded by lust. He knew she was going to try something.

"Tony." She nervously set the tray on the side table. "I know you don't trust me, and you have every reason." Hmm, assuring him of that might not work in her favor.

"What's going on, Mercer?"

"I'm asking you to . . ." No, he wouldn't believe her about Reggie. The only blemish on Reggie's stellar reputation was his association with her. And he used it in his favor! Everyone saw him as a poor older man who had been bedazzled by a wicked, amoral woman. Mercer started over. "Just keep an open mind. Tonight."

"Why tonight?"

She pressed her palms over her heart. "I have no intention of grabbing those earrings and walking out of the house."

"So you've said." He crossed his arms. "And keep saying. But why are you saying this to me?"

"I'm not asking for you to turn a blind eye. I'm not asking for help." She dropped her hands, curling her fingers into her palms, digging her nails into her skin. What was she asking? She couldn't ask for his trust: She hadn't earned it, she didn't deserve it.

Mercer's shoulders sagged as the truth slapped against her. She didn't deserve someone like Tony. She never would. Retiring from a criminal life wasn't going to change that. But now the wheels were in motion and she was stuck following through with her plans. The only thing she could hope for was leaving this house without a police escort.

"Mercer?" There was a hint of impatience in his voice.

She closed her eyes as if she was making a wish. "Whatever happens tonight, don't believe everything that is said about me, okay?" It was all she could hope for now.

Tony was silent for a moment. "Does this 'whatever happens' have the power to put you back in jail?"

Heh . . . he's good, Mercer reluctantly admitted as she wearily opened her eyes. "Yeah, it might come to that." She flashed a jaded smile. "Will you visit me this time around?"

He reached out and pulled her closer. He leaned down and brushed his mouth against her ear. "Mercer, if it comes to that, I'll help break you out."

Her breath locked in her throat as her heart beat wildly against her ribs. No, he didn't mean that. Not really. "You shouldn't tease me," she whispered.

"Who's teasing?" he asked softly.

His promise had shaken her, tilted her world. She tried to hide her reaction the only way she knew how. "Ah, gorgeous, what a shame." She patted his face and smiled. "I've been a bad influence on my knight in shining armor."

He didn't smile back. "I'm no knight."

"Good to know, because I'm no—"

"Mercer"—one of the other waitresses motioned for her as she passed through the entry hall—"act busy. Ellis is in one of his moods."

Mercer pressed her lips together and took a step back. "I'd better clean this up." Her mind clung to what Tony had said, but her hands moved at a different speed. She systematically collected the glasses and napkins from every imaginable flat surface within reach. The steps. The floor. "Were these people raised in a barn?"

When Tony didn't respond, Mercer looked back over her shoulder. He still watched her, but with a mix of knowing and . . . resignation? Was he giving up on her?

Her heart twisted at the possibility. She didn't want to give up her chance with Tony over a pair of diamonds. But if she didn't try for it, Reggie would frame her for the theft.

She hoped one day Tony would understand, would know that she didn't choose the pink ice over him. She hoped that he would eventually not think so poorly of her.

"Mercer!"

She jumped at the catering manager's harsh voice. "Yes?" she asked sweetly. She could be sickeningly obedient now. The night was almost over.

Ellis stood in the center of the hall and fluttered his hands around. "I want everything cleaned up and ready to go in twenty minutes."

Never going to happen. "Yes, sir," she said as he turned his back on her.

He stopped and whirled around. "Excuse me?"

"I'll get right on it." She crouched down to grab a few more napkins stuffed between the railings on the bottom steps.

Ellis stared at her as if she had sprouted another arm. He drew back his head. "Are you feeling okay?"

"Never better." She snuck a look at the main door. Lindsay and Dominic were organizing a ride for one of the tipsy guests. From this angle, she couldn't tell if Lindsay was still wearing the earrings.

Mercer's boss took another step toward her and studied her face. He gave a suspicious sniff. "Have you been drinking from the wineglasses?"

She looked at the stemware smeared with fingerprints and lipstick. Mercer wrinkled her nose with distaste. "I wouldn't dream of it, sir."

"Hmm." Ellis didn't sound convinced, but after a moment's pause, he turned and left.

She watched Dominic escort the inebriated guest outside. Sabrina and Ian looked as if they were the next to leave. Relief rippled through Mercer's limbs. She would be safe once those guys left.

Sabrina gave Lindsay a hug good-bye, and Mercer was so grateful that the pregnant Graham sister wasn't wearing the earrings tonight. She was already dealing with enough problems. The last thing she wanted to do was tangle with an expectant mother.

She paused from her cleaning when she saw Nicole standing between Sabrina and Lindsay. Nicole smiled at her husband, Alex. Alex was—where was he going?

Coat closet. Good. He'll be occupied. Her gaze clashed with Tony, who hadn't moved from his position. She looked away quickly and stood up.

Tony was going to be a problem. *Focus . . .* Mercer watched Lindsay from under her lashes. *Do it fast and clean, and he won't see a thing.*

Lindsay turned to say something to her youngest sister. Anticipation kicked Mercer in the small of her back.

Lindsay wasn't wearing the earrings.

The transfer had already been made. Mercer immediately focused on Nicole's evening bag. Black satin. Small. Lulu Guinness design.

Mercer smiled. She'd hit that type of purse before. She could do it again.

Now where was Reggie? She looked on the stairs. Not there. Was he out in front? Possibly, but he would have to come up with a convincing reason for hanging around on the driveway.

She saw a flash of pink and gold from the corner of her eye. Mercer turned to see Reggie and London stroll into the hall from the main formal room.

Reggie looked relaxed and partied out. London appeared tense under the practiced smile as they headed straight for the Graham sisters.

The game was on.

Now she had to get there first.

Mercer gripped the laden-down serving tray, took a deep breath, and hurried over to the sisters. "Excuse me, Mrs. Stark," she said as she walked by Lindsay. Her foot caught on the fringe of the faded Persian rug. "Would you—whoa!"

★　★　★

Tony saw it all, but he was hard-pressed to explain what happened.

One moment Mercer was picking up after the party, the next she tripped and fell on her face, taking two of the Graham sisters with her.

It had been a spectacular fall.

Napkins, glasses and a tray flew in the air. Arms windmilling, screams and cries, people rushing to help. But it was too late. Mercer, Nicole and Lindsay went down like dominos.

Tony and Alex rushed over as Ian and London helped Lindsay up. Reggie assisted Nicole to her feet.

"I'm sorry. I am so sorry." Mercer's voice trembled with mortification. She gingerly got up on her knees.

Dominic Stark appeared at the doorway. "What happened?" He saw Lindsay's disheveled appearance and wrapped his arm around her shoulders.

Mercer jerked in surprise when she felt Tony's hand on her back. "I'm okay," she told him in a low voice, "but I need to pick this up."

"You're sure?"

"Yeah." She looked at the stained rug. "Uh-oh," she said under her breath, and hastily blotted a large spot with a tiny napkin. "Is everyone okay?"

He heard Ellis's footsteps before the man rushed in. The catering manager clapped his hands on his cheeks as his gasp rang throughout the room.

Mercer cringed and hunched her shoulders. Tony got the sense that she was tempted to hide under the ruined rug. He didn't blame her.

"Mercer!" Ellis sounded beyond scandalized.

She quickly collected the balled-up napkins and stemware that littered the floor. "Yes, sir?"

Tony shook his head. Nothing—not even prostrating herself in front of Ellis—was going to get her out of this one. He wanted to comfort her. Needed to stand between Mercer and Ellis, but something stopped him. Some sixth sense that getting involved could cause Mercer more harm.

"This is it! You're fired!"

"Now wait a minute," Nicole said. "It was an accident."

"No, no, no!" Ellis waved his hands around. "I warned her: One more mistake and she was O-U-T, out!"

Ellis was getting on Tony's nerves.

Lindsay raised her hands in an effort to gain silence. "Everyone, let's calm down."

"I need to get some club soda and salt before this stain sets," Mercer said as she got up on her feet.

"You're not touching that rug again!" Ellis announced.

Tony raked his fingers through his hair when he really wanted to gag Ellis with that scarf.

"Don't worry. It'll be good as new." She bumped against London. "I heard that club soda mixed with salt will take any wine stain out," she said confidentially, as if the trophy wife needed household tips for future reference.

"Enough!" Ellis roughly grabbed Mercer's arm. "It's time for you to leave."

Okay, the guy had crossed the line. Tony reached out and grabbed the back of Ellis's jacket and gave it a good twist. "Let go of the lady," he said very softly.

"Lady? Aiii, yes-s-s." Ellis dropped Mercer's arm. "Of course."

Tony reluctantly let go of the catering manager's jacket.

"I'm going, I'm going," Mercer announced, her face bright red. She headed for the front door, cautiously walking past Ian and Sabrina. "I'll go get my purse out of the van and leave."

Tony watched Mercer walk to the door, hating every moment of her discomfort. He looked away and saw Nicole stiffen as if realizing something.

"If I have my way, you'll never work in this town again!" Ellis said.

"Fine by me," Mercer said without breaking her stride.

"Wait a second." Nicole grabbed for her purse. "Nobody move."

"What's wrong?" Alex asked his wife.

Nicole opened her purse and rifled through the small bag. "They're gone."

A sickening dread flooded through Tony as he walked toward Nicole on autopilot.

"What's gone?" he asked, noticing that Ian West blocked Mercer at the threshold.

"My pink diamond earrings," Nicole said as she shook out her purse, her compact and lipstick clattering onto the floor. "They're missing."

CHAPTER SEVEN

"Mercer," Tony said. "Put your hands up and keep them where I can see them."

To his surprise, Mercer did what he ordered without saying a word. Tony pressed the electronic device in his ear. "There's been a possible theft. Call the police and get two guards at the front door now."

"Got it," his communications guy replied cheerfully.

Tony couldn't believe it. He almost fell for Mercer's trick. He frowned, barely noticing Ellis taking one look at his fierce expression before backing away. Heh. What was he thinking? He had fallen for everything Mercer said.

Keep an open mind, she had requested. *I have no intention of grabbing the diamonds and walking out of the house.*

And what did she do? She . . .

Tony's head spun and the world crystallized in front of

him, Mercer had been very specific about what she wouldn't do. Too specific.

He looked at Mercer. Her hands were up, but she was doing her best not to look at anyone or anything. She kept her gaze on the floor and her mouth shut. No declarations of innocence. No sudden moves or breaks for escape.

It took a very confident thief to do that. Or one who didn't have the stolen goods on her.

Two of his security guards came in. "Anderson, frisk the woman in the red vest," Tony said, motioning to Mercer. "See if she has the diamond earrings on her."

Mercer showed no emotions as Anderson skimmed his hands over her body. No muscle twitched. Tony was almost positive now that she didn't have the diamonds. Which meant someone else in this room did.

Tony turned his attention to the group. "Everyone, please empty out your pockets and handbags."

"Why?" Ellis asked, affronted. "I did nothing wrong."

"Even us?" Lindsay asked.

"Even you."

"I can't believe you put those earrings in your purse," Sabrina whispered to Nicole as she opened her bag. "What were you thinking?"

"Hey!" Nicole didn't see the need to keep her voice down. "I needed them for my trip tomorrow."

"No one *needs* earrings," Sabrina said with a trace of exasperation.

"Right," Nicole responded. "Look who's talking."

Tony ignored the bickering and approached London, who

hadn't followed his directions. "Ma'am, please open your purse for me."

London gave a start, as if she suddenly realized someone was speaking to her. "Yes, of course." She fumbled with her purse.

Reggie tried to step in between Tony and London. "Why are you questioning my fiancée? You have the culprit right there." He pointed to Mercer.

Tony's mouth twisted. *Nice way to publicly refer to your ex-wife.* "I'm searching everyone."

"She's clean," Anderson announced as he backed away from Mercer.

"Impossible," Ian said. "They have to be on her."

"Frisk her again," Tony told the security guard. He watched Mercer's reaction. She didn't say anything. Nothing sarcastic or suggestive. Nothing at all. She definitely didn't have the earrings on her.

But that didn't make her innocent.

Tony watched London unlatch her purse. He bet the diamonds weren't in there, either. The design of the purse made it too difficult to slip in earrings.

"Becker," Tony told the other security guard, "have Mr. Whitley-Cooke empty his pockets in front of you."

"This is ridiculous," Reggie said as he dipped his hands in his jacket pocket. He paused. "Ludicrous, even. I won't participate in this farce anymore. Come along, London. Let's not linger."

Tony blocked Reggie. "Empty your pockets or Mr. Becker here will do it for you."

Reggie looked him directly in the eye. His gaze didn't waver. "Don't you know who I am?"

"A very uncooperative man," Tony answered, taking a step away. "Becker, frisk him."

The security guard patted down Reggie's jacket and stopped at the outer left pocket. "What do we have here?" Becker asked as he pulled out a white jeweler's box.

"What is that?" Reggie asked.

"Open it," Tony ordered. He didn't feel relief. He didn't feel anything. He was on autopilot because he knew Mercer had something to do with all of this.

Becker lifted the lid. The pink diamond earrings twinkled under the chandelier lights.

"I don't know how those got there." A twang crept into Reggie's smooth voice.

"How could you?" Lindsay said as she walked up to Reggie and London, with Dominic at her back. "Why would you steal from your neighbors?"

"I didn't." He pointed at Mercer. "She must have put them in my pocket."

"How could she?" Ian asked, stepping away from the door and heading for Reggie. "She went nowhere near you."

"In fact," Nicole said, "you were the one who helped me up. You had plenty of opportunity to take the box out of my bag."

Tony cast a questioning look at Mercer. She didn't get into the finger-pointing or accusations. She didn't say a word, but kept her gaze downcast.

"Sir"—Tony motioned for Reggie to go into the living room—"let's sit down while we wait for the police."

"I'm taking Sabrina home," Ian said over Reggie's objections. He held his wife's hand and headed for the door. "If the police need our statement, they can contact us tomorrow."

"Aw, but Ian . . ." Sabrina reluctantly followed him.

"I'm staying," Nicole said as she scooped her items back into her bag.

"We have an early flight tomorrow," Alex reminded his wife.

"We'll make it," Nicole said with breezy certainty as she closed her purse with a snap.

"What about me?" Ellis said, flipping his scarf over his shoulder. "I have a schedule to keep."

"You can leave." Tony turned and saw that London had not moved. She looked lost, uncertain. "Ma'am, it might be awhile."

"I'll wait here." She watched Reggie reluctantly enter the living room. "No . . . I think I need—I should leave. I'll call a taxi."

"Of course. Mercer?" He glanced at the entryway. She wasn't there. Tony walked to the open door and peered out into the darkness.

She had disappeared.

Mercer stirred when she heard a car. She blinked her eyes open, shielding her eyes from the early morning sun. She saw Tony walk up the path to the office building and stop.

She had been right on her hunch. She knew once Tony left the Starks' house, he would start hunting her down. His office would have the technology to get it started, and he wasn't going to waste a minute.

"What are you doing here?" he asked sharply.

"And good morning to you, too," Mercer greeted him with a sunny smile.

Tony didn't smile back. "You didn't remember to say good night to me before you left the Starks'."

So, he's going to be nitpicky about it. "You were busy," she said as she got to her feet.

He headed for his office door, not looking very happy to see her. "You didn't answer my question. What are you doing here?"

"I have a couple of reasons." She motioned at the door with a tilt of her head. "Can we discuss them inside?"

"I'm surprised you didn't break into my office," he said when he shoved the key into the lock.

"Not part of my repertoire," she replied, rubbing her arms, which were chilled from the rainy, cool morning.

Tony gave a sidelong look at her as he opened the door. "How long have you been waiting here?"

"I've been walking most of the night." She hurried inside before he could shut the door in her face. "You would have to have your offices on the other side of town."

"Of course. Have you seen the real estate prices by the lake?" He flicked on the lights.

Mercer whistled as she saw the modern decor. "Nice." The guy was doing well for himself, but the look of the office didn't quite fit him. The colors were muted, simplistic.

Tony shut the door behind him and leaned against it, studying her with an intensity that made her nervous.

"How did you know I worked here?" he finally asked.

"I memorized the address on your I.D." She wandered around the reception area. She wasn't too sure about the picture hanging over the couch. A little too boring. Too safe. Too corporate.

"You knew you were going to need it even then?"

"Hmm?" She turned and faced him. "What are you talking about?"

"I know you took the earrings."

She didn't say anything. She couldn't tell from his expression or tone what Tony planned to do about it. Did he expect a confession? Was he going to take her to the authorities?

"There are a couple of things I need to know," he continued. "Like, did you really trip? Or was your clumsiness an act?"

Mercer chuckled. "I was really bad at that job, but I used my . . . lack of grace this time to work in my favor. What else?"

"Are you still working with Reggie? That's why you pretended to be married, isn't it?"

"Oh, please." She made a face. "I would rather go back to jail than work with him again."

"Let's hope it doesn't come to that," he said wryly as he followed her through the suite of rooms. "Why did you plant the earrings on him?"

"I was nowhere near Reggie." And it was true. She didn't touch the man, which was difficult to do when you're in a human pile of pick-up-sticks.

"Mercer, don't you realize that the charges on Reggie aren't going to stick?" Tony tossed his hands in the air. "So *what* if he had the earrings in his pocket? That doesn't mean he's going to take the rap."

"I never said it would stick." She opened up a door and saw it was part kitchenette, part copy room. All beige. "But people won't be too sure of his innocence the next time some jewels are missing."

"And London?"

Mercer shrugged and closed the door. "I don't know much about her."

"She's no pickpocket, I can tell you that." He was silent as she opened the next door down the corridor. "You gave the earrings to London, didn't you?"

"Why would I do that?"

"Because you knew she would plant them on Reggie."

Mercer closed the door and leaned against it. "You're stretching it, gorgeous. Why would I trust a stranger with a pair of diamonds?"

Tony crossed his arms. "Because you never intended to keep them."

She gave a shrug. "That doesn't mean I would purposely incriminate an innocent young thing."

"You knew she would pass them on to Reggie."

Yep, Tony was good. "How?"

"She had nowhere to hide them on her in that skintight dress."

"Oh, you noticed." She withstood the flash of envy and wished she wasn't still wearing her ugly catering uniform.

"Her job was clinging onto Reggie's arm, and it wouldn't seem odd that she was close enough to slip the earrings in his pocket."

Mercer clicked her tongue. "I don't know about that theory."

"Why? You knew she would do it because Reggie trained you to do the same thing."

Mercer smiled. Tony was smart and faster than she gave him credit for. "You're good, but don't let it go to your head." She continued her way down the hall. "London is still wet behind the ears. I knew she would panic if she had to improvise. She'd do her best to get the earrings off her."

"Why didn't Reggie get rid of them?"

"Because he's arrogant about his expertise. He would have bluffed his way out the front door." She peeked inside a messy office and paused at the doorway. "And, just to let you know, the only reason I put them on Reggie was because he was going to steal those diamonds and frame me."

"Ah. So that's it."

"Yeah, that's it. I had to protect myself." She opened the last door in the hall, looked at the room filled with file cabinets and shut the door quickly. "I wanted to tell you what was going on, but, quite honestly, I didn't know if you would go with my plan."

"You're probably right."

"You didn't have to agree to that so quickly," she said as she turned and passed him in the hallway to go back to where they started.

"Just telling the truth," he said as he followed her again. "Well, that leaves me with only one more question."

She stopped in the middle of the reception area and placed her hands on her hips. "What's that?"

"Why are you here? To turn yourself in?"

She scoffed at the idea. "Not likely. Are you going to turn me in?" He didn't have any proof, but that never stopped him before when he knew he was right.

Tony sighed and ruffled his fingers through his hair. "No, I'm not. Then why are you here?"

She clasped her hands behind her back and shuffled her foot. "You said something about a job?"

CHAPTER EIGHT

HE STARED AT HER. BLINKED. "ARE you kidding me?"

"No, not really. Actually, I'm thinking about renting some office space." She looked around the reception area. "This will be perfect."

Tony's mouth dropped open. "You really are serious."

"We can draw up a contract, and I could work with you on a consulting basis in exchange for a desk and use of your office equipment," she offered.

He squinted at her as if he couldn't comprehend what she was saying. "You want to work for me?"

"Ah, no. I want to rent some of your office space. No one else would. Now, see"—she walked into an elegant room situated right off to the side of the reception area—"this space is exactly what I need."

"This is my conference room."

She looked around and nodded. "It's the best-looking room in the office suite."

"It's supposed to be," Tony said, walking into the room and heading for the large brown desk. "I don't want clients seeing how messy my real office is."

"Where's that?"

"Through there." He pointed at the door in the back of the room.

"Perfect. We'll practically work side by side."

"This isn't what I had in mind." He sat down in an executive chair. Mercer eyed the chestnut-brown leather and intimidating size. Now that was all Tony. It suited him more than anything else she'd seen.

Tony continued to study her as if she was some rare, exotic creature. "I don't want any criminal activity going on in this office."

"I wasn't suggesting such a thing." She held her hand up as she pledged. "I am a retired thief. I figured I had to give it up if I wanted you in my life—er, bed." She grimaced, not wanting to scare him off. "I meant bed."

Something hot and mysterious flickered in his eyes. "Is that right? And what do you plan to do for a living?"

She perched on the edge of the desk, her leg bumping against his knee. If only she was brazen enough to sit on his armrest. In his lap.

Mercer cleared her throat. "Well, I was thinking about that during my long and lonely walk here. And I have to face the fact that I'm only an expert in pickpocketing and jewels."

Tony rocked back in the chair, and interest flared deep in her abdomen. The chair rocked back. And swiveled. Hmmm . . .

"I don't like where this is leading," he said. "I thought you were retiring."

"I'm an expert on the jewels that I, uh, allegedly stole. I'm sure some of those items have a finder's fee. They were big-ticket items. Some had cultural significance."

Tony held up his hand. "Stop right there. You want to go after the jewels that you stole, steal them back and make money off it?"

Mercer smiled. "The ideal job, don't you think? And legitimate, too."

He rubbed his eyes with the tips of his fingers. "Only you would be ballsy enough to come up with a plan like that."

She wasn't sure if that was a compliment or not. "So"—she nudged his knee with the toe of her shoe—"what do you think?"

"You're not getting my conference room."

Her eyes widened at the unspoken promise. That sounded like she was going to get her way and get an office. Then again, she liked this room the best. It was the closest to Tony. "But I like it."

"I use this room, and you're not getting it." He sounded firm about the matter.

"Come on." She rubbed the side of her foot against his leg. "Think of all the fun we can have."

"Fun?" His gaze focused on her leg.

"Yeah, the two of us, side by side." She jabbed a fist in the air. "Fighting on the same team."

He rose from his chair and sighed. "I don't know, Mercer."

"Why not?" She braced her hands on the edge of the desk.

Tony stood close, towering over her. It wasn't fair. "You're the one who made the offer."

"Yeah, but I don't think I want to live with—er, bed," he said, deadpan, "a woman who works for me."

Excitement burst from her chest, radiating through her body. "First of all," she said, trying to sound sophisticated as her stomach fluttered, "it's *with* you, not *for* you. And second of all, we've never been to bed. You were never quick enough to catch me," she boasted.

"Do I need to catch you, Mercer?" he asked, raising an eyebrow. "Are you still running?"

The sassy comeback died on her tongue. She hadn't seen it that way, but yeah, she was still running. She was acting brazen and in control, but she kept her distance from Tony. But the chase was over. No sleights of hand or running in circles were going to help her now.

"No, Tony," she answered, trying to sound carefree and breezy. "I've stopped running. Now, what are you going to do about it?"

He rose from his chair and stood in front of her. She never realized how intimidating his size was. Mercer swallowed nervously as she tilted her head up to meet his gaze.

She was still trying to appear brazen, but it didn't seem to do much good. Mercer found it difficult to breathe. Her lungs felt tight, and the urge to bolt was fierce. She flinched when Tony cupped her knees and parted her legs.

"Sorry," she muttered, hating her telltale reaction as she watched him step between her legs. What was wrong with her? This was *Tony*. She had faced real danger many times and didn't blink an eye. Why was she acting like this now?

Because it was Tony. A wry laugh bubbled in her throat as

she figured out the answer. He had her now, and he wasn't going to accept anything less than complete surrender.

Tony kissed her, and the tension squeezed her chest. His mouth gently opened hers, and he darted his tongue inside. He continued to kiss her until she clung to him and the beat of her heart matched his.

She wasn't the "surrender" kind of girl, but it was more than that. She wanted him more than anything, but now that he had caught her, what if Tony discovered she hadn't been worth the chase?

"Don't be nervous," he whispered against her lips. Her vest sagged open in his hands.

"Me? Nervous?" The scoff caught in her throat. "Maybe just a little."

"Why?" he asked as he unbuttoned her shirt.

She couldn't remember. Her mind was a blank as she watched his eyes darken with pleasure as each button slid free. It was not unlike the moment when a thief knows he's cracked the code to a safe. Tony then reached for the bra fastening between her breasts.

Mercer held her breath as he flicked it open. He gently, almost reverently peeled back the lace to expose her tightly furled nipples. She heard Tony's groan before he took her into his mouth.

She arched back as the sensations zoomed and collided inside her. Mercer went rigid when he laid her down on the conference table. It felt hard and smooth against her back. Her shirt parted, exposing more of her to him.

Tony placed kisses along her ribs and stomach. Her muscles bunched under his touch. Heat seeped inside her, pushing away her vulnerability. She slowly encouraged him to kiss her

there, swirl his tongue over there, and press his fingertips—
yes!—just like that.

By the time Tony shucked the rest of her clothes, she was
beginning to wonder what was taking him so long. Beads of
sweat formed on her skin, and she panted with anticipation.
Her arms were stretched wide along the table as she wiggled
her hips when she heard him draw his zip down.

"Stay like that," he said softly against the underside of her
breast. "Keep your arms out wide." He skimmed his hands
down her bare hips and held her still.

She couldn't think straight with his hands cupping her bottom. Her knees trembled as he caressed and squeezed her before
sliding one finger along her cleft. "Tony—" she said in a gasp.

Heat streaked through her pelvis as he pumped his finger
inside. She met each move with a roll of her hips as the wild
sensations rippled through her.

Tony withdrew and she could feel the heat emanating
from his cock as it nudged her wet slit. She bit her lip as Tony
slowly filled her. She rocked against him, and her skin tingled.
She swayed her hips, and her world spun.

The white-hot lust drew tighter and tighter. She wanted
to grab his shoulders but instead stretched her arms over her
head. She knew he wanted to watch her reactions. Show him
how she felt without any pretense.

She bucked and rolled her hips against him. Mercer felt
dizzy. Alive. Free. Tony's fingers dug into her bottom as he
thrust deeper. Harder. The pleasure exploded, taking her by
surprise. It whipped through her body as Tony's release triggered her own.

She sagged against the table as her body continued to
tremble. Mercer glanced up at his face and saw the wonder.

She smiled, knowing that look. It was like a hunter finding a long-lost treasure.

Yeah, she thought as she closed her eyes. *They* were definitely worth the chase.

"So, Tony," she said some time later, looking down as his head lay on her breast. She threaded her fingers along his hair. It was amazing how much enjoyment she got from having the freedom to touch him. "When can you get your stuff out of this room?"

"I didn't say yes," he said as his hand wandered to her side before cupping her breast.

"You will." Mercer knew her smile was smug.

"I have to admit," he said as he pondered the problem, absently brushing his thumb against her swollen nipple, "working together would be the easiest way to keep an eye on you."

"That's the spirit." She pulled at his hair and felt his chuckle vibrate against her chest. She still couldn't believe she had fallen for an ex-cop. Maybe she was rehabilitated. Maybe she was on her way to becoming one of those bad girls gone good.

She inhaled sharply as Tony tweaked the tip of her breast. She immediately squeezed her inner muscles that surrounded him. Mercer felt the moan in his throat as his cock leapt in response.

Naaah . . .

ABOUT THE AUTHOR

Susanna Carr lives in the Pacific Northwest. Visit her Web site at susannacarr.com.